Yours Eternally

Once Upon a Time, Italian Style

by

A. K. Doran

Printed in the United States of America

First printing, 2016

A.K. Doran Publishing

Dedication:

Life can take you many places but your heart will always lead you to where you need to be. If you are lucky, some people can be with you a lifetime but sometimes there are those who can't stay but shall remain forever in your heart. When people ask me why I wrote this novel, I tell them, 'I have my own Sarah and my own Eugenio. They are forever in my heart.'

Yours Eternally
(Once Upon a Time, Italian Style)

Chapter 1

Molly took a deep breath and walked up to the podium. She looked over at the casket and turned to face the congregation.

"Sarah has been my best friend for the last twenty-five years and she will remain my best friend for the rest of my life. We are not going to let a little thing like death come between us." Her voice broke and she stopped for a second before going on. "Sarah was a beautiful lady and she died with dignity. And she did it on her schedule. The morning she passed she had made scones, those wonderful sweet scones of hers. Her daughter, Emily, Sarah, and I sat in her kitchen by the window and talked of all the things Sarah loved most in her life. We talked about her granddaughters and she told Emily how proud she was to have had the honor to be her mother. And we talked about Atlanta and how she missed the magnolia trees blooming. These were the things Sarah loved the most. Emily and I ate scones but Sarah could only sip a cup of tea. She said it tasted especially sweet and soothing that morning.

I asked her what I could do for her and she said I had done quite enough. I had accidently locked her in the storage room at the college. I had made her laugh until she peed her pants in her favorite restaurant. And I had allowed her, after too much wine one night, to lie on the sidewalk outside her apartment and make snow angels in the newly fallen snow. But she took my hand and said I had also eaten more chocolate with her than any two women should consume in

1

a lifetime, I had sat up all night and cried through old movies, walked with her in the rain, and been her best friend. And yet, looking back now, it doesn't seem like nearly enough.

Later that day she said she wasn't feeling well. She guessed most people who were dying of cancer didn't feel that great most days but she wasn't going to let it take her. She was curled up in her chair looking out the window and she asked Emily to make her another cup of tea. When Emily left the room, she said quietly, 'Take care of my babies, Moll.' I promised I would and she just smiled and closed her eyes. The doctor said it was her heart. She had done it her way.

Sarah loved Atlanta. She was going to retire at the end of this school year and go home. She always looked at Atlanta as home. She said she had had enough of the windy city and she was going home to be close to her girls. I look at Emily and the girls and I know them as well as I know my own children. I have been part of their lives since they were born. Sarah loved them more than life itself. There was always a light in her eyes when she spoke of them.

On the flight down here, I tried to think of what I could possibly say that would do Sarah justice. And then I thought of her hands. Sarah had beautiful hands. They were slender and graceful, but they were strong. She could change a flat tire and I have seen her open the most impossible of jars with ease. These hands were gentle and comforting when wiping away a child's tears and when she ran her fingers across the pictures of her girls as she spoke of them. She made the most amazing scones. And she could write one hell of a grant!

Tonight I have to fly back to Chicago and tomorrow I will have to get up and go to work. And she will not be waiting in the lounge for me. It is her turn to bring Starbucks because the coaches make the coffee and neither of us could handle it. I hate the idea of going to sleep tonight knowing that I will have to begin a life without her when I wake up in the morning."

Molly walked over and looked into the face of her friend. She leaned in and gently touched her face. "I love you, Kiddo, Tesoro mio," she whispered quietly and then walked back and took her seat. She did not remember anything else the minister had to say. She sat with her hands folded in her lap and wondered, as we all do, why such an extraordinary person, only 55, had been taken away from those who love her so dearly…and why God had chosen to take away the only person in Molly's life who truly got her.

The skies had opened and the rain was coming down in torrents by the time Molly had left for the airport. She looked up at the darkened skies and wondered if this day could possibly get any worse. She dashed into the airport and checked her bag. She went through security and was met with a barrage of frustrated passengers. She glanced at the departure board and saw the endless list of delayed flights. She walked to her gate and seeing no empty chairs, she stood by the window and wished she was on the other side of the heavy glass so no one would see the tears come in a steady stream down her face.

When she re-gained control again, Molly checked her phone, realizing she had not turned it on since she had entered the church this morning. There was a long text from Adam hoping she was okay and sorry that the U.S. Marine

Corp did not consider the passing of his mother's best friend as a reason for an emergency leave. He said they just didn't consider "like an aunt" worthy either. And he added, "You are still my best friend, Mom. I love you."

The airport was operating in slow motion. Tired and disgusted travelers waiting for delayed flights filled every seat at every gate. Molly had taken a walk, not wanting to just have to stand there alone. People were busy texting or talking on cell phones, reading, or sleeping. Small children, restless, were running while weary parents were trying to calm them and keep them from annoying other passengers.

Molly realized she hadn't eaten anything all day and she was suddenly very hungry. She had noticed a man in fatigues sitting quietly across the walkway at an adjoining gate. He was staring out at the rain pounding against the window. Seeing he was in uniform made her think of her own son. Molly had not been happy with Adam's decision, with all the problems in the world, but she felt very proud he was doing so well and how much he loved being a Marine.

Maybe it was because he seemed so alone or maybe because she was suddenly feeling very lonely herself that she found herself walking over to the man. "Excuse me. I am going to get a bite to eat. Could I buy you dinner or at least bring you something? Even a cup of coffee?"

The man stood and looked very surprised. "I am sorry. I think you are mixing me with another person."

Molly realized that he was not an American but military all the same. "You are in the military and I would still be

4

happy to buy you dinner. My son is a Marine and I would like to think strangers would offer to do the same for him."

"Thank you but I will buy you dinner for your kindness if you will let me." He extended his hand. "I am Eugenio. But my English is not always so good. I have been in the United States for a seminar so I have a lot of practice lately. Should be no problem."

"I am Molly and it is very nice to meet you. Dinner would be lovely."

They walked down to one of the nicer restaurants where there was not such a crowd and were seated near the window. When he took off his hat, she noticed that he was older than she had first thought, not much younger than herself and Molly suddenly felt embarrassed that he might think she was just trying to pick up a stranger in the airport. Molly said nothing, feeling very foolish.

"Molly, have you changed your mind? Would you rather not eat with me?"

"No, it isn't that. I just do not want you to think I am being, ah, bold."

"No, I understand. You were being nice and I like." He smiled.

Eugenio spoke softly and often asked if she understood. He had been at Fort Benning to participate in a seminar but now he was en route back to Italy.

"Have you ever been to Italy, Molly?"

"No, I have always wanted to go. I want to see Rome and the Isle of Capri and all those wonderful places I have read about. My friend and I were planning to go soon. It is on my bucket list."

"I no understand bucket list."

"It is a list of things a person makes that he or she wants to do or see before dying."

"Why do they do this?"

"So we can cross off each thing, an accomplishment to fill our heart's desire. We blame Jack Nicholson. He was in a movie about it."

Eugenio was thin and a bit shorter than Molly, wore his hair very short, and he had tattoos – all those things Molly usually did not find appealing and yet here was this charming man with all those traits and she found him very attractive. He had piercing azure eyes but there was sadness in them.

"How long have you been in the military?"

"Forever!" He smiled, "I joke. I was a paratrooper for twenty years and now I am Carabinieri, it is military police. What do you do, Molly?"

"I teach." Usually she would have ended it there but for some reason she wanted this man to know her secret. "And I am writing children's books."

"I think you must be a woman of many talents, I like." And then he added, "I am sorry. Did I offend you?"

"No, of course not."

"Do you live in Atlanta?"

"No, I live in Chicago. My best friend passed away and Sarah wanted to be buried in Atlanta. She is home now. Her funeral was today and now I am returning to Chicago."

He reached out and took her hand. It was nice to have someone comfort her after spending the last three days being a comfort to everyone else. Tears welled in her eyes and fell silently down her cheeks. He reached over and wiped them away with his fingertips. "Please, Molly, I am sorry I make you cry."

"No, Sarah was, is, my best friend and I shall always cry for someone so wonderful. I miss her so very much."

"But you have a son, yes? And a husband?"

"A son, a daughter, and an ex-husband."

"I like that you have an ex-husband, no married."

Molly smiled. "I like that he is my ex-husband now too. Are you married?"

"Separated. Is very complicated for me. Italian and Catholic…very strict."

For some reason, Molly had hoped that he would be single as well. Molly noticed that it had stopped raining. They would be calling her flight soon and his. She would never see this man again and yet, she wished that he was single.

It was so easy to talk to this man and over dinner they talked of so many things. Molly dreaded every announcement, knowing any minute that they might have to leave. The waitress came over and asked if there would be anything else. Eugenio said at home he would ask for tiramisu, but here it would have to be something else. "Gelato, ah, ice cream, we would like ice cream with…" he looked at Molly for a second and then added, "with chocolate."

"How did you know I like chocolate?"

"I just know, Molly. You like chocolate as I do."

"Yes, too much."

Molly had expected two sundaes but the waitress brought one and set it in the middle of the table and laid down two spoons.

"It looks like we are sharing."

"Is nice."

"Yes, but I must warn you. I will fight you for the last bite."

"No fight. For you."

Before they finished, they heard "Flight 0125 to Chicago O'Hare will be boarding shortly. Please proceed to Gate 17. We will be boarding anyone with small children, anyone needing assistance, and anyone in uniform."

Molly remembered hearing that same announcement when she had left O'Hare on Thursday. She liked that they were treating the military personnel with respect. She made a mental note that she would fly U.S. Air from now on whenever possible.

Then she looked at Eugenio and the smile left her face. "That would be me."

Time to leave all this beautiful Georgia sunshine and head back to Chicago. "Why could it not have rained just a while longer," they both thought as they gathered their things to leave.

Eugenio walked her back to her gate. "Thank you, Molly, for your company. It was very nice meeting with you."

"Yes, it was lovely to have dinner with a friend and not alone."

"So, we are to be friends?"

"I believe sharing a hot fudge sundae and you letting me have the last bite constitutes friendship."

"Molly?" his voice was quiet. "Would you write to me?"

Molly had wanted to ask but was afraid he would say no and ruin the two lovely hours they had just spent together.

9

She dug into her purse and held out a card. "This is me. I would love to hear from you and I promise to write back."

Eugenio reached out but took her hand instead of merely taking her card. "I very much enjoyed this time."

Molly leaned over to give him a quick hug but Eugenio took her face in his hands and if he had attempted to kiss her, she would have gladly let him, but instead, he looked into her eyes. "Ciao, Bella. I will write."

She put her travel bag over her shoulder and started through the gate, but then stopped and turned. Eugenio was still standing in the same spot, watching her. She smiled and waved and then hurried down the ramp. In her seat, she stared out the window.

It was only three days ago she had stood on the tarmac and watched as they had taken Sarah's body from the plane. She had stayed seated until all the other passengers had disembarked and then the attendant had come and escorted her off the plane. The pilot had come out and stood beside her and silently waited with her until the hearse had pulled up and security guards had carried her out. The pilot had taken Molly's arm and escorted her to the back of the car. Molly walked over and put her hand on the coffin. She leaned over and quietly whispered, "You're home, Sarah."

Now she was leaving, this time without Sarah next to her as always in all those times in the past. She leaned back and closed her eyes and a feeling of total loneliness washed over her. She did not see the man who was standing by the window watching as her plane moved away from the gate

10

and began to make its way to the runway…he too suddenly feeling very much alone again.

Chapter 2

It rained on Monday or maybe it had just followed Molly home. Not one of those soft gentle rains the Irish speak of, but one of those with winds whipping down between the tall buildings and blowing debris along the sidewalks. Three stories up, Molly found a plastic bag caught on the wrought iron railing of her tiny balcony. Sarah always complained that the rain made her hair collapse while even the slightest of raindrops turned Molly's hair into thick beautiful curls. On sunny days, Sarah had sleek shiny hair and Molly's was a mass of wispy curls. Sarah used to say that between the two of them, they had perfect hair!

"Sarah," Molly whispered out-loud as she wrapped her fingers around her hot cup of tea and felt the same emptiness in her chest she had fallen asleep with. She hated the idea of even having to walk into the college today knowing Sarah would never again be there. Sarah had only been on medical leave for three weeks before she had died, but every day Molly was sure she would go into remission and things would be back to normal. But now, she was left with only the constant reminders that she was gone.

She set her cup down and turned on her computer to check her mail. Her inbox had several messages, condolences, and a lovely letter from Sarah's Emily. A long message from Adam and a brief, "Sorry about Sarah" from her ex, and a noticeable absence of anything from Amanda.

Then it caught her eye: Eugenio! It was short and sweet. "Molly, I hoped you traveled and returned home safe and sound. Mine was good...very long but I had nice thoughts of meeting you. I worry you are too sad for your friend. I hope that you want to continue our friendship. This is important to me. Ciao, Bella. Eugenio."

Molly read it over and over. "Yes, I want as well," she thought, "I wonder what Sarah would say. No, I know what she would say. She would say, 'See, if I hadn't died you wouldn't have met this charming man. I am taking credit. Now quit sitting there and get ready for work. You have to stop and get your own coffee from now on.'"

"Oh, Sarah, I miss you! But you are right. I need to get ready for work."

Molly walked into the office to get her mail. Sarah's name had already been removed and all that remained was the empty cubby where it had been for the last 30 years. Molly suddenly felt angry that someone had taken it upon himself to remove it so soon.

Molly sat and watched her students ponder over their tests. She could always tell by the looks on their faces which of them had bothered to study and which ones had partied away the weekend and were now silently praying for some miracle to happen which would give them a passing grade.

For almost 30 years, Molly had watched so many young men and women come and go. She had always loved her job; in fact, in recent years it had often been the best part of her days. And she had attended every graduation of every one of her students, hoping she had made even the slightest difference in their lives. Over the years, thanks to modern technology, she had heard from so many of "her kids" and stayed in touch, often getting updates about further educational endeavors, weddings, and later, family pictures.

She had even gotten a few "sorry I was such a horrible student" emails over the years from some of her "more challenging" students. But she loved hearing from each and every one of them.

She glanced at her watch, another 45 minutes! A couple students had already handed in their tests and left. Sadly, these are the ones who should have stayed until the bitter end, but they will learn in their own time. Molly leaned back in her chair and took a sip of her Starbucks, lukewarm now but still much needed to get through this day.

"And what of your own life?" Molly thought. Over the years, Molly had found time to nurture her own love of literature and she realized her ability to know what was good and what wasn't. Plus, her own talents had moved past just grading sentence structure, irregular verbs and spelling.

Her grandmother had told her a lady always needs a bit of "pin money" of her own. Grandma had a small change purse in her sewing basket that held over $100.00, which was unheard of in her day. She had saved a bit of the egg money, and here and there she had done sewing and ironing for other ladies. Each time she tucked it away, not even telling Grandpa, in case the time would come when she or one of her children would need some quick cash. She wanted the peace of mind to know she could help. For some reason that had stuck with Molly and from the time she and David had married, she had always had her own bit of ready cash tucked away. Adam knew of it, but not Amanda. If she had known, it would have quickly dwindled into nothing more than a stack of IOUs. Over the last three years, as a single woman, Molly had used her talents to do some extra work tutoring and writing grants and some online textbook editing. Each time she tucked the money away, thinking how proud her grandma would be. And then she began to write a book of her own, children's stories, the ones she used to tell Adam and Amanda when they were younger. Sarah had convinced her she should start writing them down. So, Molly would write and Sarah would edit. Molly could always tell when Sarah would have a problem with what she had written by the look on her face and if she didn't care for it at all, she would say, "I think I will make some scones and we can go over this."

In fact, they were getting ready to launch their first major effort when Sarah became ill again. With more important matters to attend to, the book now sat in Molly's desk, forgotten for months. And her "pin money" sits in the bank untouched. They were going to take their "successful venture" money and use it for their trip to Italy in the summer. Now, without Sarah, a trip to Italy would never happen. Just another part of her life that had lost its charm.

Many times in the past, Molly would come from work to find a note on the table that David and Amanda had gone out for Chinese or pizza because they were starving, but they would bring something home. They liked their father/daughter times together so Molly had learned to accept the situation and often times she and Adam would sit at the kitchen table later those evenings and eat Chinese out of paper cartons or cold pizza when he came home from his after school job. It hadn't been a bad life, but she knew there was so much missing. But she had her work and a nice home even though she hated living in a condo, and she had her children. She decided after her own early years, that family was everything. But now David had moved on, Adam had gone to college for two years and then joined the

Marines, and Amanda was on her own, so to speak, and only came around when she needed money, help with a paper, or when she needed to feel pampered and loved. However, Amanda had fallen in love. So with a boyfriend in the picture, it was mostly money, or lack of, that brought her to Molly's door.

The rain had cleared into an almost pleasant day, even though the January thaw was just a temporary fix for the winter blues. Molly hadn't gotten groceries for God knows how long. She had spent so much of her time with Sarah and then had gone to Atlanta. She stepped off the train and one of the ladies from her apartment house was there to pick up her husband and Molly always had a standing offer for a ride home. Allyson greeted her when she walked across the platform. "Molly, I was so sorry to hear about Sarah. Richard and I would like you to come to dinner some night soon. You just let me know when." Molly thanked her and said she would be over soon to talk, but she thought she would walk home today and get some fresh air.

She really did need some fresh air after spending the day trying to smile and carry on, but the truth was that she was just suddenly in no hurry to get home. She walked along the familiar street suddenly noticing some changes. A new store had opened and the coffee shop on the corner had a new name. She had been so pre-occupied, she just had not noticed. She stopped for Chinese take-away and some milk and headed for home. There must have been a fire call because the men were still gathered outside the firehouse when she walked by.

"Hey, Molly, still have the truck out, need a lift home?" She waved and yelled back. "Thanks, guys, I can make it from here." Molly, often times over the years, had taken baked goods and sometimes a pot of homemade soup down to the station when they had been out on a call. She could see the station from her balcony and had developed a friendship with these men over the years, which started when she had first moved into the neighborhood, but had grown when two of Adam's friends had joined the department. Adam always walks down and shoots pool or has coffee with them when he is home on leave.

Now she walked home alone. She thought about Sarah and all the walks they used to take at night, window shopping and sharing their days, and making plans for their retirements, and of course, talking of their trip to Italy. Sarah had decided to learn Italian and not tell anyone else so she could see what people were really saying when they thought no one could understand. She would try and teach Molly new words and phrases as they walked, but then suddenly she stopped. One evening Molly asked her for her new words and Sarah had turned and looked at her. "It really would be a waste of time; Moll, you and I both know it." This was the first time since Sarah had told her about the cancer that Sarah had ever shown signs of defeat.

"Sarah, please." Molly took her hand, but Sarah stopped her. "It's okay, Moll. Just having a bad day. Let's see, how about 'Tesoro mio: my treasure'." Molly had dutifully pronounced the words, but her heart was aching at the thought that Sarah might be right.

Molly unlocked her door and kicked off her shoes. She had tried to stay busy all day, but now she was alone and she wondered how she was going to spend her evening, probably just force herself to get some work done. Always papers to grade. She grabbed a fork and her container of Mongolian Beef and sat down at her computer. She was hoping for a nice letter from Adam and maybe she would answer Eugenio. She would thank him for the pleasant dinner and dessert, but she thought about those last few minutes at the airport and the way he held her face in his hands. She remembered the way he had looked at her. She took a mouthful of food and typed a short note. She decided he was being polite so she would be the same, but she had barely sent the message when he came online. "Molly, I just finish long hours at work, but I wait to see if you come online. I wonder how you are and I worry you are sad for your friend. Do you have Skype?"

Molly had just taken another mouthful of food and wrote back, "Hi, good to hear from you. Yes, I Skype so I can talk to my son whenever possible. I miss his face and I like to see for myself that he is alright."

"So, will you talk to me as well?"

She wiped her mouth with the back of her hand and ran her fingers through her hair. "Just a sec." She ran into the bathroom and checked for food in her teeth and put on some lip gloss and then grabbed her perfume. "Oh, Good Lord!" she said out-loud. She set down the bottle and hurried back into the living room.

She took a deep breath and clicked the button. He was waiting for her and when he saw her, he smiled. "Ciao, Bella."

And so it began. Molly would find herself checking her watch during the day, waiting on those days when their schedules were such that she could hurry home and talk to Eugenio. They would talk of their day and chat as old friends. Often times she would find a quick message waiting when she woke up, knowing he had already gone to work. She knew it sounded pretty "high school," but she kept every message and read them over and over, always happy when she could add a new one. For now, the time change worked most days for them but he said soon he would be going home for a few days and then he would be working a different shift, but he promised that they would find time to talk. Many times after they had signed off, Molly would sit and stare at the blank screen, reaching out and touching the empty white space. She wished she could reach out and touch his face as he had hers that day in Atlanta.

She did not know that Eugenio sat quietly staring at the blank screen as well, angry that he had not kissed her that day in Atlanta. He thought about how many times he had tried to talk to his wife online after a long day, just wanting to see her face and hear her voice, but she said she did not enjoy it. Now he looked forward to talking to Molly. She was always happy to see him and her smile is what made his day. And she would send messages so when he came online and found them waiting, it made coming back to his small room in the barracks a little more bearable.

Always, the last thing he thought about before falling asleep was Molly. Two strangers meeting in a busy airport on a rainy day and yet they had found each other through a simple act of kindness. He hadn't noticed anyone else that day, deep in thought about returning home after being away from home for three weeks, knowing that his wife had been with another man the whole time. She had not returned his calls or even answered his messages. He had been sitting at the airport that day wondering how much more he could possibly handle before it started to take a toll on his career, his heart, and his soul. Being in the military, loneliness is part of life, but to have someone at home who loves you and misses you and who is waiting for you to come home, it is bearable. But nothing is worse than coming home and seeing in her eyes that she no longer cares.

And now suddenly there was Molly, sweet sincere Molly. He probably should have just said no thank you that day in Atlanta, but he was tired of eating alone and she looked like she could have used the company as well. And now it was easier to get up every morning and fall asleep at night when he had Molly to think about.

Tonight after they had talked, he lit one last cigarette and lay on his bed, thinking how easily they could talk and kid. There were times he would write something and then think better of it and delete it, not wanting to offend her or make her think less of him. He wanted to tell her how important she had become to him, but he was married and she deserved more than just the things he had begun to think about so often now. Having her near him, hearing her laugh, enjoying her smile, and leaning over to kiss her whenever he wanted and seeing the acceptance in her eyes. He took one last drag of his cigarette and put it out. He fell asleep that night wondering what it would be like to make love to this woman.

The next morning, Molly went into the bedroom to dress for work. She slipped out of her comfortable bathrobe and stood in front of the mirror. Too much tummy, legs have always been heavier than she would have liked (thanks

Mom and Gram). She cupped her breasts and pushed them up. God, I hate gravity! If she took the infamous pencil test by placing a pencil under each breast to see if it would fall, she would be writing with a pen the rest of her life. But all things considered, not too bad! She and Sarah talked about joining a gym once, well, more than once, but it was usually after they had been out for pasta. To get off to a good start, they would decide to forego the tiramisu and just have coffee. However, they always ended up each taking an order home to add to tomorrow's calorie count, forgetting the gym, and deciding to just walk home.

Molly knew this was the natural aging process but she didn't have to like it. And she refused to be one of those divorced women who had all kinds of work done, donning the skinny jeans and high heels and pretending all that foundation actually made them look younger…personally, it seemed like too much work. David used to tell her it wouldn't hurt if she took off a few pounds, but it really would not have mattered. If Molly had weighed an even 100 pounds, he would have found fault elsewhere.

She remembered the beautiful black lace nightgown she had gotten once for their anniversary. They had made love that night, but David told her she didn't have to try so hard, she already had her man. He was such a wonderful contradiction in terms…always needing affirmation but never thinking that a woman, his wife, might want and need the same consideration. Molly caught a glimpse of the clock in the mirror behind her. "Oh crap, I am going to be late for work and here I am standing here holding my own boobs."

Chapter 3

Later that night, Molly stopped, picking up a pizza and a bottle of wine, and walked home. The streets were busy with people in a hurry, finally finished with the week's work and rushing home to relax or meet friends, family or lovers. Molly's steps were slower. She was going home to a quiet evening alone. She had gotten used to being alone, but she wondered if she would ever get passed that initial feeling of loneliness she felt each time she neared her brownstone. She walked up the steps and unlocked the door. "Lucy, I'm home!" She said brightly. It always made her feel better if she pretended she wasn't coming home to an empty condo.

She needed a hot bath. She slid down in the bubbles, letting the water engulf her. She reached for her glass of wine. When she finally felt the day beginning to fade away, she dried off and put on her pajamas, warm comfortable blue flannel. She poured another glass of wine and set the pizza box on the desk next to her. She took a drink of wine and caught her reflection in the screen as she took a rather unlady-like bite of pizza. "Good Lord! All I need now is a cat."

She needed to write Adam a long letter. She felt guilty using him as a crutch when God knows he has enough problems of his own just being where he is. So, she wrote him long cheery letters, not telling him how much she missed him and Sarah and how lonely she felt sitting in this condo alone. Instead, she wrote about seeing his friends at the fire station and talked about times when he was little. Pleasant memories!

She looked at the clock; it was 1:00 a.m. in Italy. She was sure Eugenio would be in bed but almost as soon as she came online, he was there. "Molly are you there?"

"Yes, how are you?"

"Turn on your cam. I want to see you."

"No, you don't. I am in my pajamas and have no make-up on."

"Please, I want to see you."

"Okay, but I warned you."

She turned on her Skype camera and instantly he appeared on her screen, in full uniform. How handsome he looked! Usually he was in jeans and a t-shirt when they talked, but tonight he looked every bit the commander he is.

"Very nice. Very handsome, Very military."

"Thank you. And you look beautiful."

"I look like a lazy bum…in my pajamas and it is only 6:00 p.m."

"You look very cute in flannel and you are always beautiful to me. Make-up does not matter. Is late, but I wait for you."

Molly put her head down, not knowing what to say. This man had become such an important part of her life and she knew he was sincere. He always made her feel beautiful and desired, even being thousands of miles apart. He had never spoken the actual words but she knew.

"Molly, please, look at me. I did not mean to embarrass you. I only tell you how I feel. I know I should not say things to you but is important to me you know. Tell me what you think."

Molly took another drink of wine. Not having taken time for anything but coffee and some crackers she had at her desk for lunch, she probably should eat first and then drink. But she wasn't sure if it was the wine or Eugenio that made her cheeks feel flush!

"I think about us being together. I know you are married and I shouldn't but these last four months have been wonderful for me and I think of..." She stopped.

"What, Molly, what do you think about us?"

"No, it is foolish, I am sorry."

"Never foolish. And you never have to be sorry with me."

"I just can't help but think...you know; I think of us being together. It is just a ... fantasy. Do you understand?"

"Tell me your fantasy."

"I am embarrassed. What you must think of me."

"You must know I think of these things as well. I am alone at night and I think of you. I know it is not correct, but I do.

I think of making love to you. I want to make love to you, so please, tell me that you think of such things as well."

Molly took another drink of her wine and looked at the screen before her. Eugenio always looks so tired; and she hated to see the sadness in his eyes sometimes when they talked. She wanted to tell him how she felt but…but what? She had never been able to talk to David about things she wanted and needed and felt, but this man…She finished her wine and set the glass down with a clink. She took a deep breath and smiled, thinking, "Here goes!" Lean back and close your eyes and I will tell you." He did as he was asked and he listened as she began to talk, very slowly and quietly.

"I see me in Rome in an apartment I have rented. And you come to me late one evening when you get off duty. And you take my face in your hands, as you did that day in the airport, but this time you kiss me and it is everything I knew it would be. We go into the bedroom, I watch you undress and slip into bed next to me. You look tired so I begin to massage your shoulders. Your skin is smooth and warm and when I kiss your neck, there is the hint of salt on your skin. You close your eyes as I begin to explore the rest of your body, finding the textures and curves of your body with my fingertips. And when we finally make love, it is very slow and deliberate, finding our own perfect rhythm. Later, you lay with your arm around me. My head cradled against your chest, I close my eyes and feel a sense of peace wash over me." Molly remembered Sarah's lessons and she wanted to tell him "Tersoro mio," but she stopped herself. Instead, she leaned back in her chair and looked at Eugenio as he opened his eyes. At first he didn't say anything and she was afraid that she had gone too far. But then he leaned forward and looked at her, thousands of miles apart, but she felt he was looking deep into her eyes.

"Yes, Molly, this is what I think of with you. I want to make love to you. I adore you, Molly, you are tersoro mio. That means…"

Molly nodded, "As you are mine."

Just then the phone rang and Molly waited and watched his animated conversation, not being able to understand his rapid conversation. When he hung up, he smiled at Molly, "I am sorry; I have to go back to my office but is difficult right now. I am…I am…" He moved the camera down…it was obvious that he was aroused.

"I am so sorry."

"No, not sorry, never sorry. Is good and I love that you say such things to me. That you want to be with me. Please do not be embarrassed. You are so good for me. A long time since a woman wanted to make love with me."

"Not embarrassed, Eugenio. Very surprised I say these things to you, I have never…"

"I am glad NEVER before…I like just us."

"Me too."

"Molly, I have to leave now, back to my office, but we talk soon. And please, think of me as you do. Ciao, Bella."

"Bye, M."

He blew her a kiss and then was gone. After he signed off, Molly leaned back in her chair. OMG! She thought, what did I just do? Was that what they call cybersex? She realized that Eugenio was not the only one who was aroused. She had not felt like this is a very long time…horny as the kids would say, definitely horny!

"Well," she thought, "Obviously enough wine and I don't smoke so I guess that leaves cold pizza and chocolate. Where did I put that Snickers I bought yesterday?"

She started into the kitchen, but she stopped and leaned against the doorway. "Oh my God, Sarah, you are not going to believe what I did! Oh wait, yes, you would believe it." She opened the cupboard and took out the candy bar. She unwrapped it slowly and took a bite. She felt sadness wash over her. "God, Sarah, I miss you!"

Molly put the rest of the pizza in the refrigerator and decided to just lie on the couch and watch a little TV. She tried to watch a movie but her mind kept going back to her bold exhibit of exactly what she was not sure. She had never done anything like that before in her life. It had been a very long time since she had attempted the art of seduction in the bedroom and just exactly what was it that she had attempted earlier that evening? Eugenio had assured her that her recent display of whatever the hell that was, had made him happy. Lulled into a sense of well-being from wine and chocolate, she closed her eyes and soon fell asleep.

Molly pulled the afghan on the back of the couch down around her. She fell back to sleep remembering those lovely nights when she would rock Adam to sleep, kissing his tiny fingers, and promising to keep him warm and safe.

Saturday morning came all too early. The glaring sun through the patio door woke Molly. She opened her eyes and quickly pulled the afghan over her head. "Good Lord!" She thought, "It can't be morning already." She opened her eyes again, still hidden under the soft knit fabric, and gave them a chance to at least focus. Then she pulled it down and the sunlight shone on her face. She sat up and she wasn't sure if it was the entire bottle of wine or the early hour that hit her first. She leaned over and put her head in her hands. Coffee! She needed coffee. She got up and headed for the kitchen.

She opened the cupboard and reached for the Folgers when she saw the Snickers wrapper lying on the counter and the events of the night before came flooding back. "OMG! What did I do?" She said out-loud, but it was only rhetorical…She remembered exactly what she had done. She leaned against the counter, letting the can of Folgers slip to the counter with a bang. "What the hell was I thinking? Oh yeah, I wasn't." She made coffee and then went back into the living room and stood looking at her computer. She sat down and stared at the blank screen. She reached out to type in her password but stopped. She suddenly felt sad, afraid of what message she was going to find from Eugenio when she checked her mail. There would most certainly be one, but did she really want to read it? What he must think of her! Last night, he had said it was what he wanted, but things change in the bright light of day.

She went out and poured herself a cup of coffee and opened the refrigerator to take out the creamer but then stopped.

"Better take this straight and strong. I am going to need it."
She did not even notice the pounding in her head because
the pounding of her heart far out-weighed it.

She stood at the counter and took several sips. It was hot
and the smell always seemed to be the best part of that first
cup. She re-filled her cup and walked into the living room
and took a deep breath. "Here goes nothing!" She thought
and then sadly added, "More than likely, here goes
everything."

There were two messages waiting. One was from Adam and
one was from Eugenio. It was like the 'which do you want
first, the good news or the bad news?' situation. She opened
Adam's first. He wrote a cheerful letter, saying he was fine
and then going on to talk about some of the things she had
mentioned from when he was little. And he apologized for
that scar on her thumb from the time he put a fish hook into
it and then panicked and pulled it out himself, not thinking
how the barbed tip would tear her skin open. Molly looked
at her thumb, only the faintest hint of a scar remained.
Funny the things we remember!

She finished her coffee and took a deep breath and hit the
key to open her mail again.

"Dear Molly,

It has only been a few hours since we talked. I had to return
to my office to take care of an emergency situation, but I
return to my barracks now. I think about what you said to
me. Once the situation was taken care of, I sat in my office
and tried to do some paperwork, but it was hard to
concentrate, so I return to my room to write you. I know

29

you are probably asleep now, but I want to write to you before I go to sleep. I have come to know you and I am afraid that you may feel like you did something wrong tonight when you shared your fantasy with me or feel embarrassed. I want you to know that I like very much what you say to me and I like that you think of making love to me. I have much work to do for the next few days and then I go home for a short time. I will try to write you and hope we can see each other and talk, but if you do not hear from me for a day or two, please do not think for even a moment that it is because of what you say to me. Is important that you understand this. I think of you so often, Molly, often times in the same way in which you speak. You know that I am married but separated and I should not feel this for you because it is no fair to you, but please, you are so important in my life now. I do not know what will happen when I go home but I promise I will never lie to you.

Eugenio"

Molly read the letter and felt a sigh of relief move through her chest. She read it a second time just to make sure and then headed for the kitchen for aspirin and another cup of coffee. Now that her heart was beating normally again, she realized that she would have to spend at least the morning dealing with a wine hangover. She sat down and read the letter a third time and decided that this head-ache was worth it…it had given her the nerve to tell Eugenio how she had felt and worth it to have gotten his response to her wine-induced confession. She walked back to the couch and lay down again. Maybe the best way to occupy her morning until aspirin kicked in was a nap. She pulled the afghan up around her and closed her eyes, letting the warmth of the sun and Eugenio's words lull her back to sleep.

30

The following Thursday, Eugenio packed a small bag and threw it in the back of his Fiat and headed for home. Home, it didn't seem to have the same meaning as it once had. But as he got out of the city, he rolled down the window, lit a cigarette, and turned up the music. By the time he pulled into his driveway, he had made up his mind that once more he would try to save his marriage and put his life on track.

"I have to go now. Eugenio is just home. I will see you tonight, Ciao." Alessia walked over and gave Eugenio a light kiss. "Ciao, Eugenio." He gave her a hug, which she accepted with little warmth. "We are having dinner tonight with new friends I met on the beach. Carlos and his wife, Bianca, I meet them for lunch sometimes and when I tell them you are coming home, they invite us to dinner. You need to change; we are meeting them for drinks at 7:00 p.m."

"I was hoping we could stay home tonight. I am very tired and we need to talk about things, Alessia."

"I sit here and wait for you to come home so we can go out and all you want to do is stay home. I want to have some fun. This is why we have problems now. This is why we have separated. It was to be better, Eugenio, why I asked you to come. I hate this."

"Or is it me you hate?"

Alessia turned and looked at him. He was always so accepting of anything she wanted to do because he wanted to make her happy. There was something different this time.

"Why would you say these things to me?" She walked over and put her arms around his neck. "I just want to have some fun." And she kissed his neck.

"With me?"

"You are my husband."

"That does not answer my question."

She turned and walked into the bedroom and he followed. He put his arms around her and kissed her.

"Not now, Eugenio. We have to get ready. I thought you would be home earlier." Then she gave him a smile and added, "But tonight when we are home again, it will be different."

That evening Alessia was quite charming. Whenever she spoke to him, she would lean in and touch him. She told Bianca how proud she was of her husband for having chosen such a noble military career. But then she asked Bianca if she would mind terribly if she danced with Carlos. She loved to dance but Eugenio was so very tired. Eugenio watched them move across the dance floor and suddenly he knew. It was not that she was enjoying the evening with her husband; she was trying to make this man jealous. He leaned back in his chair and took a long drink of his cocktail. The hopes he had of making this marriage work faded as he watched his wife. She smiled when Carlos's hand slid off her waist and rested on the curve of her hip. Instead of the rage he should have felt, he felt numb.

When they returned home, Eugenio had tried to kiss her but she said she would be right back and disappeared into the bathroom. Eugenio undressed and lay down in the bed. When she finally came out, she was dressed in a long blue nightgown. Her hair was twisted into a long curl that hung over her shoulder. Eugenio turned on his side and looked at her, she was still a beauty and he still felt desire whenever he was with her. She slipped into bed next to him, "I am sorry to be so long. I decided to take a bath. I thought you would be asleep by now."

He put his arms around her and she responded until he began to caress her breasts and then she pulled away. "I am sorry, Eugenio. The bath has made me very tired. Maybe tomorrow." She kissed him and turned on her side. He lay in the dark and suddenly his thoughts were of Molly and how she had spoken of her desires. He thought about holding her and kissing her. And she would return his kisses and her fingertips would caress his neck and chest, then slowly letting her hand slide down and touch his thigh and she would whisper his name and tell him how much she wanted to make love, deep passionate love. He felt guilty lying there wanting another woman, but then he remembered watching Alessia and Carlos together…he needed to feel something again. He pulled Alessia to him and kissed her. First, slow kisses while he studied her face in the moonlight. When they were first married, it seemed like they could not spend enough time together, often leaving parties early, slipping away from family dinners and even movies to just be alone together. Her heavy perfume filled his senses. "I want you," he said and reached down and pulled up her gown. His hand slid between her thighs. He wanted again those nights of passion.

33

"Do you want to be on top?" he asked.

"Just finish, Eugenio." Anger surged through him, anger and frustration. He pushed her legs apart and slid over on top of her and pushed deep inside her. It only took a few minutes and it was over. He rolled over on his back and tried to put his arm around her, but Alessia swung her legs off the side of the bed and went into the bathroom. He grabbed his shirt from the side of the bed and dried himself. When she came back to bed, he turned to her. "I am sorry. I just needed to make love to my wife. I miss you."

She put her hand on his cheek. "It was good, Eugenio. Always good. Good-night." She turned and pulled the sheet up around her shoulders.

Tomorrow he would go to the church. He had not been in a while and there was so much he needed to confess!

***

For the next week, every morning Molly would wake to find a lovely message waiting. He said he was sorry that he was so busy but that they would talk very soon. She would read the messages several times and then would head out for her busy days. She knew he was busy and she loved that he took the time to write her, but she also realized that there was never a mention of his time at home.

In reality, since his return to the barracks, he longed to see her, but he just could not face her. He did not want her to see the frustration and his pain and his guilt. He would sit in front of his computer, alone in the barracks, smoking and trying to sound like everything was all right. But it could not be farther from the truth. His life was in turmoil and he did not want Molly to know.

The morning after he had made love to Alessia, he woke to find a note on the kitchen counter. She had gone shopping and would be back after lunch.

He had busied himself around the house, doing all the little things that needed tending to. He had not been home in several weeks and Alessia had left a list of things that needed to be done casually lying on the counter. Eugenio looked it over as he drank his coffee. "Fix our marriage' should be on this list," he thought, "Maybe at the top."

About 10:00 a.m., he decided to run down to the hardware store to pick up a few supplies if he was going to complete the list. The day was warm and inviting and it felt good to be out of uniform. He had on a pair of cut-offs and a t-shirt and decided while he was out, he would take a short run on the beach. It was already crowded by the time he found a place to park and walked out onto the warm sand. The winter had been mild, but people were more than ready to get out and enjoy the early warm weather and sunshine. He began slowly jogging, dodging the children as they splashed and played on the water's edge. Turning back, he walked up along the boardwalk. He decided to stop at their favorite restaurant and pick up some tiramisu to take home for lunch. It was Alessia's favorite.

As he waited for his order, he walked out to the railing and stared out at the water. Then he heard that familiar laugh. He turned and saw Alessia and Carlos sitting at one of the tables, shaded by a large umbrella. They were having lunch. He started to walk over to join them when he realized that the table was set for two, obviously Bianca was not with them. He watched as Carlos took her hand and kissed it. She leaned over and whispered something in his ear and Carlos laughed and motioned to the waiter for the check.

Eugenio took a few steps toward the table but then stopped. Did he really want to make a scene? He turned and walked away, trying to gain control of the range of emotions that were running through him. Anger that she had lied to him, stupidity because he had believed her when she said they were going to work on their problems. He thought again about last night and how she had been so loving all evening. Only to make Carlos jealous, he knew now. And the guilt he had felt making love, no, he had practically forced himself on his own wife, burned in his chest. He got back in his car and pulled out on the highway, not knowing where he was even headed. He drove along the coast, finally pulling over and getting out of the car. He lit a cigarette and leaned against his car, staring out at the water. He had tried for years to make Alessia happy, trying to compensate, almost even feeling guilty at times for his choice to stay in the military. Alessia did not want children and even though he came from a large family and wanted children of his own, he had accepted her decision. They bought a home three hours from the barracks because Alessia wanted to be near the beach instead of being close enough that he could be home most nights. But what about him? Wasn't he entitled to something more? He got in his car and drove back to the house and packed his bag. He left the tiramisu on the counter with a note that he had been called to go back early. He stood in the doorway of what had been his home for many years. He closed the door and walked away. Eugenio knew things would be very different the next time he returned.

He drove back to the barracks and threw his bag on the floor. He lit a cigarette and lay down on the bed. "Guess this is home from now on," he thought. He wanted to talk to Molly, but he could not bring himself to turn on the computer. She knew him so well. She would know something was wrong and it was not fair to lay all this on her. He checked the clock, it was morning in Chicago and she would be home. He would have to wait to write her when he knew he could just leave a message.

With the warmer weather and the passing of a very long and lonely winter, Molly had finally taken out her writing and decided it was time to get busy. It kept her occupied evenings and it always made her feel closer to Sarah. Often times she would write a while and then break for a cup of tea and ask the question out-loud. "What do you think?" Sarah was still such a big part of her life, that it surprised her when the answer was only silence. One evening after she had done what she thought was some really good writing; she turned to the first page in the folder. She took out her pen and wrote: "DEDICATION: TO SARAH, FOR A MILLION AND ONE REASONS."

Molly had also been walking home every day from the train station, enjoying the fresh air at the end of the day, well, what fresh air there actually was that survived in Chicago. She had been tempted to accept a ride home today, because for some reason she had not felt up to par. "Probably just tired," she thought, "the fresh air will do me good." She came around the corner and saw several of the firemen standing outside the station. Nick waved and shouted, "Hey, Molly, aren't we about due for a batch of chocolate chip cookies? You can't be sending them all to Afghanistan to Adam. We are on the front lines here too, ya know."

Molly started to raise her hand to wave back when a pain stopped her. She took a deep breath and felt like someone was holding her heart, preventing it from beating. She leaned against the building and tried to take a few shallow breaths before continuing on.

"Molly, you okay?"

Before she could answer, three of the men came running across the street. Donnie took her purse and bag and Nick put his arm around her and started to help her across the street. "Maybe you better let us take a look. You look a little flushed."

Molly was going to protest but instead she just leaned against his shoulder and let him guide her into the station. Nick helped her into the back of the ambulance and took her pulse. "We are just going to hook you up and see what the problem is." He started sticking patches on her back and chest while Andy was preparing an IV for her arm.

Molly closed her eyes, she hated needles, especially when they were about to be stuck into her. Nick looked at the monitor for a few minutes and then turned to Molly, "Listen Molly, we are just going to take a little ride. Nothing to worry about, but we want to have you checked out. We've got your back, so just relax."

"It is not my back I am worried about." She said and forced a smile. Molly heard the engine start and felt the ambulance swing out into traffic. She closed her eyes and took a few slow breaths but another pain made it difficult. Nick took her hand and smiled at her, "It's okay, Molly, we are not just a bunch of pretty faces, we are really good at what we do. Have you back baking us cookies in no time." He could see the tears start to well in her eyes. "Hey, I heard from Adam the other day. Said he wants to get home and kick my butt at pool again pretty soon."

Andy checked the IV in her arm and then sat down next to her. "How ya doin', Molly? Any more pain? We are about 15 minutes out."

Molly looked up at the two concerned faces next to her and tried to smile.

"Guys, think you could do me a favor?"

"Sure, Molly, what can we do?"

"Better light 'em up," she whispered.

"Molly? Molly? Stay with me, Molly!"

She heard the siren as the ambulance sped up, but she felt very calm. The last thing she remembered was that the air was suddenly filled with that all too familiar aroma. She opened her eyes. "Sarah" she said softly and smiled as the faces looming over her disappeared into darkness.

Chapter 4

Molly was awake but was afraid to open her eyes. Did she really want to know where she was? She could feel the IV in her arm and weight across her legs, making it impossible to shift even slightly to a more comfortable position. She could hear the steady beep of the machine next to the bed and she had watched enough television to know it was a heart monitor. Then she felt the warmth of hands picking up her own hand and holding it close. They were larger now and stronger, but so familiar. "I guess the Corp thought Mom having a heart attack was reason enough for leave," she whispered. She opened her eyes to see Adam sitting next to her bed. He was wearing his uniform, exhaustion and worry had left dark circles under his eyes and he was in need of a shave, but he looked wonderful to her.

"Mom, how do you feel? I have been so worried." He leaned over to kiss her and she felt his tears against her cheek.

"Better now." Her right arm was strapped down but she put her left arm around his shoulders and held him close. "My baby boy."

"Come on, Mom, I am a Marine now."

"Still my baby boy."

The nurse came in. "Well, look who is awake. How do you feel? Any discomfort?"

"My legs feel heavy."

"We have a weighted blanket on them to keep you still. We want you to have as little motion as possible for a while longer. No chest discomfort?"

"None. Exactly what happened to me?"

"The doctor will be in shortly to talk to you but he is going to be very happy. You are lookin' pretty good, Miss Molly. But I would be smiling too if I had a handsome Marine sitting here holding my hand."

Suddenly Molly began to remember the trip to the hospital and waking up with so many people around her. She had looked over once and saw two EMTs standing quietly in the corner. When Nick caught her eye, he gave her a thumbs up and blew her a kiss. Usually they just filled out the paperwork and left, but they had waited. She was sure it was Nick who had contacted Adam. Neither Amanda nor David would have acted so quickly to let him know.

Adam took the glass off the tray and held the straw for her. "They said you can have some orange juice but no food until the doctor sees you." She took a long drink. It was not cold but it tasted cool and sweet in her parched throat. Adam put the glass back and adjusted the covers around her. "Rest until the doc comes in, Mom. I will be right here when you wake up." Molly just wanted to see her son but she was very tired. She reached out and took his hand and holding it tightly, closed her eyes.

The next time Molly woke up, she would hear shouting. "I need to see my mother!" It was Amanda. The nurse in the hall was trying to calm her and the nurse who was talking to Adam pulled the heavy curtain around her bed.

"Mom, Amanda is going to have a stroke if she doesn't get in to see you."

The nurse walked out and Molly heard her say, "She is awake and you may go in for a few minutes, but you must be very quiet and not upset her."

Amanda came in and sat down next to the bed. "I have just been out of my mind with worry, Mom. How do you feel? Don't worry, Eddie and I are going to come over and stay with you when you go home."

Molly smiled but Adam saw the look on her face. "Amanda, I will be home for a few days and then we will see how Mom feels. She probably shouldn't have too many people around so she can rest. But we will take care of that later. Right now Mom just needs to rest."

"You seem to forget that I am the big sister and besides, a mother needs her daughter in times of crisis."

Molly took her hand. "There is no crisis, Amanda. I just had some chest pains. I feel better now. Honestly, you do not have to worry about me. You have finals soon. You need to study."

"But Mommy, you need me." Amanda began to cry.
Just then the curtain was drawn back and the nurse asked everyone to step out so the doctor could examine his patient.

"Good morning, Molly. You gave us a bit of a scare the last couple days, you had a heart attack and we did find some blockage but nothing we can't take care of. I want to keep you a few more days and run a few more tests and then we will get you set up for some surgery and have you as good as new. For now, I am going to put you on some medication and I want you to just rest."

"Why the weight on my legs?"

"We did an angiogram and we opened a main artery in your groin. We just wanted to keep you from moving about until we were sure it was alright. There will be some bruising but that is normal. If the tests look good tomorrow, you should be able to go home as long as there is someone there to stay with you. No steps, no heaving lifting, no standing for more than five minutes at a time."

Molly asked quietly, "Please let me tell my children. My daughter wants to come and stay with me. I would rather she didn't."

"Of course, you can make your own arrangements." He smiled, "She may not be the best thing for you right now. I will check on you later today. For now, you may have dinner and some company but please ask for assistance if you need to get up." He patted her arm, "And don't worry. I promised Nick I would take good care of you."

The nurse brought a tray in. "The doctor said you are ready for some real food." Then she leaned over and whispered, "But unfortunately, this is what you get." There were some plain mashed potatoes and a tiny piece of beef with a bit of gravy. There was grape juice and milk and a cup of green Jell-O. Molly was just happy to see food. She was suddenly very hungry.

Adam and Amanda came back in and sat with her while she ate. Adam was very quiet and watchful with every bite she took. Amanda chatted on between her texts to Eddie. Finally, the nurse came in and announced it was time for Molly to rest a while. Amanda quickly stood to go, gave her mother a quick kiss, and said she would be back in the morning. She bounced out the door but Adam waited until she was out of sight and then sat down again.

"You heard the nurse."

The nurse smiled at Adam and pulled the curtain closed as she left the room.

"Sorry, but I asked her to give Amanda a few minutes and then boot her. I have a couple things I want to talk to you about."

"Adam, I am fine, really. But, my will is in the lock box and…"

"Do not even joke about that, Mom. There are a couple things I do need to talk to you about."

"Alright, ask away. Sounds serious."

"First, I need to know how you really feel, none of this 'I am fine' stuff." I mean, you aren't just saying this to keep me from worrying? I have been concerned about you ever since Aunt Sarah died. You always sound like everything is good, but I know how much you miss her."

"I really am feeling good, Adam. And the only pain in my heart is this dull ache I have every day worrying about you and missing Sarah."

Adam took her hand. "And the other thing is…who is Eugenio?"

Molly instantly felt her face redden.

"I know those red cheeks are not because of your heart, Mom…or is it? The thing is, I was using your computer and these messages have popped up. He sounds very concerned about you."

"Adam, I…"

"I talked to him, Mom. He obviously is very worried that he hasn't heard from you. I wrote him back and told him you had a mild heart attack and you are in the hospital, but you are doing very well and will be home soon. Whatever else you want him to know is up to you. I am sorry, but he is so worried."

"Adam, I wanted to tell you about Eugenio, but I did not know where to start. To be honest, I wasn't sure what to say. I met him in Atlanta and we have become good friends. We talk a lot. He lives in Italy."

"It's good, Mom, in fact, it is great for you. And he seems like he genuinely cares for you. We talked a while and I promised I would report when I got back to the condo tonight. Is it serious?"

"It can't be. It is what it is, I guess. I really hate that expression but right now it is all we have. I should not be explaining this to my son, ya know."

"Hey, you are my best friend, remember. And I know how tough it has been for you…first Dad takes off and then Amanda moves out, well, maybe that part wasn't so bad."

"Adam, stop! She is your sister."

"I am kidding, well, kind of. And then losing Aunt Sarah. I should have never gone into the Marines when I did. I am so sorry."

"Just stop! There is no reason for you to feel guilty. You do not have to stay home and take care of old mom. I am very proud of you and I have been doing fine, well, up until last Tuesday anyway. But the doctor thinks I will be home soon."

"And what do you want me to tell this man of yours when I write him tonight?"

"Tell him…tell him not to worry. I will talk to him as soon as I get home. And tell him…"

"I will deliver the message." He smiled. "Now I am going to get out of here so you really can get some rest. I am meeting Nick for a beer and I am gonna kick his butt in a few games of pool. Or maybe I should let him win. I owe him, I was so glad he was there when you needed him."

"Have some fun and then get some rest. Just don't worry about rushing back here in the morning. Relax a while at the condo."

He gave her a kiss and squeezed her hand. "See you tomorrow. Love you."

When he left, Molly leaned back on her pillow and closed her eyes. What if Eugenio decided it best to end things rather than have to deal with a middle-aged woman with a bad heart? She missed him terribly. Tears rolled silently down her cheeks. It would be the best thing in the world right now for her heart if she could see his face.

Molly was just finishing breakfast the next morning when the doctor came in. He pulled a chair up next to her bed and sat down. Adam had just come in and taken a chair.

"And how's my patient doing today?"

"You tell me." Molly smiled. Actually she was feeling pretty good. The nurse had gotten her up earlier and they had taken their walk down the hall and back and it felt good to stretch her legs. She was more than ready to get out of there and go home. She looked over at Adam. "It's okay, he can stay."

"The tests have all come back and I think that it is time for you to give up this bed to someone who really needs it. The thing is, Molly, you are going to require some surgery. At this point, I am looking at stints, but there is the possibility of CABG."

"Cabbage?"

47

He smiled. "It is coronary artery by-pass surgery. Pronounced: CABBAGE. It relieves angina pains, reduces risk of death from coronary disease. It means I am going to repair the blockage but it would require taking grafts from your leg and putting them in your heart. I want to see how the medication is going to work over the next 6 weeks. The surgery will be later in the summer but for now, the school year is over for you. There are only two weeks left and I am sure your students can email finals in, but I do not want you to return to campus until fall. I have a list of things for you, the nurse will go over them with you, but I just want you to get rest and take things in moderation. No lifting over 5 pounds, no vacuuming, no long flights of steps. Everything in moderation…sex is okay, but no running any marathons."

Adam had been sitting quietly by. "Doctor, what about travel?"

"Are you planning a trip soon?"

"Well…"

"She is planning a trip to Italy this summer."

"Well, I want to see you in two weeks and see how the medication is working. Let's wait and see until then. You suffered a mild heart attack but there was no damage to the heart. I want a check-up before you finalize any plans for travel."

He reached over and took her hand, "Molly, I am one hell of a doctor, and I have done these surgeries a hundred times. I know you are concerned because first, it is surgery and second, because it is your heart, but you will be fine." He stood up. "Do you have any questions?"

"Not right now but I am sure I will have a hundred of them later. I just need for all this to sink in for a bit."

"If you begin to worry, just call my office or my home number and we will talk about it but for now, rest, and start making a list of what you want to pack for Italy."

When the taxi pulled up in front of the brownstone, Nick and Andy were sitting on the steps. Molly stepped out of the cab and walked over and gave them each a hug. "What a nice welcome home." She started to walk up the steps but Adam took her arm. "No you don't, you heard the doctor." With that Nick and Adam swooped her up and carried her up the steps like she weighed nothing.

Adam unlocked the door and pushed it aside so she could walk in. It felt good to be home! "Good Lord!" Molly thought. "Never thought I would think that." She walked into the kitchen but Adam followed her.

"And just what do you think you are going to do?"

"It is almost noon. I thought I would make you boys some lunch."

"Oh no, you don't. You rest and we will take care of lunch. No arguments. I am going to make you some tea. Now, go and sit." Molly did as she was told. She sat by the window, but she was looking at the computer. She wanted to see if there was any message from Eugenio and she needed to write him and let him know she was home and alright.

"Here is your tea, Mom. We are going to get some take-out. What are you hungry for? How about some under-seasoned chicken, green Jell-O, and a small glass of milk?"

Nick looked puzzled. "What kind of diet is that?"

"The one I have been on for the last 5 days. I want real food. Surprise me."

"Back in a bit." The three men headed for the door but Adam walked back and leaned over to whisper, "Write Eugenio."

There were seven messages from Eugenio. Tuesday he wrote about his day and hoped to talk to her before he went to work, but if not, they would speak Wednesday. Wednesday morning there was a brief message saying he missed her. Thursday his letter sounded concerned. Had he said something to offend her, was she doing alright, had something happened why she did not write?

Friday was a long letter after getting an email from Adam. Saturday, he wrote of his concern and was anxious for her to come home so they could talk but not if she needed to rest. Possibly her son could let him know. And then just a short 'Take care, Bella.' And today he sent a note thanking Adam for letting him have the knowledge of his mother's health and he was happy that Adam was there to take care of her. But please, let him know of her progress.

She opened her Skype and instantly Eugenio came online. "Molly?"

"Yes, I am good and I have missed you."

"Turn on your camera, I need to see for myself that you are alright."

Molly wanted to run and change clothes and at least run a comb through her hair, but she did not want to wait. Eugenio was leaning back in his chair, smoking, but he leaned forward and smiled when he saw her.

"I have been so worried. Tell me, Molly, what the doctor say to you."

"Later, right now, just talk to me. I have missed you. I don't want to talk about doctors or hospitals or nurses…or green Jell-O."

"Green Jell-O, I no understand. I know of Jell-O but why green?"

"My least favorite and what I had every day on my tray for dessert in the hospital."

"Ah, you would like a lovely sweet tiramisu?"

"I would love to share a chocolate sundae with you."

"Yes, yes, I remember. Was a good day for us, Molly, I think about often. Only one thing that day I regret."

"Regret?"

"Yes, I regret that I did not kiss you that day. I think stupid! But some day, Molly, someday I want to kiss you, many times to make up for that day."

"Yes, many times." Molly smiled but she wondered if that would ever really happen.

"I have to go soon, Molly. I will be on duty soon, but I hate to leave you."

"I know, me too, but I am home now and we can talk whenever you have time. I obviously, am not going anywhere for a while. And with Adam watching over me, I won't be leaving the condo for a few days. He would make me stay in bed if he thought he could get away with it. He acts like a mother hen."

"I no understand mother hen."

"Very protective."

"Yes, yes is good. I still worry but I know that he will take care of you. I ask him to watch over you for me…and I pray that God will not take you from me."

"Thank you. I will follow orders and we will talk whenever you have time. And don't worry. I am fine, better now that I see you."

He blew her a kiss. "Ciao, Bella." He waved and was gone.

Molly stared at the blank screen. Eugenio had such faith in God. Molly had never been devout in her religion. She and

Sarah had talked about it one night as they walked. Sarah did not approve of what she called "front pew Christians"…the ones who hurried to get the front row every Sunday so everyone would see them, but failed to practice the values any other time. Sarah believed in Christian charity and kindness and a God who listened when she needed to talk. And hopefully, He would help. Molly seemed to have lost what little faith she had when Sarah died. She asked Sarah how she could be so faithful to a God who knew she was so ill. Sarah said God answers prayers, sometimes He just says no. "Besides," she added as she put her arm through Molly's as they walked, "You don't know what I prayed for."

Just then she heard the voices in the hall. Lunch had arrived! Real food again, Molly was excited at the thought of something good from the neighborhood!

Each was carrying a bag when they came in. "How much food did you get?" Molly laughed.

"We each headed a different direction: we have Chinese and Mrs. Fong sends good wishes and extra spring rolls. Nick brought homemade chicken soup from the station and Andy brought bread sticks and pizza. We didn't know what you were hungry for."

"Anything but green Jell-O."

Molly was up early. She needed a little time to prepare herself for Adam's departure. She wanted to go to the airport with him but he insisted she stay home because he would worry about her. But they had four days together, and Molly was happy for the time. He had gone out with

Nick and Andy the night before he had to leave. He wanted to stay home but when they dropped by, Molly said she was tired and going to bed so he should go out for a while. He had barely left her side since she had gotten home and he deserved a little fun on his last night.

After he left, she had made cookies and packed them in small tins and put them in his duffel bag. She had added her little message on each cookie, the way she had done when he was little. When she packed his lunch or sent him off on Boy Scout outings, she would write him notes. One day he told her that the other guys made fun of him and now that he was 12, she should probably stop. Instead they decided she would send "the message" by putting a thumb print on each cookie. He would always be her little boy!

He had come in about 1:00 a.m. and Molly heard him come in and check on her. She was just about to tell him good-night when he gently pulled the duvet up around her and lightly kissed her hair. "Love you, Mom" he whispered and then he went to his room. Molly wondered how many times she had done that to her children as they slept. She felt blessed to have such a loving son but also a little sad that he worried so much about her. It was him who needed to be watched over. She hated the idea of him having to go back but he said it was only another four months and he would be stateside again.

Yesterday at lunch, Adam had suddenly reached over and took her hand. "Mom, go to Italy."

Molly looked surprised but he continued. "I know Dad did not make life easy for you and I know my sister. It is time you do something for yourself. This man makes you happy.

54

You should go. Aunt Sarah would want you to go, for both of you. You don't have to run around like a crazy person and exhaust yourself. You can relax and spend an entire month enjoying yourself at your own pace. And spend some time with Eugenio. But remember, sex in moderation."

"Adam, Good Lord!"

"Seriously, Mom, I think he is a good man and it is so obvious that he cares for you. He said…" Adam stopped.

"He said? First of all, what did he say? And second, just when did he say it?"

"Well, we talked last night. I got up in the night and he was online. I asked him if we could talk a while. I know how things are but he makes you happy and I understand his life. I admit that I would like to see you in a nice normal relationship but you both deserve this. And who knows what will happen down the line. We both know that life is never what we want or expect it to be. I want you to go to Italy. If you don't, Aunt Sarah will come back and haunt you. Mom, do not pass up this chance for a little happiness."

Molly looked at this man sitting across the table from her. "When did you become so wise?"

"Well, I have always been a bit of a smart ass. Maybe it is just spreading. Honestly, I worry about you. I know you are a strong woman and you can take care of yourself. God knows it was pretty much just you and I when I was growing up, but please, let this man take care of you for a while. And you go and be with him, he needs you right now as well. And another thing…"

He took a drink of his Pepsi. "Amanda still wants to come and stay when I leave. Tell her no. And when she wants you to stay here instead of going to Italy, tell her no. And when she suggests that you take her along, tell her hell no!"

Molly laughed but she knew that Adam was right. "There is just one thing wrong with this whole discussion. We have talked about the trip Sarah and I were going to take but he hasn't said COME."

"He will, Mom. Say yes!"

Molly stood at the top of the steps and waved until Nick's car was out of sight and then she went in and opened the door to her condo. "Lucy," she began and then stopped. Nothing was going to take away the feeling of loneliness that washed over her. She closed the door and looked around the room. That breath of fresh air that she had felt while Adam was home was gone now. She sat by the window and felt the tears begin to flow. Then she looked over at the computer. On the front was a white piece of paper taped to the screen. She took it off and opened it. "I am not kidding, Mom, say yes." And in the lower left hand corner was a thumb print!

She wanted to talk to Eugenio but she did not want to let him see her like that. He did not need to have to try and comfort her, and God knows he did not need to see her with red eyes and a snotty nose!

Molly took a seat in front of the doctor's desk. She hated this waiting but the nurse had seemed pleased with the stress test and Molly was happy with the eight pounds she had lost. One hell of a lousy way to do it though…must have been all that green Jell-O. Maybe she would stock up…ah, no! Dr. Temple walked in and took a seat. He looked through the file the nurse had handed him. "So, how have you been feeling?"

"Actually, I have been feeling pretty good. I have been walking every day a bit, no lifting, no marathons."

"Then I would say the next thing you should be doing is packing for Italy. And I will see you again before you leave. The medication appears to be doing its job and we will decide our next step when you return."

Later that evening Molly wrote Adam and told him the results. She wanted to tell Eugenio but she was not sure what his reaction would be. What if he did ask her to come to Italy? Worse yet, what if he didn't. She went in and took a long hot shower and wrapped a towel around her body. As she walked into the bedroom, she glanced at the computer…there was a message so she walked over and sat down. The instant she was online, Eugenio sent a request to video chat. "I need to see you, Molly."

"No," she quickly responded.

"Why no? Are you not alone? Are you alright?"

"Just out of the shower, only wearing a towel and my hair is soaking wet."

"Molly, please, I need to see you."

"Are you sure?"

"Yes, please. I want to see how you are."

Molly pulled the towel tightly around her and raked her fingers through her hair.

Eugenio looked unshaven and very tired.

"What's wrong?"

"Nothing now, always is better when I see you." He smiled. "You are beautiful."

Molly never knew what to reply when he said things like this.

"I love your hair wet, is very curly and you look very good in a towel. I wish you were here. I want so much to touch you." He leaned back and sighed. "Tell me what the doctor say today."

"He said I am doing very well."

"Did he say you could travel?"

Molly's heart quite literally skipped a beat! "Well, it really didn't come up but I am not planning on going anywhere right now anyway."

"Ask him. Ask him if it is good that you can travel. We have been talking about this for a long time now. I want you

58

to come to Italy, to come to me. Is time for both of us, Molly. I may be deployed soon. Please, is time for us to be together. Come to me, Bella."

Molly looked around her condo and at the single plate she had set on the table. Then she looked at the picture of Sarah and her, that the waiter had taken the night they had gone to La Dolce Vita Americana, drank too much wine, and made a promise that they would go to Italy in the summer. She took a deep breath and leaned close to the screen. "Yes, I will come."

"Not just to make love, Molly. I want to be with you. We will talk and eat and I will show you Roma. And we will be happy."

Eugenio smiled. "I wish I could be there with you now, in Chicago. We could have good meal and I could take care of you."

"Isn't this a date?" Molly kidded.

"But is very cheap date. I can no spend money on you. And I cannot touch you."

"But good company. We have had so many coffees and so many meals together, many dates."

"Is not enough, Molly. I want to be near you. I want to touch your skin." He leaned back and lit a cigarette. "You look so beautiful to me."

"I am wearing a towel and my hair is soaking wet." Molly laughed.

"But I like…"

"Well, you might change your mind if you ever see me without the towel." Molly was joking but suddenly she wished, as she had so many times in her life, that she had chosen her words more carefully. Eugenio leaned forward in his chair. "I want to see you, all of you." He asked quietly.

Molly put her head down. Here was a man halfway around the world who could make her feel good about herself as no one had ever done before. Before she could answer, he said, "Is okay. I am always afraid I say the wrong thing and you will change your mind and no longer want me. You are the only good thing in my life right now and I long to be with you."

"Eugenio, I am not young and I am not sexy and I…"

"Stop! You are very beautiful to me, on the outside as you are on the inside. I find you desirable."

"But you might change your mind if you see me naked," she repeated.

Molly thought about all those times David had told her he was tired and would turn away when she tried to touch him. "Please Eugenio, I could not bear to see disappointment in your eyes. It would break my heart."

"I do not know so much of your life yet, but I am angry with the man who has made you feel this way. Is okay, I do not mean to make you feel uncomfortable. I will not ask you again and you can tell me when you are ready. It is just that I want you so much." He leaned back and closed his eyes. There was a sadness in his voice and it made Molly want to just hold him, feel close to him.

"Eugenio." She said softly. He opened his eyes. She stood up with no reservations. She unfolded the top of her towel and let it fall. She turned slowly and then cupped her breasts and let him see her nipples, hard with desire.

"Oh God, Molly, you are so beautiful. I want you, no, I need you. When you come to me, I will show you my desire for you. It has been a very long time since a woman wanted to make love to me."

Molly pulled her towel around her and sat down. "Not disappointed?"

"Why do you say such things? You are a woman with a lovely heart and soul and body. And seeing you only makes me want you more."

It has been such a long time since Molly had felt desire or desired. Could she actually be falling in love with this man? Someone she had shared a few hours in an airport with months ago and had not even kissed yet? Yet, Molly smiled, suddenly "yet" is becoming a reality.

***

Molly used to love the sunrise when she lived in the country, the shades of purple and pink and blues that blended together and then burst forth in that first bright ray of sunlight, making the world a place of peace and hope.

61

But here in the city, there was always that gray that hung over the city unless the sun was directly over-head and then it was all too soon gone again, hidden once more behind the tall buildings. There are no sunrises and sunsets when one lives in the city.

She had mentioned her unhappiness to Eugenio one evening and he had asked her what she had disliked about the city. She said she wasn't sure because the diversity and excitement and the sounds and tastes were amazing. Sarah used to say a person could be happy anywhere with the right person. Maybe she had just come to the city with the wrong person.

Eugenio reminded her of her unhappiness now. "What of Rome, could you be happy in Rome, Molly?"

"Yes," she answered, without any reservations. "I will be happy in Rome."

Eugenio smiled. "Is good for me to think of then, until you come. I have to go to work now, but we will talk tomorrow of your trip."

"Yes, tomorrow. I will see what I can find for an apartment. I have looked before but until now it was always just 'someday.' Have a good day at work. I will sleep tonight dreaming of Rome...with you."

"Ciao Bella...and Molly, thank you. You make me happy." He blew her a kiss and was gone.

Molly hadn't really thought about "Someday" for a very long time. She had stayed in Chicago because that is where

David wanted to be. And now, after all these years, it was where she worked and where she was paying for this condo. "SOMEDAY" disappeared after Sarah died and Molly had resigned herself to the fact that she would remain there. Where else would she go? She was close to retiring and maybe she would have grandchildren who would come to visit. But for now, she had a trip to Italy to plan...suddenly her mind began to race and tomorrow she would need to start making a list...so many things to do. She lie in bed that night letting the fantasy that began to manifest, take over. She would be published, she would love living in the city, but the city was Rome and she would be with Eugenio. And her children would bring her grandbabies to Rome to visit. Hey, she thought, this is my fantasy!!! She slipped out of bed and sat down at her desk. She opened the drawer and took out the calendar Sarah had given her. Actually Sarah had left it for her among some other things. It was in a manila envelope. Sarah's daughter had given it to her one afternoon. "Mom left this for you."

There was a note on the front: "MOLLY, you have to do this for both of us now! I am counting on you, Kiddo. Love, Sarah"

It was a calendar of Rome. She had shoved it into a drawer, not wanting to even look at it. She made a cup of tea and sat down on the couch. She slowly flipped through the pages. Some months were of places Molly knew, but some were just quiet city scenes. She turned to May. Tomorrow she would hang it over her desk. She finished her tea and took one more look at the picture. It was a simple scene of a stone wall with a single window. There was a flower box over-flowing with red flowers and ivy. Trastevere, somewhere in Trastevere, somewhere in Rome. She slept that night dreaming of her "someday"… when she would finally be able to collect that kiss she longed for since that day at the airport.

After Eugenio had returned from duty, he lit one last cigarette and stared at the blank screen. A feeling of relief came over him. He had been so worried, but Molly looked good, didn't she? Tired, but still his Molly. Soon he would be able to hold her close, look into her eyes and kiss her the way he wanted to that day in Atlanta. He took one last drag from his cigarette and put it out. He turned off the light and in the quiet of his small room, he thanked God again for not taking her from him.

Chapter 5

McGinty's Pub on East State Street had been the meeting place for the faculty at the college for many years. On Friday afternoons, co-workers would gather to celebrate birthdays, holidays, and sometimes, just because it was Friday. Being a small college, many friendships continued outside the walls of education. Molly and Sarah had joined in for years and most times their husbands would meet them later. After Matthew and David were out of the picture, they would still enjoy an occasional celebration. Now Molly looked at McGinty's as one of her safe havens just as the college had been for many years.

Illini College had become more than just a job to Molly over the years. She realized she was happy there. She was good at what she did and she was acknowledged there for her abilities and talents. A couple years ago, she was doing a visit to one of her students who was finishing up her teaching semester in a special education classroom. She helped as teachers and paras gathered up end of the year bags for the students. One young girl was sitting in the corner crying. Molly had inquired why she was so upset and the teacher said because she knows it is the end of the school year and she won't be back all summer. She doesn't want to go home. It is not good there and this is where she feels loved and gets attention and fed well. Later that afternoon, Molly stood at the window and watched as two teachers and two paras struggled to literally carry this girl out and put her on the bus. She was begging not to go. As Molly watched, tears ran down her face and she saw her own reflection in the window. Over the years, many times Molly had known exactly how this young girl felt.

One of the faculty had called and said they were sending a taxi for her at 3:00 p.m. to meet everyone at McGinty's. Finals were over and they were having a good Irish craic to celebrate. It would be good to see everyone again and she needed some time out. She had finished grading essays and posted her own grades and now her days and nights were spent in front of the computer planning her escape. A good glass of wine and some great company would be just what the doctor ordered, well, so to speak!

After a couple hours of laughing and telling year-end tales of woe and eating the best corned beef sandwiches Chicago had to offer, things had settled down. Some of the crowd had left for home, but a few had stayed around, no hurry to get out and face the rush hour traffic.

Molly took a sip of her wine. She knew that an Irish pub was probably not the best place to order wine, but sipping wine reminded her of Eugenio. She felt quite contented at that moment although she felt a small excitement growing in her to think that soon she would be sitting in a small sidewalk café sipping wine with Eugenio IN ROME!

Martin Astor came over and sat down next to her. He slid his arm across the back of her chair. "So, how are you, Molly?" Martin was a coach, a very married coach, who seemed to forget that after a few drinks. Before she could answer, he continued, "Been a pretty rough time for you." He let his hand lightly touch her shoulder. "David leaving and Sarah dying and the old ticker giving you problems. If there is anything I can do…"

Molly slid away. "Thanks Martin but I am fine. David has been gone three years now. I miss Sarah every day and the old ticker is fine. In fact, I am leaving soon on a trip to Italy."

"One of those bus tours? Maybe I should go along and add a little fun. Otherwise you are going to be stuck with a bunch of old ladies and in bed by 9:00 p.m. every night." His arm moved over and touched her shoulder again.

"Actually, Martin, as much as I appreciate your offer, it is not a tour. I am renting an apartment for a month in Rome."

"Well then, I definitely should come along."

"And" she continued, "I am meeting a friend there." She took a sip of her wine.

"Well, it looks like our little Molly is going to have an Italian booty call," he said much too loudly.

Molly finished her wine. She turned and smiled, "Ya never know, Martin." She slid out of her chair. "Time for me to head for home. It's been great to see you guys. I will get in touch when I get back." She picked up her purse and made her exit before there could be any questions. Over her shoulder she could hear Martin, "I think our little Molly has been keeping secrets."

"No, you jerk," she thought. "I just don't get drunk and tell everything I know." She hailed a taxi and climbed in. She was anxious to get home. She had things to do!

Molly spent the next day looking into apartments to rent. She was afraid that it was too late for her to find anything decent. But there were several places… running from a studio garret, that she was pretty sure she would never be able to stand upright in, to a three bedroom with a garden and swimming pool. She did a few virtual tours and had contacted a booking agent. Just as she was starting to feel overwhelmed, Livia sent an email. It was actually a place that belonged to her own cousin. The apartment was in Trastevere, the medieval part of the city, nestled along the south bank of the Tiber. It had a tiny patio and back yard. Her cousin had not even decided to rent it out yet, but Livia explained Molly's situation and she agreed to talk with her about the possibility. The problem was the one-bedroom situation; maybe she was being too hopeful that this trip would be more than it was. She should probably talk to Eugenio first. Eugenio! What if this was one of those, "I am inviting you because I know you will never come" invitations? No, this man was not one to play games. She stopped and leaned back in her chair. "Just stop!" she thought, "You are going to make yourself crazy!" Like Adam said, it is a month in Italy! She sat down and began to type.

"Dear Mrs. Rossini…"

It was early afternoon when she received an answer. The apartment was available and very reasonable since she was taking it for a month. The back yard connected to her own, but there was a gate between the two. She added that she did have two children and Molly could easily shoo them home and close the gate if they came to visit. She sent pictures and Molly was very happy with what she saw. She wrote a reply, took a deep breath, and hit SEND. It was

68

probably the bravest thing she had ever done without Sarah. She wondered what Eugenio would say when he read her next email. Well, with or without a lover, she was going to Italy. "Well, my darling Sarah, I am going to Italy just like we planned. God, I wish you were going with me." Molly felt her chest beginning to tighten but she wasn't worried. She knew the difference between a heart attack and the ache caused by loss. She looked up at the calendar above her desk. That lovely quiet window somewhere in Rome. Two weeks from today, I will be there!

It was as if he knew because suddenly a message came on her screen. "Molly? Are you there?"

"Yes, but only for the next two weeks."

"Why, what has happened? Are you alright?"

Molly felt guilty for a moment. She shouldn't tease a man who struggled with English as he sometimes does. She quickly answered. "No, I am fine, but in two weeks I will be in Italy."

"Do you have time to talk, Molly, I need to see you."

Molly ran her fingers through her hair and turned on her Skype.

"Tell me, tell me everything."

"Well, I found an apartment and I talked to the woman today and told her I would take it for a month. I leave the first of June. It is in Trastevere and has a small patio and back yard."

Eugenio smiled. "I will like anywhere I can be with you. And I will pay for half of your rent. I want this to be for both of us for a whole month. I insist. You know I can only come to you for three days a week, but I promise I will make them happy times for you. The other days you can rest and write and have no worries. I promise I will not ask anything from you that you are not wanting.

Molly laughed. "And I will promise you the same thing."

He read her reply and then stopped for a moment as if he did not understand and then he smiled. "Si, Si, but there is nothing you could ask of me that I would not do for you. Or with you. This makes me very happy. And you, does it make you happy?"

"Very."

"Good, then we have many things to talk about if you are not too tired. I know is late for you. I just return from work, but suddenly I am not tired. This is something I have thought about many times."

"Me too. And yes, many things to talk about and do. Two weeks doesn't give me a lot of time."

"But the doctor is very sure you will be alright to travel. I do not want you to come if it could cause you harm."

"My darling Eugenio, don't you know, there is nothing better for my heart than you. Now, I have many questions for you."

***

Molly dreaded the conversation she knew she was about to have with her daughter. Amanda had come over a couple times since Adam had left. She had been pretty frazzled with all the studying for finals but now it was over. Molly hoped that Amanda had gotten some sleep and was now excited that in just three days she was graduating. It has been a long hard battle for everyone concerned but Amanda had done well. Molly would be a very proud parent on Saturday when she sat in the audience and watched her daughter graduate. Molly also hoped that she was going to take her mother's news without too much drama.

Amanda came into the restaurant and waved when she saw her mother. Molly was glad that Eddie had not invited himself along. Molly really wanted to talk to her daughter without feeling it was a two against one battle. "Mom, you are looking great. How are you?"

"Good and how are you now that finals are over?"

"Relieved. I didn't think I would ever get through all this."

"Are you excited about graduation?"

"Yeah, I really am. You always said it is your own personal 'look what I did' and I am really looking forward to having the diploma in my hand. I talked to Daddy and he and Tiffany are coming. I wish you had someone to be there with you, Mom. But we will all be together later for dinner afterwards. Daddy is taking us out, but he said you are welcome to join us. I wish Adam was home. It would be easier for you since Tiffany will be there."

"Actually, that is what I want to talk to you about."

"You are coming, aren't you? Mom, please, you have to have dinner with us." Molly knew that tone and was well acquainted with that pout.

"Yes, Amanda, I will be there and we will all have dinner together. And then I am going away for a while."

"Away? What do you mean away? You just had a heart attack."

Molly took a sip of her ice tea. "My heart is fine and I am going to take that trip to Italy that Sarah and I had talked about."

"Mom, are you asking me to go to Italy with you? Is that my graduation present?" There were two things that would always ring true with Amanda. First, she loved presents and second, she assumed everything was about her.

"Amanda, you know I love you, but no, it is not an invitation and it is not your graduation present. I have a friend I am going to be with."

"A friend? Who is she? Someone from work?" Her voice was full of disappointment.

"Here we go" Molly thought. "My friend is a man, a lovely man who lives in Italy."

"MOTHER! What are you thinking? Where did you meet this man? No, wait, please tell me you did not meet him online."

"Amanda, calm down. I met him in Atlanta. His name is Eugenio and he is in the military. He is 50 and…"

"Fifty? Mother, he is 6 years younger than you. What are you thinking?"

"Have you forgotten that your father is thirty-five years older than Tiffany?"

"What do you REALLY know about this man? Have you ever thought that he only wants your money?"

"I doubt it, I don't have much thanks to your father and your education. And is it so hard to believe that he may just want me?"

Amanda's voice softened and she reached over and took her mother's hand.

"Mom, I know it hasn't been easy for you since Daddy left and it has been awful since Aunt Sarah died, but you can't just travel halfway around the world because you are lonely. Certainly, there is someone here you can date."

"My dear sweet daughter," Molly began, "I could date here if I wanted to. I do have men ask me out. But none of them have interested me."

"I know it must be hard to replace Daddy."

"Not that difficult" Molly thought but instead she just smiled and said, "Your father and I have both moved on. He has Tiffany now and I am off to explore my options."

"But do you have to go so far? What if, Heaven forbid, you fall in love with this man? How are you going to be able to come back here and forget about him? You have a life here, Mom."

"Whatever happens, I will be okay. I promise you. Now, let's order lunch."

"Well, Eddie and I are going to come over and stay at the condo while you are gone. It is the least we can do."

"No, Dear, you will be busy finding a job and getting your own life organized. I have paid your rent until the end of June, but after that you will be on your own. The condo will be fine while I am gone. My neighbors will keep an eye on it for me."

The waitress walked up. "May I take your drink order, Ladies?"

"Yes, I will have another ice tea." Molly smiled at Amanda, ignoring the frown on her face. "And what would you like, Amanda?"

Later the next day when she received a letter from Adam, she had to laugh when he said he was proud of her that she didn't give in when Amanda pouted. Amanda must have gone straight home and emailed him.

On Saturday, Molly sat quietly and watched as Amanda made her way across the stage and took her diploma. She saw David looking at her out of the corner of his eye, but she did not turn her head. She had glanced over a few times and Tiffany was busy texting while David's eyes were focused on the stage. Molly smiled and turned back to listen to the speaker.

Molly did give David credit; he had taken them to a very nice restaurant for dinner. And again, Molly had to smile when they brought Tiffany's food and she had taken her gum out and put it on the side of her plate like a kid. David asked Molly how she was feeling and she had told him she was fine. When she mentioned she was not teaching any summer classes, he said that she would have plenty of time to rest over the summer. It was then Molly could have kissed Eddie. He said, "Hell, Molly is heading for Italy next week. She found herself a fifty-year-old Italian stallion."

That seemed to get Tiffany's attention. "Molly, do tell!"

"There really isn't much to tell. I met Eugenio in Atlanta and he asked me to come to Italy. Sarah and I had talked about going this summer and Adam convinced me I should go."

"Molly, what are you thinking? You can't go running off to Italy to meet a man you barely know."

"David," Tiffany said, "Where is your sense of romance? I think it is romantic. I am so jealous."

"Well, I think it is ridiculous. Mom is an older woman and here she goes off to spend a month with a man she hasn't

75

even slept with yet. What happens when he sees you naked? You are 56 years old."

Molly set her fork down and looked across the table at her daughter. "Amanda, this is not the time or place for this discussion. Nor is this a conversation I am going to have with my daughter in front of her boyfriend and my ex-husband. And he has seen me naked and thinks I am beautiful. So please, let's change the subject." She took a bite of her shrimp. "They do a wonderful scampi here. I will have to remember that."

"Hey, I think your mom is pretty hot for her age." Eddie added between bites.

"Shut up, Eddie," David and Amanda said at the same time.

On the taxi ride home, Molly thought about her evening. It was really the first time she had had to spend any time with David since he had moved out. Most of their conversations had been about the kids or something that he had decided he wanted after the divorce. Molly probably would have given in if it wasn't for Sarah. She told her to stop being so nice and get pissed off. The man was a cheat and a liar and he gets exactly what the judge gave him and nothing more…oh, and Tiffany, which is gonna come back to bite him in the ass someday. Tonight, she had looked at this man who had been such a big part of her life and now she realized she felt nothing for him. At 10:00 p.m., he was complaining about being tired and wanting to go home. Tiffany, on the other hand, had been smiling coyly at the handsome young bartender. Yes, Sarah, "and he has Tiffany…and she has David." She leaned back and smiled to herself… "And I am going to Italy to be with Eugenio. I win."

***

There is a brief few seconds in the morning that Molly would lie in bed with her eyes shut, those few seconds between consciousness and dreams with the light beaming across her face and the sunlight feeling warm on her eye lids. White lights, tiny explosions. Most people try to clear their heads and wake up but Molly would lie quietly and enjoy the array of illumination before she opened her eyes and started another day. For such a long time, it was the best start of her days. But today was different. Today, even though she had tossed and turned all night, the instant the sun streamed across her face, she was awake. The most she had slept all night was about three hours. At one point, she got up for a drink and felt like a kid, too excited to sleep the night before a vacation or school trip. She glanced over at the suitcase on the floor. Yes, today was different. Today she was flying to Italy…to Eugenio!

Molly sat on the edge of her bed and stared at her suitcase. The last time she had taken her suitcase out, it had been to fly to Atlanta. Seven months, well six months and 26 days, but then who is counting. How she had managed to survive those long months and an entire cold winter without Sarah, she didn't know.

The joy she had felt just a minute ago suddenly dissipated. Would Sarah have taken this trip without Molly? Molly had to smile, she knew exactly what Sarah would say, "You bet your ass! And Italy with a man like Eugenio waiting for you. I love you, Kiddo, but I'm dead. Go for both of us and have the time of your life."

An hour later, there was a tap at the door. Nick had insisted on taking her to the airport. He picked up the bags and looked around. "Got everything?"

"I hope so."

"Well, I promise to keep an eye on everything while you are gone. And water the plants. Now come on, Miss Molly, you have a plane to catch."

Chapter 6

After the pilot had turned off the sign, Molly sat quietly and waited until most of the passengers had moved quickly toward the exit before she reached up to take her bag from the over-head rack. For the first time since she left Chicago, she felt anxious. As she had looked out the window as the plane lifted and she saw Chicago disappear as they rose through the clouds, Molly felt very relaxed. She leaned back and closed her eyes. The last two weeks had been busy and it was almost a relief to finally hear Nick close her door and check the lock. But the realization hit her when she felt the wheels touched down…she was actually in Rome!

She waited in line to go through customs. "What is the purpose of your visit?"

"Holiday."

"And how long will you be staying?"

"A month."

The lady stamped her passport and slid it back through the tiny window. "Enjoy your holiday," she said without even looking at Molly again, she motioned for the next person.

"I wonder how many times a day she says that?" Molly thought. "And how many times she really means it?" It didn't matter. She said thank you as she followed the rest of her fellow travelers to get their luggage.

She moved through the terminal, following the signs to the train station. She walked through the glass walkway and looked out…looked pretty much like every other terminal she had ever been in, but the people around her happily chatting in Italian made her think, "Toto, I don't think we are in Kansas anymore."

She bought her ticket and took a seat on the train. As the train began to move toward the city, Molly began to worry. What if he didn't come? What if he changed his mind? Ok, just stop! He is not David, she reminded herself. He will come! She watched as each stop brought her closer to Trastevere…and Eugenio!

Molly stepped out of the terminal into the warm morning sun and looked around. It was a busy square. The train station dominated the area, but buses also made a stop there. There was a small grocery store and a café. On the corners there were two makeshift shops. One was selling purses and sunglasses under an umbrella and the other had several racks of cool gauze blouses and dresses under a long awning. She crossed the street, waiting for the tram to pass and began to follow Livia's map to the apartment.

It was a beautifully-shaded residential street and transportation was certainly near-by. Just as Molly crossed the street, a young woman on a small motorbike pulled up. "Molly?"

"Yes."

"I am Livia. We have perfect timing." She parked her bike along the sidewalk and walked over and gave Molly a kiss on each cheek. "Welcome to Roma." She opened the wrought iron gate to a small walkway leading up to a heavy wooden door. She opened it to reveal a charming apartment, bigger than Molly had expected.

The living room had a cathedral ceiling and two ceiling fans. The kitchen was a small cove and the counter had a number of appliances. The bedroom had a lovely queen sized bed. There were two sets of patio doors, from the kitchen and from the bedroom that opened onto a small patio and back yard. The entire area was closed in by a tall brick wall covered with ivy. There were huge pots with lemon trees and cactus.

"Does it meet with your approval?"

"Oh yes, it is perfect."

"I have another appointment but Gina said she will give you a chance to get settled in and then she will come over and answer any questions and help you with any needs you may have. There are drinks in the refrigerator and some pastries on the counter that she brought over this morning. Here is my card and we will talk soon." She headed for the door and then turned, "You will be happy here, Molly, this is a nice place." And she was gone.

Molly kicked off her sandals and pulled her suitcase through to the bedroom. She stopped and looked around the room. It was decorated in cool greens, very peaceful. Then she looked at the bed…even the sight of it made her suddenly nervous. What if he doesn't come? Molly leaned against the doorway… she was being silly. She knew he would come and then…she went over and sat on the edge of the bed. And then??? She lay back on the bed and closed her eyes. Yes, and then…

Molly suddenly realized that she was hungry and she went to the kitchen. She opened a Coke and took the plate of pastries out on the patio. It was warm, but the covered patio was pleasant. There was a note attached to the plate with a bow. "Prego, Molly." Yes, she decided, she was going to like it here.

The gate at the back of the yard opened and Molly turned to see a young dark haired woman walk through. "Molly, are you busy? I am Gina."

"No, please, come and sit. I was just having the snack you left for me. Thank you. It was very kind of you."

Gina leaned over and kissed Molly on each cheek. "It is lovely to meet you…I hope everything is suitable."

"Yes, it is more than I expected."

"I wanted to have something here for you before you go to the store for groceries. There is a small shop at the train station, but also, very near there is a large more modern plaza with a supermarket. I left you directions for everything on the desk, but if you have questions, please just ask."

"I am just excited to finally be here after all these years of dreaming, and the apartment is more than I ever hoped for."

"When my husband and I were first married, we lived here. My husband's parents built it as a separate home next to theirs for his grandmother after his grandfather passed away. They wanted her to be close, but wanted her to have a home of her own. When Grandma Eva died, we moved in. About the time my daughter was born, my in-laws decided to move to Sorrento and we moved into the big house next door. They bought an apartment house near the beach so we have a home there as well. My husband works very long hours Monday through Thursday, so we may have long week-ends out of the city with the children and family. In a few years, we will move to Sorrento as well. My husband's family are barristers, lawyers, and when his father retires, he wants his eldest son to take the main offices in Sorrento. It will be good to leave the city. I love Rome but a small city will be better for all of us." She walked to the refrigerator and took a Coke.

She took a long drink. "One of my guilty pleasures when the children are not near-by. I am sorry if I go on but it is nice to speak English with someone. I came to Rome as a student but I am from Manchester. Marc won my heart and I have lived here eight years now. I do miss English. I teach my children and Bea does very well and Alex is beginning to learn now. It makes my mother happy. She was very sad when I first came but she knows I love Marc and he gave her two beautiful grandchildren for her to come and visit. She has even learned some Italian. He gives her big hugs and she frowns and pretends to be annoyed but they adore each other." She took another drink. "Mr. Marino, has he been your friend a long time?

"I met him last fall in Atlanta."

"Do you plan to marry? Oh dear, I am sorry, Marc says I ask too many questions sometimes."

"No, it is good to have someone to talk with. My best friend passed away last year and I miss her very much. And then I met Eugenio and we became friends. Sarah and I had planned on coming to Italy and I gave up the dream, but Eugenio said I should come for both of us."

"I notice when you spoke of your friend, you touched the necklace you wear."

"Yes, it was Sarah's favorite. When I told Sarah's daughter I was coming to Italy, she sent it to me to wear."

"I think your friend will be happy that you have come and you'll have someone here to share the time with."

"Yes, I am sure she is. And she would approve of Eugenio. He is a dear sweet man and he is very lonely as well. I am divorced, but he is still married. I know that sounds awful but…"

"Oh no, I should not have asked. Italians, they do not divorce as much as in England or America. They separate and divorce only as a last resort. They are living too close to the Pope, I think." She smiled.

Molly laughed. "Yes, that is probably it. I was married for 30 years and it seems like a lifetime ago. The thing about never really being in love, like you should be when you marry, is that you aren't sure what you should be missing. When it ends, and you are spending your Saturday nights alone, eating Ben & Jerry's out of the carton and watching old movies alone, it is no big deal, because you have been doing it for years. It makes you wonder how many others there are just like you. Who have been dumped or worse, traded in for a younger model."

"Or women stay because they feel it is their duty."

"Yes, those women who cared and nurtured and waited, hoping for their turn. And then one day, they realized it was never going to happen, but they stay…out of loyalty or maybe even love. But THEN, there are all those older couples you see, still holding hands and happy just to be together. Still obviously in love. You never know."

"Did you date after your divorce?"

Molly laughed. "Well, I did go on a few dates because my friend insisted. Let's see, there was Larry, who cried whenever he spoke of his ex-wife and he spoke of her all through dinner. There was Tony, who called me at 3:00 a.m. the night after we had gone out for dinner and wanted to come by. Mike, the man who lives in my brownstone, who thought we would be perfect together. I could join his bowling leagues, all three of them. Oh, and he is a vegan and he thinks chocolate is the invention of the devil. Oh yes, perfect! I haven't dated in a couple years."

"Well, I hope that your Eugenio will be your happily ever after."

"I am afraid I am too old for fairy tale endings."

"No, Molly, never too old for love, because true love is like Roma, it is eternal."

A young girl poked her head through the gate. "Mrs. Rossini, we are back from the park," she said in Italian.

"Molly, I have wonderful children but they are very social and if they come to visit you, please just shoo them home to their mother. Bea will probably be over asking if you would like to have tea."

"Well, then, maybe I will have to have you and your daughter over for tea soon."

"I miss my English teas. My mum and I were in London once and she took me to Harrods' for High Tea. I remember wearing my favorite dress and she let me wear a touch of pink lipstick. I felt very grown-up. I hope to do that with my own daughter someday."

"Well, until then, I shall invite you both for High Tea here and we shall do it right with hats and gloves."

"Oh please, do not bother. You are on holiday."

"Gina, please, I am alone for three or four days a week and it would be fun. Maybe next week."

"Then we would love to come."

"I will send an invitation."

Gina finished her drink and stood up. "Motherhood calls. It was lovely to meet you, Molly, tomorrow we go to Sorrento but I will stop by and answer any questions before we go."

She leaned over and gave Molly a kiss on each cheek and smiled. "Relax and enjoy the time with your Eugenio. We are right here if you need anything." Molly stood and as they walked to the gate, Gina slipped her arm through Molly's. "I am happy you are here." She turned and walked through the gate. "Ciao, Molly," and was gone.

Molly took the other pastry from the plate and took a bite. She hoped that Gina had not made these herself and that she had purchased them at a nearby bakery. They were delicious and she would love to have more over the course of her stay.

"Men," she pondered. "Of course Sarah and I did have men in our lives." Sarah used to say they had Ben and Jerry and then there was Mr. Cherry Garcia. Even on the nights when they were at opposite ends of the city, they would sit in their pajamas and talk online or on the phone and eat ice cream. But Molly remembered the night Sarah had just shown up at her door. When Molly answered the door, Sarah held up that all-too-familiar white bag. "Sorry about the hour."

"What's going on? You okay?"

"Ben and Jerry and Mr. Garcia first." She headed for the kitchen and came back with 2 spoons. She took a seat on the couch and handed Molly a carton. "Have you ever wondered how many gallons of this stuff we have shared over the years?"

"I wonder how many new flavors they will invent to tempt us."

"That's the thing, Moll," Sarah said quietly. "You will have to carry on the tradition without me. I have cancer and it's bad."

Molly felt like someone was holding her heart so tightly that she couldn't breathe. It would be too painful to take even one more breath. "Oh, my God." Molly got up and walked over and put her arms around her friend's shoulders.

"It's okay, Moll. That's why I am here. I spent the last four hours crying and being angry with God. Now I feel like throwing things…so I came to your house. No sense busting up my own things." She forced a laugh. "Now sit down and eat your ice cream. Tomorrow we will deal, tonight we eat!"

They had spent the rest of the night watching 'P.S. I Love You' and pretending that the tears were over the movie they had already seen a dozen times. Sarah had finally gone in and lay down in the guest room. Molly went in and lay down next to her. "I wish…"

"I know." Sarah reached over and took her hand and that's the way they fell asleep. They really didn't need the words.

Sometime before daylight Molly had slipped off the bed and gone into the kitchen. She made a cup of tea and sat by the window, watching the early rays of light struggle up through the tall buildings and send a tiny stream of light across the room before falling asleep in the chair.

She woke again to that wonderful scent of Sarah's baking. She walked into the kitchen to see Sarah wiping flour from the table. "What on earth are you doing?"

"I needed to. I needed to punch something so the scones may be a little tough from over-kneading. And we need to eat because we need to make plans and we can't do this on empty stomachs. Make coffee."

They had talked all day and they made plans to finish Molly's book. Later that night they had gone out for pizza and Sarah had chatted happily about their trip to Italy. And later they had just walked, arm in arm, around the quiet streets, not talking, just walking. Finally, Molly asked if she was getting tired. Sarah stopped and turned to her, "Do not do this, Molly. Do not baby me. I'm okay and when I am no longer okay, I will tell you. Don't watch for signs. I will tell you. I promise."

It was a week later when Sarah called and asked her if she wanted to come over for pasta; she was working on a new recipe. The moment Molly had knocked, the door opened. "I am going to lose my hair, Moll! I love my hair!"

"You can have some of mine. I have enough for both of us." Molly held up the white bag and her copy of 'P.S. I LOVE YOU.' She walked in and put her arm around Sarah's shoulder and kicked the door shut with her foot, shutting out the rest of the world for a few hours.

Molly wiped the tears from her face and looked at her watch. Eugenio would be here in four hours. And she needed to get busy!

Molly took a quick shower and fixed her make-up. It had been a very long day with the time change, but the idea of Eugenio being there soon excited her.

Molly walked past the train station, down the steps and through a wide tunnel. It was like she had stepped out of ancient Rome and into a modern city. The traffic was heavy at that time of the day and the sidewalk cafes were full of people enjoying cool drinks and coffee. The scent of strong Italian coffee caught her as she walked by. "I could use one of those!" she decided.

She walked over to the big supermarket and bought meat, olives, wine, cheeses, and two bottles of Moscato. Three euro and seventeen for a bottle of Moscato. She hoped it was good because at that price, she would be making that a staple at the apartment. The Moscato she drank at home was $18.00 a bottle. She passed a small fruit and vegetable market and stopped for some cantaloupe and lemons. Again, she was accosted by the smell of coffee. There was a small café next door. Molly stopped for a quick cup of coffee. She decided she needed to just sit and relax a moment. She took her latte and was about to take a seat under the awning on the sidewalk when a large woman took her arm.

"Darling, y'all don't wanna sit none in Italy. They make you pay more. And the coffee is like drinkin' pure chicory."

"Thank you," Molly said politely and then watched as the woman walked away before going over and taking a seat. Even in the heat of the day, the coffee tasted good. AND, she was drinking it IN ITALY. She watched the people hurry by, some stopping at the coffee bar for a quick "shot of coffee" and then went on their way. But Molly wanted to savor the moment and the taste. She raised her cup and didn't care who was watching, "Here's to you, Sarah, God, how I wish you were here."

"The waiter came out to clear the table next to her. He smiled and in broken English, he introduced himself and extended his hand. "I am Marcello. Are you a tourist?"

"Actually I am here for a month. I am Molly."

She extended her hand to shake his but he took her hand and kissed it lightly. "Very good. You come often."

"I think I am going to like it here," she thought as she walked back to the apartment. She arranged the lemons in a bowl and set them on the patio table. She loved the lemon trees in the back yard but she didn't want to pick the fruit. She checked her watch, still two hours until Eugenio was due to arrive. She unpacked her suitcase and went in and brushed her teeth again and ran a comb through her hair. The time was crawling. 6:15, 6:20…he said between 6:30 and 7:00 p.m., didn't he? She went into the bedroom and put on some more perfume. "Perfect," she said out-loud. Now I officially smell like a French whore."

Across the street, Eugenio was leaning against a street light, looking at the door to the apartment. What if she hadn't come? Or what if he sees disappointment in her eyes when she sees him again in person? He took a last drag of his cigarette and threw it down. It was too late now! He threw his backpack over his shoulder and walked across the street.

Molly jumped at the sound of the doorbell. She ran through the living room and then stopped and took a breath and reached for the doorknob.

Eugenio stepped in, leaving his bag on the sidewalk. He stood in front of her and looked into her eyes. "You are so beautiful. I worry you would not come. That you changed your mind."

Molly reached out and touched his face, not even knowing where to begin.

"Now I fix what I did not do in Atlanta," he cupped her face in his hands and kissed her, a soft gentle kiss, more like a whisper than a touch. And then he put his arms around her and held her close. "I worry that the trip is too much for you."

"I am fine. In fact, I have never felt better. Bring your bag in and I will show you the apartment."

He stood looking out at the patio. "Do you like it?" Molly asked.

"I like anywhere I am with you, Molly."

They walked into the bedroom and Molly sat on the bed while he set his bag down. He sat down next to her. "Is okay?"

Molly smiled, "Is okay."

Eugenio took her in his arms and laid her gently back on the bed. The worry and embarrassment that had caused so many restless nights for both of them disappeared. It began with soft sweet kisses. Molly was silent, watching his face as he began to unbutton her blouse to expose the lace beneath. As his lips moved slowly across her neck, his fingertips slid gently over her nipples and she could feel the heat of his hands through the thin lace.

All the months she had dreamed of this moment and now it was finally just the two of them. Molly pressed her head back into the pillow, enjoying the sensation as his fingers ran across the top of her bra and then slid back the material so his lips could kiss her bare skin. He cupped each breast, running his tongue slowly over her hardened nipples before moving his lips down across her stomach until his cheek brushed against the top of her waistband. Again he asked, "Is okay Molly. Is it what you want?"

Molly scooted off the side of the bed and Eugenio lie quietly watching as Molly stood before him. She unhooked her bra and leaned forward slightly, letting her breasts fall free. She had been so worried about taking her clothes off in front of Eugenio at all, much less in the light of day. So many years with David, thankful for the heavy drapes in their bedroom, shutting out the lights, feeling self-conscience of her own body. But here, with this man, she felt desirable. She stepped out of her skirt and lay next to him.

"I need to make love to you, Molly. I have wanted this for a very long time."

Molly moved close to him and began to kiss his neck. "And I need you," she whispered. Eugenio moved to the side of the bed and took off his heavy boots. Then he stood and removed his shirt and camo pants before moving over and sitting next to her on the bed. "Close your eyes," and he began exploring her body, touching her hair and face with

93

his fingertips. He caressed her neck and her nipples and her stomach. He ran his hands down the outside of her thighs and calves. And then, as if he was trying to memorize every inch of her body, he slowly began to move his hands up her legs. She parted her legs slightly and his fingers moved up, feeling the heat from her skin as they made their way between her thighs.

He pushed aside the thin strip of lace and Molly felt a wave of desire rush through her as his fingertips brushed against the soft damp hair and then, as if he were afraid it would break at the touch, he let them slide over her clit and find their way inside her. Molly opened her eyes and reached down and took his hands.

She pulled him down next to her, feeling his need for her as she pressed her body against his. She reached down and caught the band of his underwear with her thumb and pulled them down slightly and let her hand slide down inside. She had known since that night online when he had become aroused that he was well-built but she had no idea. She lifted slightly as he pulled her panties down. She began to stroke him, slowly at first, feeling him grow harder in her hand. Eight inches, perfectly shaped, and all hers!

He rolled over and lifted himself over her. His cock slid down her stomach and pushed deep inside her. Molly drew her legs up and wrapped them around his waist and arched her back, wanting him deeper inside her with every stroke. "Oh fuck!" escaped from her lips.

"I cum for you, Molly. Only for you."

He rolled over on his side, holding her close, and kissing her hair. Molly was quiet, still feeling as though something had stimulated every nerve in her body. Suddenly Eugenio rose up on one elbow and turned her face to him. She could see the concern in his face. "I am so sorry; Molly are you alright? I should have been more gentle."

"Eugenio, please, I am fine. In fact, I have never felt better." She smiled and kissed his cheek.

"Was good for you?"

"Worth that long trip I made to get here. And not just this, Eugenio. Being here with you is unbelievable, but of course this makes it perfect."

Eugenio brushed the hair from across her cheek and kissed her. "Yes, for me too. You make me happy. Next time we will take more time and I will not cum so quickly. I want this to be right for you. We have the next three days to be together. But now we need food. To keep up our strength."

Molly laughed. "This is going to be a fabulous month."

Chapter 7

The sun was down so the yard was a quiet shaded place, where the city was blocked out by the tall brick wall. It was as if they had found a place just for them. Eugenio opened a bottle of wine while Molly put together a light meal. It was as if no time had passed since their meeting in Atlanta. The difference is the looks and the smiles that passed between them now, and the fact that Molly's heart pounded in her chest every time he would lean over and kiss her.

"Tomorrow I show you La Citta Eterna."

"Why 'the eternal city'?"

"Has been that name since the beginning. The story is about twins, Romulus and Remus. Their mother was Rhea Silvia, the daughter of Numitor, King of Alba Longa. Before their conception, Rhea's uncle killed his brother and took power. He killed all male heirs and forced Rhea to become a Vestal Virgin, sworn to chastity. But Rhea gave birth to twins, whose father was either the god Mars or the demi-god Hercules. When the twins were born, Uncle Amuluis had them abandoned in the Tiber River to die. A she-wolf finds them, suckles them, and then a woodpecker feeds them. When they are older, they decide to build a new city. Roma was founded April 21, 753 BC. So much of Rome today is very old or built around ancient Rome and legends and myths. Lord Byron wrote, "When the Colosseum falls, Rome shall fall. And when Rome falls – the World.""

"You have read Byron?"

"And Keats. He is buried here. If you would like, we visit his grave tomorrow."

Molly smiled, "So, you aren't just another pretty face. Tell me more."

Eugenio leaned over and kissed her. It was good that he would teach her of Rome, first because it is the city he loves, but also because he wants her to think he is a man of education.

He continued, "For nearly 3,000 years, Rome has been the center of love and life at its best…and its worst, and a million in-betweens. It is called the Eternal City because to visit Rome and not fall in love and not hold it in your heart forever is nothing less than a miracle. Some cities are female in nature, but Rome is masculine. He is like a haunting memory of a lost love. He will invade your thoughts, fill your senses, fulfill your desires, and awaits your return with hope and anticipation."

Molly could not wait to begin her exploration of this city. She wanted to experience Rome and feel all those things, but she knew when she returned home, it would be Eugenio who invaded her thoughts and filled her senses. But for tonight, she was quite content, no happy, just to be with this man. They talked and finished their wine. Molly stifled a yawn.

"Is not late, but I think you should rest for now. I don't want you to tire yourself. It has been a very long day for you. I worry about you, so please, is time for bed."

When Molly came out of the bathroom, Eugenio was already in bed. When she lay down next to him, he turned and took her face in his hands. "Molly, thank you for coming here to be with me. I will try to make your time here good for you."

She leaned over and kissed him. "It is already perfect." Molly was very tired and as much as she would have loved to have stayed awake every minute she was with Eugenio, not wanting to waste even a second with him, she closed her eyes and feeling him close to her, she fell asleep.

Sometime before daylight Molly woke and looked over at the man sleeping next to her. He was lying flat on his back, all tucked in, looking very military even in his sleep. She slid over and carefully put her arm under his pillow and pressed against him. He stirred slightly. "Are you feeling alright, Bella?"

"Yes, I am fine. Go back to sleep." and she kissed his shoulder.

He turned and kissed her, first a soft kiss but then he felt all those urges he had felt so often as he lay alone at night in the barracks move through him. He put his arms around her and covered her face with kisses, then moved down her neck. Through the sheer material of her nightshirt, he began to caress her breasts. She sat up and pulled the nightshirt over her head and leaned back. This time he began to kiss them, feeling the soft, warm flesh against his lips. He let his fingertips find each nipple and guided it into his mouth. Molly moaned and the sound of her pleasure made his hands tremble. He began to nibble lightly, feeling each nipple harden with longing. Eugenio rose up and pushed back the covers. They slid off the end of the bed into a pile on the floor. He kissed her thighs and then moved them apart with his hands. He let his tongue wander upward until his cheek touched the soft hair and let his tongue slide into the warm wet flesh that he had longed to taste and savor. When neither of them could wait any longer, Eugenio rolled over on his back and Molly slipped her leg across his and sat looking down at him. Without a word, she slid up and sat across him. He pressed against her stomach and she raised her hips slightly and let his waiting cock find its way home. Her hips rising slowly, she arched her back and felt him deep inside her. For all the reasons why they shouldn't be there together, there was only one that trumped all the others. This just felt right! Moments later, Eugenio whispered, "Sleep well, Bella, tomorrow I show you Rome."

The next morning, they left the apartment early. It was still cool and they took the tram across the river and then walked through the narrow streets that led to the Piazza della Rotunda. In front of her was the Pantheon. All those pictures she had seen over the years did not do it justice.

"It was commissioned by Marcus Agrippa during the reign of Augustus and was dedicated to "pan theos" which means "all the gods." It was re-built by Emperor Hadrian about 126 AD. You like, Molly?"

Austere and yet over-powering, it is still the world's largest non-reinforced concrete dome. Molly walked past the tall Corinthian columns and felt like she was walking into another world. So much activity around her and yet the only thing she saw was the oculus in the ceiling overhead. With the sun directly overhead, beams of sunshine hit the floor below, offering a spotlight for anyone caring to stand within its rays. Molly was overwhelmed with the idea of standing there amidst the ghosts of all those who had come before her, all those remarkable Romans who had influenced the world. Standing in the exact spot, and maybe wondering, as she did now, at what lies above, through that tiny portal to the Heavens. Was it like Alice looking into the rabbit hole or perhaps, it was the Heavens peering down through the hole, like scientists looking through a telescope, examining the mere mortals who wandered under their lens?

"Yes, I like very much."

"The height and diameter of the interior circle are exactly the same, 43.3 meters. One hundred and forty feet." Eugenio watched as Molly walked slowly around the room, trying to take in all the history, stopping before each crypt. She waited patiently for a group of people to move away from one and then she stood quietly, studying the writing, trying to read what she could although she knew it well. Raphael, one of her favorites, had been given a place of honor here. Molly thought about all of his paintings she had admired for many years. Always like him, she had told Sarah once, because the man loved women with a little meat on their bones.

"Michelangelo came here to study the dome before he began his work on St. Peter's dome. And many other places have used it as a model. The British Museum in London and in the United States, the Jefferson Rotunda in Washington, DC and at the University of Virginia. The basilica dome at the Vatican is actually two feet smaller than this one. The bronze doors weigh two tons each and the walls of the Pantheon are twenty feet (six meters) thick. It was a pagan

100

temple, is now a church, and is considered to be the historic center of Roma."

As if he knew what Molly was thinking, Eugenio leaned over and said, "You stay alone, Bella, I leave you for a little time. I will be out waiting at the obelisk. No hurry." He turned and walked away leaving Molly on her own.

Molly reached up and touched her necklace. "Well, Kiddo, we made it." Tears welled in her eyes as she walked around the vast room once more, lost in a mental conversation. When she walked back out into the bright sunshine, Eugenio was sitting on the steps leading up to the fountain, smoking a cigarette. She sat down next to him. "Thank you."

"Are you tired? Do you need to rest for some time?"

"No, I am good. Where do we go next?"

"Coffee first and then Trevi Fountain."

It was very crowded as they made their way through the narrow streets toward Fontana di Trevi. With images of "Roman Holiday," "Three Coins in a Fountain," and maybe even "Gidget Goes to Rome," in their heads, tourists flock to the fountain. Molly had seen them all, many times, yes, even the Gidget movie, just to get a glimpse of Rome, but the fountain is one of the three places she most wanted to visit. Molly had read about the building of the fountain, beginning in 19 BC and completed in 1762 and considered the most beautiful baroque fountain in the world. Pictures could never do it justice. Now she was going to see it for herself.

As they stepped around the corner, despite the people crowded around, Molly had to stop and take a minute to enjoy her first look. Eugenio stepped back, giving her a moment, knowing that Molly needed to have this time to share, not with him, but with her friend. He watched her face as she held the necklace in her hand and saw her wipe the tears away from under her sunglasses. He wanted to go to her, but he knew this was not his place and time right now. She would come to him when she was ready.

Eugenio lit a cigarette and leaned against a wall, out of the way of the crowd. When Molly finally walked over to him, he smiled. "Is beautiful, no?"

"Is beautiful, YES."

"Our Trevi Fountain is very popular. Is 86 feet high and is very helpful. Tradition says that if you throw a coin with your right hand over your left shoulder, it will assure your return to Rome. But I know that you know this already. You have seen the movies." He smiled.

"Yes, many times. But why helpful?"

"Over 3,000 euros a day are thrown into the fountain and they are used to stock the food bank for the needy. And yet, people try to steal the coins. Give me your camera so I may take your picture. When you are home, you will be able to look at and remember this day."

"I shall always remember this day. I won't need a picture. But I have a better idea." There were some obviously American tourists near-by. Molly walked over and asked

102

them to take a picture of her and Eugenio together. Molly smiled into the camera but when she looked at the picture later, she saw that Eugenio was smiling as well, but he was looking at her.

It was getting warm and Eugenio was worried that maybe the heat would be too much for Molly. They had lunch at Tre Scalini in Piazza Navona.
"I am thinking about tiramisu."

"Please, let me order something else, something special I want you to try and maybe it will remind you of our first day in Atlanta." He spoke to the waiter in Italian and a few minutes later he brought over a plate with a lovely ice cream dessert. It was almost too pretty to eat…a ball of chocolate sliced in half, showing the inside with layers of ice cream, caramel bits, cake and hazelnuts."

Molly took a bite. "This is amazing." Eugenio leaned back and watched her, enjoying the idea that he had given her this special treat.

"Is zuccotto. In Italian means, "little pumpkin."

"I suppose you want to share this with me?"

"No, is for you."

Molly picked up his spoon and handed it to him. "No, we share."

"But you have the last bite."

Molly smiled, he remembered!

As they walked along the street markets, Molly noticed that Eugenio was watching her closely. Finally, she stopped and turned to him. "I am fine, stop worrying." But he continued to watch for signs of fatigue or pain.

Back at the apartment Molly took a glass of ice tea and went out and sat on the patio. As much as she loved the city, she enjoyed their quiet little place, away from the hustle and bustle. Eugenio joined her. "Good day for you?"

"Yes, but I have a question. Everyone goes to see the Colosseum first, why didn't we start there?"

"Do not be upset. I want it to be special for you when you first see. Tonight, when it is dark, we will go to the Colosseum and you see in the moonlight. But for now, is too hot and you should rest for a time. You are not used to the Italian heat."

"Mother hen." She said quietly.

Eugenio laughed. "I know mother hen. But is very hot this time of the day so is best we relax here and we will go out much later in the night."

Eugenio had fallen asleep on the couch watching a movie and Molly had gotten up and quietly gone out and sat alone on the patio. She turned on the speakers on her computer and leaned back and closed her eyes. The music filled the night air. Vittori Grigolo. The man's voice was enchanting. She had listened to him so many times, but sitting here, it was almost magical.

"Molly?"

"Eugenio was standing in the doorway. "Are you okay?"

"Yes, just listening. Do you like Vittori Grigolo?"

"Yes, very good and very young."

Molly looked up at the night sky. It was clear and she could see the stars and planes coming in to the airport. She took a deep breath. She could not get used to the idea that Eugenio was close enough now that she could touch him any time she wanted. No more waiting and wondering. Playfully, she took his hand and headed for the doors leading into the bedroom, but Eugenio suddenly stopped.

"I am sorry, am I being too demanding?"

"No, I like but I think you want to make love to this man who sings and you only have me."

Molly laughed, thinking he was kidding, but then she saw his face. "Seriously?"

"Then why do you want to make love to me now?"

"Oh gee, I don't know. Let me think…I am in Rome under a star-studded sky in a lovely private garden, listening to an Italian tenor and sipping Moscato with a man I came halfway around the world to see. And I want to make love to him. What was I thinking?"

"Do you think I am a foolish man?"

"No, my love, what woman could not look at Vittori Grigolo and not think what a little hottie he is, but Eugenio, I love to listen to his music, it touches me, but I love you, only you." It came out so naturally, as if she had spoken it 100 times but the actual words startled her. "I am so sorry. I didn't mean to…"

"No, do not be sorry. You love me, Molly? You never say love to me before. I am a foolish man, but I am happy you love me. Come Bella, I want to make love to you. As they walked past the computer, Eugenio closed it… "No Grigolo. Only you and I."

Molly laughed and squeezed his hand.

Eugenio was lying on his side and she could hear his breathing begin to slow down. She thought about the day, waking with Eugenio, coffee on the patio, and this wonderful day. She tried to relax but she suddenly began shaking. At first she thought it was her heart, but she knew it wasn't that. She pulled the sheet around her but it didn't help. It was still warm and there was only the hint of a breeze but she was shaking uncontrollably. She could only remember two other times in her life feeling like this, those hours after she had given birth to her children…those uncontrollable tremors when her hormones were running rampant, like fevered chills, while her body tried to gain control after having accomplished such miraculous feats as giving birth. But here? And now? She slid off the edge of the bed and picked up the comforter from the floor. She wrapped it around her and went out and sat on the patio. She rocked back and forth and hugged her knees, trying to regain her composure. Slowly she began to feel her heart beat slow down and the shaking began to subside.

What was it about this man who set her whole body into such a state? Or maybe it was all those emotions that she had held inside for so long. She thought of the unbridled love making, the lack of inhibition and asking for and telling of what she wanted and needed from this man and his willingly offering and complying with her wishes and desires. And her own willingness to do whatever fulfilled his wants and desires as well. And afterward, how he had gently let his fingertips wander across her nipples, soft lazy circles encircling her skin and how she had selfishly laid back on the pillows and let the sensation of fulfillment sweep over her. Was this what it should have been like all these years? Had this been what she had been missing?

She had had a couple of lovers in college, no one special, just the usual brief relationships one has, experimenting with that first freedom in life. And then there was David…hmmm. But this man…this man managed to touch every nerve in her body, sending shock waves through her with every touch, every kiss, every exploration with his tongue and hands. He seemed to awaken places on her body she never knew could be aroused to those heights. She wanted to devour every inch of him and the thing is, he let her. There was no grabbing her hands or giving her accusing looks or telling her to stop. And when he rolled over on his side, turning his back to her, she did not feel that he was turning away from her, but merely had turned and pressed against her, taking her arm and wrapping it around his waist, wanting to keep her near. It wasn't that feeling of being dismissed as she had so often felt in all those years of her marriage. With Eugenio, it had been physical exhaustion and contentment, but he still wanted her close, to fall asleep together, their bodies still warm and melting together to form one in the early morning light.

She began to relax and she let the comforter slip from her shoulders and she breathed in the warm night air. The air smelled sweet and she looked up at the stars. She knew by now Eugenio had relocated himself, even in his sleep, into his military sleep, arms at his side and tucked in. She smiled and wondered how he would react if he woke up and she was listening to Vittori Grigolo once again. Instead, she carefully lay down next to him and closed her eyes.

When she woke, she could feel the sunshine on her face even before she opened her eyes. For a brief moment she felt a panic. "Oh no! Please don't let this be a dream." She opened her eyes and felt relief at the sight of the pale green walls that surrounded her. Then she started to laugh. She slipped out of bed and walked into the kitchen. Eugenio was standing at the kitchen sink and she could hear the all too familiar "O SOLO MIO" coming from the patio. She walked over and slipped her arms around his waist and kissed the back of his neck. "Grazie, Eugenio." She whispered. "For these last two days and nights. I adore you."

"But I am not Vittori Grigolo."

"No, but he can only sing and is just another pretty face. But you, you are all I could ever ask for."

"But I promised to show you the Colosseum by moonlight and we only sleep."

"Well, not only sleep." She smiled. "I think we need a good American breakfast. I will make omelets."

"Yes, Italians, we have coffee and little breakfast. I like American."

By the time they were ready to head out for the day, the skies had clouded over and the air felt sticky.

"Maybe we should wait and see what happens before we go too far," Eugenio suggested. "When we have summer rains, they are very heavy but do not last too long. Do you mind, Molly?"

"I am perfectly happy just being here with you. In fact, if we did not leave at all until you have to leave on Sunday, I would be content."

Eugenio just smiled. "Is good for me as well." He settled back on the couch and picked up the remote.

"Some things must be universal." Molly thought, but then he added, "I want to see the weather and then please, will you read for me some of what you write?"

"Let it rain. Let it rain, let it rain," ran through Molly's mind as she slipped off her shoes and curled up next to him on the sofa.

It didn't matter that it poured rain the rest of the day and early evening. They spent the afternoon talking and just being together. Rome could wait. Today it was just them. Molly had read Eugenio some of her stories and he listened intently and smiled. "Good for young adults, Molly. I like your work. They can learn many things from you."

"These are stories I began to write when my children were young. Things I wanted them to learn and understand." Suddenly she stopped, "I am so sorry, Eugenio. I wish you had the opportunity to be a father. You would be a wonderful father."

"May I ask you a question?"

"You may ask me anything."

"Why do you never ask of my wife?"

"When you are ready to tell me, you will."

He suddenly looked very tired. He leaned back in his chair. "Is sad to mourn the loss of love. You feel alone and you try and nothing works. You wonder how much sadness you can endure to do the right thing."

"I know. I was obligated to mourn the end of my marriage because no one else did. It was not a good marriage the last few years, but it wasn't always like that. There were good times and laughter and I had my children. Those are the things I cried for. And when it ended, I wondered what I was going to do with the rest of my life, except wait for grandbabies to fill my life again."

"I have no children so I will have no grandchildren. I have my work and I have my family but at the end of the day, I am alone and I am tired of the loneliness. This time with you has been so important to me. For the next four weeks, I

110

can come home and find you waiting. I no expect a woman to be here to just wait for my return but now I have something to look forward to, even for a short time. I took the metro and then the tram and the closer I came, the more I could not wait to open the door and find you waiting for me. I do not mean to be selfish but is important to me. I will hate when you leave and I only have loneliness again. Is good I have such a strong family but is not enough at my age."

"Tell me about your family."

"Oh, that could be a very long talk. I have a large family."

"And we have a rainy afternoon and a bottle of Moscato and some wonderful bread and cheese. Tell me, I want to hear all about them."

"My grandfather's name was Nikolas and we always called him PaPa Nick. My great-grandfather did not like him for a very long time. Great-Grandpa Carmine had three sons of his own and he wanted them to all become priests but they said no. Uncle Carmine was the oldest and named after his father. He said he was too handsome and there were too many beautiful women in the world. It would be a shame not to marry one of them and have beautiful children together. The next oldest brother was Damarco, not as good looking but every bit as charming. They had many women in their youth, which really upset my great-grandmother. She wanted them to settle down. Antonio was the youngest. Very handsome, but very quiet. And all three boys loved to cook. They talked of opening a restaurant together. They knew with their family recipes and love of cuisine, they would have a success. Their papa said no, he wanted strong boys who did the work of strong men. But their mama said to do what was in their hearts so when they were in their 20's, Carmine and Damarco opened a small restaurant and it became very successful. It was just a few years later when they bought the building next to them and it became even more successful. And they married beautiful women and had beautiful children, which made their mama very happy. And eventually their papa decided a good restaurant where they did not charge him to eat and beautiful grandchildren to sit on his lap were good and there were already enough priests in the world." He stopped and took a drink of wine.

"My grandmother was younger by several years so she was treated like the baby. Her name was Isobella and when she was old enough, she would work week-ends at the restaurant, under the watchful eye of her brothers. One evening a tall handsome Greek student came in with some friends to have dinner. The next night he came back alone and sat quietly eating and smiling every time Isobella passed by his table. On Monday, he came back but she was not there. Tuesday and Wednesday and Thursday, he walked by hoping to see her. On Friday, he decided to come one more time, worried that he had met her at the end of her waitress career. He thought sadly that maybe she had quit to be married and his heart sank. But Friday, he saw her pass by the window and when she saw him standing outside, she smiled and waved. And so it began. He would come late on the nights she worked to eat and then they would sit on the patio and talk until one of her brothers would come out to take her home. Finally, one night Nikolas asked Uncle Carmine if he could walk Isobella home. It was only across the bridge. Carmine had been watching this young man, seeing the way he looked at his little sister and how she would smile when she saw him in the doorway each night.

Carmine said yes, but two things, straight home and no tell PaPa. They walked down the side street onto the busy Lungotevere degil Anguillara and started to cross Ponte Garibaldi.

That night they stopped on the bridge to enjoy the view of St. Peter's and he kissed her for the first time. It was also the night that he asked her to marry him. He said she had to marry him because he was getting fat and going broke from eating at the restaurant just to be near her. He said he did not want an answer until he asked a second time but would she please think of it. He still had six months until he graduated but then they could marry and he would stay in Rome instead of returning to Greece. Isobella could not bear the thought of not seeing him, during the week she would study and look out over the city and wonder where her darling Nickie was. And on the nights when he had studied late and could not sleep, he would walk across the bridge and look up at the large building that loomed in the darkness and he would wonder what Isobella was doing. And then he would pause on the bridge and make plans to make a life with this young Italian beauty who had won his heart.

When Nick finally graduated, he was offered a job at the company where he had worked during his last year of school. He went to Isobella that night and asked again if she would marry him. If she said yes, he would stay in Rome. Isobella knew the time had come that she must tell her papa the truth. She asked her father to take a walk with her and together they strolled along the river one evening after dinner. She told him of this young man she loved, but he kept shaking his head, saying "Why you no marry a nice Italian boy?"

But Isobella said because this man was kind and gentle and that she loved him, the way that her mother loved her father. And even at the wedding, as they stood at the back of the church, Isobella in her beautiful gown and her father looking very uncomfortable in his new suit, and he saw how happy she was, as they started down the aisle, he whispered, "But why does he have to be a damn Greek?" My grandparents were married for 65 years and they were very happy. I remember they used to hold hands and PaPa Nick used to call her "Mia Bella." She was holding his hand when he passed.

The rest of the family was near-by but at the end, it was only the two of them holding hands and whispering their good-byes.

We would go and visit her and on Sundays we would take her to the restaurant, which is run by Carmine's and Darmarco's and Antonio's boys now, but without PaPa Nick, she always looked sad. It was only a year before she was gone too."

"What about Antonio?"

"Antonio was tall and handsome. He had a plan in life. First the military and then come home and run the restaurant with his brothers. When he was sixteen, he was making some extra money working part-time for a man who had a small moving company. Antonio was big and strong for his age and willing to work hard for little money. One day, he was hired to help a family. He had already worked most of the morning carrying boxes and furniture and was taking a break when the family arrived. The daughter, AnnaMaria

114

was sixteen as well. He went home that night and told his mama he had met the girl he was going to marry. MaMa smiled, wondering how many times she would hear that before he finally chose the right bride. But AnnaMaria remained the one. For four years, they dated and saved their money. Antonio and AnnaMaria now had a plan together. She was going to become an accountant and he was going to have the restaurant with his brothers and they would marry when he returned from the military.

When he enlisted, Anna was broken-hearted, but she knew it was what he wanted. She also thought it was foolish to buy her an engagement ring because she would be happy with a plain gold band. But Antonio had been saving for a long time and one day he saw the ring he wanted. It was a simple gold band with an amethyst stone, elegant and graceful like his Anna. He had taken her for a walk after they had had dinner at the restaurant. They walked up onto the bridge and stopped, as they did so often to enjoy the view of St. Peter's and suddenly Antonio stopped and knelt on one knee. People walked by and smiled. We Italians do appreciate love.

'Anna, the first time I saw you, I knew you were the one I wanted to spend the rest of my life with. You walked up the steps past me and into the apartment and every time I saw you the rest of the day you pretended not to see me, but I saw the blush in your cheeks. You made my heart stop the first time you looked up at me and smiled. And I know I am going into the army for some time, but when I come home we will marry, if you will have me.'

Anna said nothing but held out her hand to him and he pulled the ring out of his pocket and slipped it on her finger.

Then he folded his hands around her fingers and kissed them. 'We will be happy together, Anna – forever you will have my heart.'

And she replied, 'And you shall have mine.'

The first time Antonio came home on leave, Anna told him she wanted to be married while he was still in the service. She thought he would be so handsome in his uniform and she would wear her grandmother's wedding gown. Antonio agreed so they planned to marry the next time he came home on leave. Anna said she wanted a small wedding but Antonio laughed and told her even if it was only family, it would not be small. That night they made love for the first time and in the morning Anna stood on the platform and watched as he left, waving and blowing kisses until the train was out of sight.

Anna planned a very simple wedding, just family and it would be, of course, at the church where she had been baptized, but the reception would be at the restaurant. But the next time Antonio came home, it was very different. The morning she was to marry, Anna stood in front of her closet and stared at the beautiful gown hanging there. She ran her hands down the smooth silk and across the beading at the neck. This was to be her wedding day! Then she quietly reached over and took out a simple black dress and shawl and closed the door on the dress and her dreams. Antonio had been killed by a sniper. That day she sat in the church, surrounded by family, staring at the altar. It should be them, standing there holding hands and taking their vows to love each other forever.

One by one the family passed by the coffin to say good-bye. Anna remained seated until all the others had left. Then she walked over and stood looking down at the handsome young man in his uniform. She leaned over and kissed him and touched her hand to his heart. 'I will love you forever.' She whispered. And then she turned and walked away, not wanting to see them close the coffin and take away the man who was taking her heart with him wherever his next journey led. Almost to the church door, she felt the room begin to spin and she reached for a pew to steady herself, but collapsed on the floor.

My great-grandmother had always considered Anna part of the family long before she and Antonio announced they would marry. She took Anna's hand that day and told her she understood. And that Anna was her daughter-in-law in her heart. And when Anna's family heard her news, they told her she had disgraced the family and told her she would go away from Rome and give the child up for adoption so no one would know. But Anna went to my family and they told her that she and Antonio's child were their family now. So, Anna became the accountant for the restaurant and she gave birth to a son. Of course, he was named Antonio. Anna worked and watched her son grow into a tall handsome young man. His mother and grandmother would watch him at play and deal with their grief together. When Little Antonio was about ten, Great Grandma told Anna she was still a beautiful woman and she should re-marry. Antonio would not want her to be alone any longer but Anna said she had just never found anyone who could ever take his place. Now she is a quiet little woman who still comes to the office at the restaurant in the mornings sometimes and then she has lunch with Antonio before they are busy. She still wears her amethyst ring; it has never been off her finger since the day Antonio placed it there. She says Antonio gave her a beautiful son and wonderful family, and now she has grandchildren, but most of all, he gave her a love to last a lifetime.

Most days she takes the tram home, but sometimes she likes to take her time and walk across the bridge and stop to enjoy the view of St. Peter's and remember. And at night, before she closes her eyes, she looks over at the picture of her handsome soldier, always on her nightstand and whispers 'Good night, my love.'" Eugenio took a long drink of his tea. "I am sorry, Bella, I go on but I know these stories so well. Is important to me that you know of my family. It is a good family and I want to share with you."

"Oh no, Eugenio, I love hearing about your family."

"For now, has stopped raining and the time is good for us. We go out for some time. We have dinner and then I show you the Colosseum."

As they stepped out the door, they could hear church bells. "It must be close." Molly commented.

Eugenio took her hand, "Yes, I show you." They walked only a block when Molly suddenly stopped. She looked up as they turned a corner and there it was. A tall brick building with a single window with a flower box over-flowing with red flowers. It was the picture on her calendar. That "somewhere in Trasteverve" was almost in her own backyard. She took Eugenio's hand as they continued to walk but she could feel him start to jerk his hand away.

"What is it?" Molly suddenly felt a panic. Did he not want to be seen with her? She had noticed that he usually was two or three steps ahead of her when they walked and now it was like he did not want her to touch him in public.

He could tell he had done something that hurt her. He could see it in her eyes. "I am sorry. I am not used to this. My wife, she did not like to touch me when we were out. And never hold my hand."

"It's okay."

"No, I see it hurts you."

"I just worry. Yesterday you walked ahead of me most of the time."

"I would never hurt you, Molly, I just am used to military, I think."

"You aren't marching. Stop and smell the roses. Do you understand?"

Eugenio looked around but there were no roses. "No, explain to me."

"It means to relax and enjoy. Slow down."

Eugenio reached out and took her hand. "Yes, slowly and touching. Is better."

They stepped into a small piazza. In front of them was a small church, white during the day but with the lights of the piazza, it gave off a soft glow against the night sky. Eugenio pointed up, "The bells."

They walked back and took the metro and when they walked out into the terminal Eugenio said, "Close your eyes and let me lead you." He took her hand and she followed him about 15 steps. She felt the night air on her face just as he said, "Open your eyes, Molly."

Across the street, lit against the clear Roman sky was the Colosseum. Eugenio was right, this is the way one should see the Colosseum for the first time. It was more than she could ever have imagined.

"Stand here, Molly, I want a picture. I want to capture, I think is the word, that look on your face."

Molly stood looking at the massive structure and Eugenio took his picture before they walked across the street. It was late but there were still many people milling about, but nothing like during the day. Molly knew it was the largest amphitheater in the world but to actually stand there and see it all before her! It had been named the Colosseum after a colossal statue of Nero that once stood near-by. Now only the base of the statue remained but the Colosseum's grandeur was over-powering. The moon had become visible in the now clear sky and Eugenio took several pictures of Molly and her latest fascination. Eugenio said he was going to sit over on the brick wall and smoke if she didn't mind. He took deep drags from his cigarette as he watched her clutch her necklace once again and have her private conversation with her friend.

When he joined her, he took her hand and she squeezed it tightly. "You are right; the first time should be at night."

"We will come back and spend much time later." And then he smiled and added, "But is getting late. We must eat soon. Is the week-end but we cannot dine too late."

Molly suddenly felt hungry as well. They walked up the street and entered the patio of a restaurant. The roof was made out of beams that were covered with grapevines. Small lights had been laced into the vines and they set off a soft glow over-head. It was late but the area was still very lively. They took a table near the street and the waiter had attempted to seat Molly on one side of the table until Eugenio spoke to him and he gestured for her to sit on the other side of the table. When she sat down, she realized she now had a perfect view of the Colosseum over Eugenio's shoulder. Now it was her turn. She took the camera from her bag and took a picture.

Molly looked at the menu. There were so many things that sounded so good that it was hard for her to decide. She finally decided on a simple carbonara penne but Eugenio ordered a prosciutto and melon starter for them to share.

He said the prosciutto was much different in Italy than in the United States. In the States it is very salty and dry, but here, where it was born, it is very different. And he ordered a bottle of Moscato. "I do not drink so much these days but with you, is special to share a lovely bottle of wine."

When the waiter set the plate down, Eugenio cut the contents in half and set it down before her and watched as she took her first bite. He was right, the ham was wafer thin

121

but it was soft and combined with the sweet taste of cantaloupe, it was perfect. He could tell by the look on her face that she was pleased. "The cantaloupe is wonderful. The sweetest I have ever tasted and we grow pretty good melon in Illinois."

"Many countries claim cantaloupe is theirs, including Italy. Columbus took seeds to America in 1492 but Italy still claims it belongs to us. In the late 14th century it was cultivated in the Papal Gardens in Cantalope, Italy so it was named after the city."

"And what about the prosciutto? I know it is an Italian specialty."

The waiter opened the wine and allowed Eugenio to taste. A small sip and he nodded, which signaled the waiter to pour the glasses.

"The prosciutto, yes, is special and very protected."

"Protected?"

"It takes a very long time for prosciutto to cure, nine months to two years. The word comes from the Latin word meaning 'before and to suck out the moisture.' There are many steps and the temperature must be just right. Italians wanted their prosciutto to be their own because of the time and love they put into making it just right. The Common Agricultural Policy of the European Union controls the product and its name. Prosciutto crudo di Parma and Prosciutto crudo di San Daniele are the most famous and most expensive."

"I did not care for it when I have had it before, too dry and salty, but this is sweet and soft and has a nutty flavor. It is wonderful."

"Italians don't just eat food to live, Molly, we have a romance, a relationship with food." He took a bite and nodded his approval. He continued, "When I was young, on Sundays we would go to MASS and we would come home ravenous because we could not eat. We no receive Holy Communion unless we fasted. And then we would go home and the minute we opened the door, we were welcomed with smells of rich gravies. They are called sauces now, but they were gravies when I was a child. And there would be warm bread. I used to call my grandma my nonnina, which means "little grandma." This is funny because she was about as tall as I was but that is what my older cousins called her. We would all gather in her kitchen, not in a big dining room, but around the kitchen table. No kids' table, we all sat together. There would be aunts and uncles and cousins and grandparents and sometimes someone new, a friend or new girlfriend or boyfriend who had been invited for one of two reasons. First because someone had truly fallen in love and he or she needed to be slowly introduced into the family to adjust to the fit. Or second, because of the constant barrage of questions about "Why you no have a girlfriend? Why you no give me grandbabies?" so one of us would bring a friend to give our parents and grandparents hope and us a little peace.

My grandparents' home was a large apartment, two floors. The kitchen was on the second level but there were steps down to a small yard and garden on the ground level. It was not flowers or flowering bulbs or neat little rows of vegetables. It was pomodoros… tomatoes. Nonnina would

123

buy her vegetables at the market and once in a while, if she knew the local vendors, she would buy some tomatoes but she said her gravies had to have her own tomatoes to give them love. Her back yard was filled with a long table and enough chairs for the whole family, and the back fence was lined with tomato plants.

In the warm weather, we ate in the tiny yard, crowded together, elbow to elbow, laughing and talking loudly. In cold weather, it was in the kitchen, but always together."

Molly sipped her wine and smiled. Eugenio felt embarrassed. "I am sorry yet again to go on about my family."

"No, no, I was smiling because I love what you tell me." She got up and walked around the small table and put her arms around his neck. I love your stories."

Eugenio felt his face redden, but then he looked around and saw others who might have been looking on, smiling as well. "Yes," he thought, "and we Italians love love."

The waiter waited until Molly sat down again and then set two large bowls of pasta before them.

"Good Lord! I will never be able to eat all this." Molly exclaimed, but as they chatted and drank and ate, Molly suddenly realized she had eaten every bite. "There goes that 8 pounds I just lost," she said. "We will have to walk home tonight." Home, home with Eugenio, what a lovely thought. She knew all this was like living in a fantasy but she was going to enjoy every minute of it as long as it lasted.

Eugenio signaled the waiter and Molly assumed it was to ask for the bill, but soon he returned and set down yet another fabulous dessert in front of her. "Oh no!" Molly leaned back in her chair.

"Is tartufo."

"Well, it looks too good to eat."

Before her was a ball of chocolate, sliced and laid open on the plate. Inside was a soft ball of chocolate ice cream and inside that was a ball of raspberry ice cream and inside that were raspberries. A raspberry sauce was drizzled in the shape of flowers around the chocolate.

"Okay, one bite." She took one spoonful. "Oh dear!"

"You no like?"

"I no like, I love." She handed Eugenio the spoon. "But we share."

And when they were almost finished, she put her hands up. "You may have the last bite. I quit."

When they left the restaurant, they strolled a few blocks, walking around the Colosseum, viewing it from every point. "It truly is unbelievable."

Molly stifled a yawn.

"Molly, I am sorry. We have stayed out too long. You must be very tired."

"A little. I didn't get a nap on the sofa this afternoon." She smiled and squeezed his hand.

Eugenio put his hand up to hail a taxi.

"Wait, I thought you said taxis are very expensive in Rome?"

"Yes, but you are tired. We need to go home now."

Molly lost her smile. She suddenly had flashbacks to all those times she had tried to dote over Sarah, constantly questioning her. "No, please, let's walk."

"Too far and too late for the metro. Tonight, we take a taxi. Special night."

Molly didn't argue. She really was too full and too tired to put up much of a fight about anything.

Chapter 8

It was almost 1:00 a.m. when they returned to the apartment. Molly went in and kicked off her shoes, lay back on the bed, and closed her eyes.

"Are you alright, Molly? Did we do too much today?" His voice sounded full of concern.

Without even opening her eyes, she only smiled, "I couldn't be better." She heard Eugenio moving around the room but it was just so lovely to just let her mind wander through the day's events. Finally, she stood up and started to undress. She threw her skirt over the back of the chair and giving him a quick kiss on the cheek as she passed, she headed for the bathroom. When she came back in her nightshirt, she noticed he had carefully hung her skirt up on the rack and her shoes were lined up next to his by the door. She slid between the cool sheets and scooted over next to him.

He put his arm around her. "Was a good day for you, Bella?"

"When I came to Rome, to you, I didn't know exactly what was going to happen but I never imagined this."

"What do you mean 'this'?"

"All of this, Eugenio, falling asleep next to you, waking next to you, and all the lovely moments in-between. The talking and walking and EATING. Seeing so many places I have only dreamed of."

"And the nights, Molly, have they been good for you?"

"More than you will ever know."

"Will you never forget me?"

"I am pretty sure I am going to think about you every day for the rest of my life."

Eugenio rose up on one elbow and touched her forehead. "Not here." He slid his hand down her cheek and neck and let it rest on her heart. "Remember me here."

"As long as it beats, it will remember."

"You will be okay, Molly, you will be okay no matter what the doctors decide to do. I want you to love me for a very long time."

Molly closed her eyes and fell asleep with his hand still resting on her heart. When she woke, it was still dark. She looked out the patio doors. Eugenio was sitting at the table. She could see the glow from his cigarette as he put his head back and exhaled, watching the smoke as it dissipated into the night air.

"What's wrong?"

"We have not talked of this yet but I have to leave tonight. I work an early day shift."

"I hate that you have to leave but I understand. And we both knew this was going to happen the whole month I am here."

"I just hate to leave you. You know this."

Molly walked over and put her arms around his neck. She leaned over and kissed his shoulder. "I will be all right. There is all of Rome for me to see on my own. And I have work to do. And...I will be here waiting when you come home."

He took one last drag of his cigarette and put it out. "Come."

Molly was almost asleep when Eugenio's hand found hers. She put his fingers to her lips and kissed them gently. Taking the tip of each one into her mouth, running her tongue along the roughness of his skin. His hand guided hers down to find his longing for her waiting for her touch. Without words, as none were needed, they made love, very slowly, very deliberately, savoring each moment.

Molly woke to one of her moments of illumination, enjoying the sunshine on her face and the explosions of light as the heat touched her eyelids. She finally opened her eyes and tried to focus on the clock. It was almost 10:00 a.m.! Good Lord! What would Eugenio think? She sat up, expecting to be alone, but she found him still asleep beside her. She slipped out of bed and quietly closed the door. Coffee! She sat down on the patio and reached over and clicked on YouTube. She knew what she needed to hear. Etta James! She sipped her coffee and listened to the music. "I WANT A SUNDAY KIND OF LOVE, A LOVE THAT LASTS PAST SATURDAY NIGHT!" How many times had she sat in her condo and listened to that song. And now here she was, as if every word Etta sang had been granted. She opened her book and began to read. "It just doesn't get any better than this!"

"Shall we go to the Colosseum today?"

Molly looked up to see him standing in the doorway. "Nope, not today. I didn't hear you get up."

"Military training. Where do you want to go today?"

"Nowhere."

"Yes, is good. I like this nowhere."

They spent a quiet afternoon, letting the busy world outside carry on without them. After lunch, Eugenio watched a movie while Molly curled up next to him on the sofa and read. Every now and then she would reach out and touch him, just content he was near. But about 6:00 p.m., he got up and went into the bedroom. She knew he was packing but she decided she would not show him how sad she was. She walked in and sat down on the bed. "Getting to be about that time, I suppose."

"Yes, very soon." He carefully folded his clothes and slipped them neatly into his backpack. When he finished, he sat down next to her. "I hate this."

"I know." She touched his cheek. "When will you return?"

"Late Thursday night when I finish. I will drive in and I leave my car at my uncle's and take the Metro into the city. I will arrive here about 10:00 p.m. unless you think it is too late for you. I can wait and come early Friday morning."

"Are you serious?"

130

"Yes."

Molly laughed. "No, I mean, are you kidding? And miss even one night with you. Whatever time you arrive, we will have a late supper here. Just come as soon as you can."

"What will you do this week?"

"First of all, I will miss you every minute. But I do have plans. I am having a very formal tea party with Gina and her daughter and I have some museums to visit."

"I will miss you."

"When I came, I was hoping for one perfect day, one to remember for the rest of my life, and you have already given me three."

"But now I go for four days."

"We knew this would happen when I came but it is only four days and they will go quickly. You will be very busy. She slipped her arm through his and leaned against his shoulder. "And I will be here waiting for you," she added quietly.

An hour later, Eugenio opened the door and then turned and put his arms around her, holding her close, trying to memorize the scent of her hair and the warmth of her skin. "You call if you need anything or if you feel ill at all. And I will write you when I am in the barracks. Ciao, Bella."

He picked up his backpack and gave her a quick kiss and then one that lasted much longer and walked out the door. Molly stood and watched as he walked across the street. Just before he disappeared into the crowd of people waiting for the tram, he turned and waved, knowing she would still be in the doorway, watching. As the tram pulled up, she blew him a kiss and closed the door.

Molly picked up the camera and began to flick through the pictures. She was amazed that he had captured that look of awe when she saw the Colosseum for the first time. And he had taken several pictures of her, deep in thought at each place they visited, each time holding her necklace. And then she saw the one she had taken of Eugenio at the restaurant with the Colosseum looming behind him. What an extraordinary shot! She touched the screen gently, touching his face with her fingertips. She turned off the camera and walked into the bedroom. She lay down on the bed and reached for Eugenio's pillow. She closed her eyes, trying to memorize his scent. When she woke, it was almost dark. She thought she would feel alone but instead, there was only contentment. She took a peaceful breath and sat up. Food!

She walked out into the night air. She wasn't sure where she was headed but she hoped to find a nice restaurant nearby for a quiet dinner. A few blocks from the apartment she saw a sign. *THE NEW STATION*. She walked over and looked at the menu posted by the door. Yes, pasta! One of the waiters had been standing nearby, smoking. He walked over and opened the door for her. "Please, come in. I am finished with my time. I will serve you. I am Alex." Molly followed him to a booth and slid in.

The building had obviously been an actual train station at one time she could tell by the architecture. It was beautifully decorated like an old station, ah! The name!

She looked around the dining room. She was the only one dining alone. There were two tables with large families. It was getting late so it was the end of their meals. The smaller children had re-located to laps of parents and grandparents as the adults finished their desserts and coffee. Molly had never been blessed with a large family and David never liked to "dine out" with the kids until they were older. She watched as one man shared his cake with his granddaughter, pretending to take a bite before giving it to her. She remembered her dad pretending not to look when Molly would sneak her fork over and take the last bite off his plate. She smiled. She wished things had been different with her father, especially when it had been just the two of them after her mother died. Molly sighed and then she saw a young couple who were sharing a tiramisu. She did not understand what he was saying but she recognized the gesture. He pushed the plate over in front of her to have the last bite and smiled. It was a universal gesture of affection and she remembered that day in the airport when Eugenio had offered her that last bite. A gesture of affection between two strangers.

The Pasta Primavera was excellent. Primavera means "Spring" in Italian and it was evident by the fresh crisp vegetables blended with the thin pasta. She had never had it with asparagus before and she made a mental note to add it on her next attempt to make her own. Alex came over more than once to inquire if she needed anything. She knew he was being especially attentive since she was dining alone. She hoped she didn't look pathetic as she ate alone. In

Chicago, there were people alone everywhere, reading, texting, talking on their phones, or sitting quietly. She wondered how many of them would rather have had company or if they were escaping to have some quiet time to themselves. But here, there were very few loners at this time of the night. She ordered a tiramisu even though she had eaten every bite of pasta. As Alex had started to walk away, she touched his arm. "Could I have two spoons, please?"

"Two spoons?"

"Yes, please." He looked puzzled but he nodded his head. He returned and set the dessert in front of her and made a gallant gesture to present her with two spoons. After he walked away, she was sure he was watching curiously, but he seemed to understand. She ate the dessert slowly, savoring the rich cream. When she was down to the last bite, she pushed the plate to the middle of the table and set the second spoon next the plate. For her dad or for Eugenio, she wasn't sure. Maybe she should have left two bites but it was just too good! When she stood to leave, Alex walked her to the door and pushed it open for her. "Come again, Bella."

"Molly. I am Molly." She extended her hand which he took and kissed lightly.

"Ciao, Molly."

She stepped out into the night air. She was glad she had a chance to walk a while. She decided this was definitely a place she wanted to bring Eugenio. And next time she would try the Carbonara. "Good Lord! It is a good thing I am only going to be here a month. I will weigh a ton at this rate." Suddenly, she felt sad. Only a month! She walked back to the apartment and opened the door "Lucy, I'm home!" she said out-loud. She picked up her computer and went out to the patio. She began to type, "Thinking of you..."

It was almost midnight when she finally went to bed. She had done the dishes and written out a nice invitation for Gina and her daughter. She decided Tuesday would be a good day for a tea party. Tomorrow she would go shopping. She had walked past a small shop that had lights and decorations in the windows and several portable stands on the sidewalk full of party favors. That is where she would start. And maybe a gift for Beatrice. She went in and lay down on the bed. She missed Eugenio being next to her but she made plans of her own for the next few days and the time would pass quickly. It was going to be a good week. She set the alarm for 6:00 a.m. She wanted to get an early start!

Molly was awake before the alarm even went off. She rolled over and looked at the empty side of the bed and smiled. "Soon!" She slid out of bed and went out to make coffee. She knew there would be a message from Eugenio waiting.

"Molly, I worry on the way back to the barracks that you had times when you were not pleased with me. But I hope it is so minute that you were still happy to be with me. It was such a good time and we did see many things in Rome but I most like the times when were in the apartment alone together. I left with remorse to leave you even for a few days and I think of making love with you again when I

135

return on Thursday but I worry about this. I hope you see much of Rome while I am away from you. Molly, my heart is full now that you tell me that you love me. There were many times I want to tell you but think I do not have the right yet, but you must know. Kisses, Eugenio."

Molly took a drink of her coffee and began to write: "The thing about two people who spend time together, even if they are identical twins, is that they are two different people and not going to agree on everything. And honestly, think how boring that would be if we had no differences in thoughts and ideas? We will only learn from each other and grow closer. There was not a time when I was displeased with you but I worry that you can't relax and slow down so you may "stop and smell the roses." But you have to know that I enjoyed every second of our time together. I am sure that we will have things to work on but it does not mean that I don't adore you. And if you are honest, you will admit there were some things I did that bothered you. We are close enough that you can tell me and we can get past them. It is human nature and do not worry. I will be more careful about hanging up my clothes from now on. Our time together is all I dreamed of and so much more. Here we are back to writing again but now we have so much more to talk about and our time apart is very limited. Miss your face. And yes, Eugenio, I know. M."

The day was going to be warm so Molly showered and headed for the piazza to do her shopping. When she walked through the tunnel, she saw Marcello standing in the doorway of the café. He smiled when he saw her approach.

"Good morning."

"Good morning, Marcello."

"Ah, you remember. And you are Molly."

Molly took a seat under the awning. "I think a large latte and a croissant will be good today."

"Are you enjoying Roma?"

"Yes, very much."

"And you have seen the Colosseum?"

"Yes, in the moonlight. Now I want to see it in the daylight."

"And Trevi?"

"Yes, and I still have a long list."

"Take your time and enjoy. Do not rush as many tourists do. Experience the city and these things."

"That is my plan."

"And you come and have coffee often with Marcello and tell me what you have seen."

"Yes, often."

Molly walked into the little shop and walked through the crowded aisles of decorations for every occasion and holiday. She soon had a small basketful before heading to the supermarket. She found Cadbury chocolate, Earl Grey tea, tea cakes, and the makings for her sandwiches. She wanted Gina to enjoy her afternoon as much as Beatrice. When she got back, she took her invitation over and lightly knocked on the back door.

She heard running feet and then the door opened. Before her stood a little girl with long dark hair, she was a delightful blend of Gina's gentle smile and those dark alluring Italian eyes Molly saw in so many of the young children. Before Molly could say anything, Gina appeared at the door. "Molly, come in. This is Beatrice, my daughter. Bea, this is Mrs. McMillian, the lady I told you about."

"Please, it's Molly." She held out to her hand.

"And the little man who is about to burst though the doorway behind me is Alexander."

Just then a face appeared around the corner, curious about the stranger. Carefully, he moved over behind his mother and peeked out again.

"Alex, this is Molly."

Molly bent down and put out her hand, "Buono Griorino, Alex."

The little face peeked out from behind his mother and smiled, "Buono Griorino, Molly." Then he smiled and added, "Hello" before putting his chubby little fingers into her hand.

"I did not want to bother you but I wanted to bring this over for Beatrice." She handed the invitation to Beatrice, who quickly opened it.

"Is a tea party for us, MaMa. Di Martedi, for you and I and Molly's friend. Please, may we go?"

"Oh, will Eugenio be back so soon?"

"No, this is a ladies' tea and I have a special friend coming for Beatrice."

"Yes, we would love to come. What may we bring?"

"Oh no, I have everything. Please, just come at 3:00 p.m."

"May I offer you a coffee?"

"No, I have some things to do today but I will see you tomorrow." She knelt down and extended her hand again. "Ciao, Alex."

"Ciao, Molly."

Beatrice opened the door for her. "Grazie, Molly. I will see you tomorrow."

Molly walked toward the church. Along the piazza she had seen several small shops and she was sure she would find the perfect friend for Beatrice. Maybe a stuffed animal. She wandered through the tiny shops, wondering how many pieces of that beautiful Venetian glass she could take home without breaking. One shop reminded her of the variety stores she had grown up with; it had food and clothes and dishes and toys and so much more. She walked around and scanned the shelves. Ah, just what she was looking for...a stuffed doll that reminded her of a Raggedy Ann doll. She had rosy cheeks and she was wearing a hat with a flower on the side. Perfect for an afternoon tea! She carefully took her off the shelf and carried her to the counter.

As she stepped outside, the bells of the church began to ring. It was noon and people were walking through the open doors. Molly wanted to go but she felt she wasn't dressed right and she wondered what people would think when she walked in with a big doll. This was not one of the more elaborate churches but Molly seemed drawn to it. As she walked home, she looked up at the window they had seen the night she and Eugenio had followed the bells. She took her camera and took a few pictures of it. She would make her own calendar next year!

The heat was beginning to bear down and Molly decided she should head for home. "Home," she thought again, "I like."

She turned on the ceiling fan and curled up on the sofa with her computer and turned on the TV. She worked a while and then set it on the coffee table and leaned back and closed her eyes. Maybe she would rest just a minute. "I really need to stop napping," she thought, but the couch was just so comfy and she was just following doctor's orders. About four o'clock, she woke when she heard English. She had left the TV on and NCIS was on in English. She made herself a light snack and went back to the couch. Off-line messages were waiting from Adam and Amanda, and Eugenio.

"Mom, just because you are on vacation does not mean that you do not have to stay in touch. I hope you are resting but I hope this trip is everything you want it to be. See the sights, eat all that wonderful food, and enjoy your time with Eugenio. Love you, Adam."

"As you wish," she said out-loud.

"Mother, why haven't we heard from you? Are you alright? Daddy says to be very careful because you cannot trust Italians. I do not know why you had to do this but since you did, have some fun but get lots of rest. And Eddie says not to do anything he wouldn't do. LOL."

"That Eddie is such a clever wit," Molly thought.

She had saved Eugenio's for last. "Ciao, Molly, I just take a break for supper and I wanted to write. I hate that you are in Italy and I cannot be with you. Working very long hours so I can be finished early on Thursday and come to you again. Is very hot here and I have to wear a dark uniform. I am happy to be back in the barracks. I think of you when I am alone and I wonder if you miss me as I do you. I go to eat now and rest but I think of you all the time. Thank you for alleviating my concerns. Ciao, Bella."

Molly wrote Adam, telling him about the Colosseum and Trevi Fountain and all the food. And she assured him the trip was everything she had hoped for and more. To Amanda she wrote that it was time she stopped listening to her father. The Italians she had come to know are all sweet and charming and go out of their way to make her trip wonderful. And she added that maybe she and Eddie would have to compare notes when she gets home. And she added her own LOL...let them wonder!

She waited until later to write Eugenio. In the early evening, she went out on the patio and took a deep breath. The air was still warm but sweetened by the flowers and scent of the lemon trees. "I had a lovely quiet day and my thoughts were of you. I walked to the church this morning. I seem drawn to it, maybe it is the bells. One day when I am dressed more appropriately I will go inside. I met Gina's children today. Tomorrow we are having a tea party. Work hard, stay cool, and hurry back to me. M." She wished they would be able to Skype for a while because she wanted to see his face, but she knew he was busy and when he was off, he needed to sleep.

Molly fell asleep reading. She had set a glass of peach tea on the night stand and when she reached for it, it was warm. She looked at the clock. It was 3:00 a.m. Good Lord! She finished the tea and put her arm around the empty pillow next to her and fell back to sleep.

When she finally got up, Molly felt a cool breeze through the patio doors. She made coffee and began her preparations for her party. By the time Gina and Beatrice came through the back gate, Molly was just putting the final touches on the table. She had tea and iced peach tea, finger sandwiches, and biscuits, (well, cookies but the British preferred biscuits), tea cakes, and some cool mints. Molly loved them but she seldom made them because she would eat them all herself. She used to always tuck some in a napkin when she attended a wedding to take home. These she had made round and carefully carved a G, M, or B on the top of each.

Beatrice handed Molly a small bouquet of yellow flowers. "Thank you for inviting us." Gina saw the doll sitting at the end of the table.

"And who is this guest?"

"This is Annie. I thought she might like to join us."

Gina talked about her childhood in England and Beatrice told Molly about school and about a boy at the park she thought was cute. But she added that he acted like a baby sometimes. Molly and Gina laughed...if she only knew that often lasts well into adulthood. Molly talked about her mother and how much she missed her. It was a pleasant afternoon and they laughed and sipped tea like proper ladies. About 4:30 p.m., the nanny stuck her head through the gate and said Alex was up and very upset he was not included.

"Of course he may join us. If you think it is alright." She turned to Gina.

Gina nodded and Kara quickly appeared with Alex in hand. Molly asked Kara to sit and have some tea as well. Alex sat on his mother's lap but he was eyeing the plate of cookies, waiting for someone to offer him one. Molly held the plate out and he studied for a moment and then chose a small tea cake.

When they were leaving, Molly leaned over as if whispering to the doll.

"Oh dear, Annie, I don't know, I will ask." She turned to Beatrice. "Annie says she is lonely for another little girl to play with. She has no friends here. She would like to go home with you, if you would like."

"Oh yes! I will take her and be her friend."

Just before they walked through the gate, Alex let go of his mother's hand and ran back and gave Molly a hug. What a lovely afternoon. She had not had a tea party since Amanda and Sarah's daughter were young. They would wear hats and gloves and carefully hold out their pinkies as they drank. Sarah said, being from the South, tea parties were very important for young ladies. Manners, that was how young girls learned proper manners.

As she was finishing, she heard the church bells. She was dressed up a bit so she left the dishes sit, grabbed her purse, and hurried out the door.

People were filing in through the open doors and Molly walked in, prepared to take a seat at the back, but as she walked in, her eyes were so taken with the majesty and she had walked halfway up the rows of pews before she realized. She slid into a pew and quietly continued to scan the beauty before her.

From the outside, one could never imagine anything like this. She had picked up the pamphlet in English near the door. Basilica of Our Lady in Trastevere dates back to 340AD. Good Lord! Molly smiled, "How fitting!" Believed to be where the first MASS was openly celebrated in Rome and the first church in Rome dedicated to Mary. The stained-glass windows and granite columns with frescoes of saints were over-whelming and Molly was glad she had been beckoned by the bells. Of course, she did not understand the service but she sat in reverence. And at the end, Molly walked out into the early evening air with a great sense of peace and awe. She looked back at the humble exterior and thought how that applied to people as well...some go through life without anyone realizing the beauty and power that lay within. She walked back to the apartment, passing under that familiar window and stopping to look up for a moment before walking on. That night, curled up in bed, Molly wrote Eugenio a message to find when he got back to the barracks. She didn't want to write of her day. She wanted to be able to sit and tell him in person, sharing her experience at the church over coffee. Then she fell asleep early, long before the moon rose high over the city.

She was rather pleased at the ease with which she was able to find her way to the Spagna Metro. She had spent many years traveling the Chicago EL but it was much different when she was faced with directions in Italian. Still, she was soon standing in the small piazza looking up at the Spanish Steps. "Do not do long steps, Molly," rang in her ears as she looked up at the MANY steps before her. Maybe not, she decided. Instead, she ordered a latte and paid the extra charge and took a seat outside a coffee shop. As impressive as The Steps are, what she came for was the pink house to the right.

The Keats Museum. John Keats was one of Molly's favorite poets and she told Sarah when they got to Rome, she was going on a pilgrimage of sorts to honor one of the trilogy of Romantic poets: Lord Byron, Percy Shelley, and John Keats. Keats wrote "The great beauty of poetry is, that it makes everything and every place interesting." Molly loved to teach Keats. For a man who had no advantages in life, not through birth, money, or education, a man who lost his parents early in his childhood, he was able to enrich the world. Molly told her students that being able to read the works of a man who had a true passion for poetry was a gift. She hoped one day they would understand.

And Keats had one of those love affairs that held a story of its own. It was years after his death that the literary world learned the truth and depth of his love for Fanny Brawne. And her real identity had been a secret until she passed years later and her children made Keats's letters to Fanny known.

When Keats was diagnosed with TB, he wrote Fanny, "I have left no mortal work behind me, nothing to make my friends proud of my memory - but I have lov'd the principle of beauty in all things, and if I had had time I would have found myself remembered." Keats died with a broken spirit, never to know the impact his words and passion left on the world. She walked through the rooms, reading and enjoying the exhibits. Loyalty, love, and a shared passion kept artist Joseph Severn and Shelley staying with Keats in Rome through this pain and suffering, to the sad end. Molly was glad this was a place she had come on her own.

From there, Molly took the Metro to the Piramide exit. The idea of a real "occupied" pyramid built in 30 BC in the middle of Rome fascinated her but today she walked around Porta San Paolo until she found a small flower shop and then walked passed Pyramid of Cestius and entered the cemetery behind it. This is Cimitero Acattolico, meaning non-Catholic, and the only Protestant cemetery in Rome. It is known as "The Englishmen's Cemetery." It didn't take long for her to find the headstone. It just read "YOUNG ENGLISH POET".

Molly sat down in front of the headstone and brushed away the dried grass and leaves and placed her bouquet of daisies at the base. She knew that Keats had loved daisies and Shelley had had daisies planted at the site. "A thing of beauty is a joy forever." Molly said out-loud, one of her favorite lines from the young poet himself. "You have not been forgotten," she whispered before she moved near-by to visit the graves of Severn and Shelley as well. She took pictures, sure they would not have minded. As she left the cemetery, Molly held her locket in her hand. Sarah would have come with her but again, poetry was her passion and she was glad this was something she had done alone.

Molly stopped once and turned to look back at Keats's headstone, "I wonder," she thought, "had you not died at age thirty, what would you have left as your legacy? And what would have become of that great love you and Fanny once shared?"

With the afternoon heat bearing down on her, Molly caught the tram and headed back to the shaded streets of her own little piece of ancient Rome.

She spent the evening working on the patio. It was hard at first to really get into it again because she was used to having Sarah's constant input. Tonight, she worked until it was almost dark and then sat alone and read what she had written. She played with the locket around her neck as she read out-loud, correcting and editing as she went. Finally, she took off her cheaters and laid them on the table and rubbed her eyes. Not bad, she decided!

Gina opened the gate and poked her head around the corner. "Molly, may I come over?"

"Yes, of course."

"I heard you talking and I thought you may have company."

Molly laughed. "No, I write and then I read out-loud. I have told my students for years it is better to hear out-loud what you write. I am taking my own advice. My friend used to do the editing but now, I am on my own."

"You must be a very good teacher. That makes sense to me. It is better to hear what is good or is wrong. Our minds play tricks on us that our ears will tell us. We see what we want to see but we hear our mistakes."

"Exactly."

"I just wanted to thank you for the tea party. It was very nice of you to go to all that trouble. I quite enjoyed it as much as Bea did. She has named the doll Annie Molly. It has been difficult to keep the children from coming over to visit you all evening."

"Please do not worry. The children are always welcome to come and visit."

"But this is your vacation and when your Eugenio is here, I do not want them to bother you."

Just then Molly saw a little head peek around the gate over Gina's shoulder. "I think we have company."

Gina turned and motioned for Alex to come in. "You may come for a bit but you must never come through the gate without me. If you do, you have a time-out." Alex nodded and then smiled at Molly. She put out her hand and Alex took it. He scooted over and crawled up on her lap. "Molly," he said, "Mio Molly."

Gina and Molly tried not to laugh because he clearly was very serious.

After they left, Molly was feeling anxious. Tomorrow Eugenio would be back. The time had gone quickly! It would be late evening before he returned so she had the whole day to herself. Early the next morning she walked through the tunnel and saw Marcello waiting on a couple as she approached. He smiled when he saw her. "Molly, good to see you. Where are you going this fine morning?"

"Actually, just here. A large latte and a pastry. You choose for me."

As she took her first sip, she looked over at the small news stand next to the coffee shop. There was a rack of postcards out on the sidewalk. She hadn't even thought of sending postcards to anyone back home but she decided she might buy a few to maybe send later. She chose, of course, the Colosseum and Trevi Fountain and the Pantheon, but also some of the other places she still wanted to visit. She wondered if she should send a card to Sarah's daughter. Would she be happy to hear from Molly or would it only be a reminder that her mother had never been able to go?

She wandered around the neighborhood for a while, taking a few pictures, strolling up one street and down another. She had only been here two weeks but already it felt like home. She had been lucky to find that apartment, in that neighborhood, and then there was Gina and the children, Marcello, and of course, Eugenio. It was everything she could possibly have asked for, well, if Sarah could have been there, it would be perfect.

Molly stopped at The New Station for a late lunch. Alex came to the door the minute he saw her come in. "Miss Molly, is good to see you. We are happy you like our food. Come, I give you a seat by the window."

"Why do I eat like this?" Molly thought as she walked home. The Penne Alfredo was perfection on a plate, that's why! Her plan had been to have a light meal and take the rest home for later but once again, she had finished every bite.

By 5:00 p.m., Molly had bathed, so she headed for the kitchen to prepare a dinner she could just re-heat when Eugenio arrived. He had left a message that he would be working but leave for Rome as soon as he finished, anxious to begin their time together again.

She pulled a lounge chair out of the sun and set a glass of tea next to her. She wanted to close her eyes just a minute and relax. The faint sound of the traffic soon lulled her to sleep and when she opened her eyes again, she reached for her tea and it was warm. She sat up; the sun was down over the wall. "How long have I been asleep?" She looked at her watch, it was almost nine. Eugenio would be home soon. She smiled. She would never get tired of the sound of it, even if it was all pretend for them. She headed for the bathroom to brush her teeth and hair once more when the doorbell rang.

When she opened the door, Eugenio was standing there. "Are you the lady of the house? I come to sell vacuums." He stepped inside and kissed her. "I joke. Do you understand?"

"Yes, Sir, come in. My husband is not home. We could have a glass of wine..." and then she leaned over and whispered in his ear, "and make love."

"Yes and make love. Forget the vacuum." He kissed her again, this time more slowly and more passionately. "I miss you. Was it good days for you? Tell me about your days and nights." He took her by the hand and they walked out to the patio. "I want to hear everything you did."

"Well, I wandered the neighborhood, had a tea party, did some reading and some writing, had coffee with Marcello, and ate way too much at my favorite restaurant. And I went to church and, Eugenio, it was amazing."

"Who is this Marcello? Should I be jealous?"

"A very handsome man who works at the coffee shop near the supermarket. Very young, very sweet and a bit of a flirt." She leaned over and gave him a kiss on the cheek. "But he doesn't hold a candle to you."

"I do not understand 'hold a candle'."

"It means he does not come close to you. I prefer you."

151

Eugenio smiled but he felt his heart sink at the idea that he had to work while other men spent time with Molly.

"Dinner, I will make dinner. You must be hungry. You relax."

"No, is late, you do not need to cook for me."

"I have everything almost ready. It will just be a minute."

The night had cooled and the lights from the city filtered through the trees, giving off a soft glow. It was as if they had been together forever as they chatted about their days apart. Molly cleared the dishes and brought back coffee and some tarts she had picked up at the bakery. When he took his last drink of coffee, Eugenio leaned back in his chair and Molly waited for him to say something but he just looked around the tiny yard and then at Molly. Finally, he said so quietly that she wasn't sure if it was meant for himself or for her, "Is good."

Molly walked over and stood behind his chair and began to rub his shoulders. He leaned back and closed his eyes. She bent down and kissed his neck, putting her face into the curve of his neck. She could taste the hint of salt on his skin. This was all make-believe but for now, make-believe was enough. She knelt down in front of him and took his hands. "You must be tired." She could feel the tension in his hands and she had to laugh. "It is true; Italians talk with their hands." She held them tighter but he pulled free and took her hands gently in his.

"Then no words, I will show you." He helped her to her feet and led her to the bedroom. She started to say something but he put his fingers to her lips.
"No talking, showing."

The next morning, they were sitting on the patio when Eugenio pointed behind her. A little face was peeking around the gate. As soon as Molly turned, Alex came running and crawled up on Molly's lap. "Eugenio, this is Alex. And Alex, this is Eugenio." Eugenio extended his hand but Alex put his arms around Molly's neck.

"Mio Molly." Alex looked directly at Eugenio.

"Looks like I have even more competition." Again he put out his hand "Ciao, Alex."

"Alex is just learning English. And I really need to start learning more Italian."

"It will come in time. I learn because I work with American troops and I liked. But it took me a long time and I still have trouble when I do not speak so often. I have to think first sometimes but I will teach you Italian if you like."

"As I remember, we did just fine last night without English or Italian."

Before he could reply, Gina came through the gate. "Molly, I am so sorry." She put her hand out. "ALEXANDER!" Her voice was sharp. She walked across the grass and put her hand out to Eugenio. "It is nice to meet you. Please, I apologize for my son. I say no but I am afraid he has a bit of a crush on our Molly."

"I understand. Would you like to join us?"

"No, thank you, we are leaving for Sorrento. But it is nice to finally meet Molly's Eugenio." She turned, "Come Alex, we go now. When we return, I will get a chain for the gate." She smiled but Molly knew she was serious.

Alex gave Molly a kiss on the cheek and slid down and ran to take her mother's hand. The gate clanged behind them.

"What will we see today? What is on your list?"

"Are you sure you are not too tired? We can stay here and relax."

"I promised to show you Roma."

"And I just want to be with you. I do not care where we go or what we do. So, if you want to stay home and relax all morning it is fine. We can go out later. In fact, I want to take you out to dinner tonight."

"You are good for me, Molly. I would enjoy to just stay at home for a few hours and relax."

A quick rain about noon took the heat out of the day. With the gentle rain against the patio doors, they made love. Molly had gone in to get her book from the night stand. When she turned, Eugenio was standing in the doorway. "Molly," he said quietly, a question in his voice, but before he could finish, she held out her hand. And later they slept, Molly liking the idea that the pillow next to her was no longer empty.

Eugenio woke and looked over at Molly. She was lying there quietly reading. "Michelangelo…" she said before he had even asked.

"You are reading of Michelangelo?"

"No, today I want to see Michelangelo. The statue of Moses at San Pietro in Vincoli. It is near the Colosseum. I know there are others and I will see some at the Vatican but I love this statue. Could we please go?"

"Yes, of course."

"The thing is that I am a tactile learner. I would love to touch it."

"No touch, Molly. They have guards and railings to keep people away. Is not possible."

"I know, don't worry. I won't get arrested."

"I am police. I would have to arrest you." He laughed.

"I promise, no touching. But can you imagine being able to run your fingers over that cool smooth marble, knowing that Michelangelo created this and most certainly ran his hands along the gentle curves when he finished, not just looking at his work but feeling the sense of perfection. And then standing back and viewing his own genius with pride. But I will stand quietly with my hands behind my back and just look."

"And then tonight we will have a special dinner."

"Yes, I want to take you to dinner."

"Molly, please. I want to take you somewhere very special for me. My family restaurant. Is time you see and meet my cousins. And the food is the best in all of Roma."

"Are you sure? How will you explain me? And what will they think of me?"

"My cousins, they know of you and they know of my marriage trouble. They want to meet you. You will like them and they will adore you as I do. But I worry, my cousins, they are like their papas, handsome Italian men, charming and tall."

"I am afraid that all other Italian men pale in comparison to you in my eyes, well, except for Dean Martin and Vittori Grigolo.

"Yes, I know, you tell me...but also, I am here!" He smiled.

"Well, if I am to meet MOSES and your family, I need get ready." Molly took out a white dress she bought at the end of last summer. Sarah had insisted when they had seen it at Macy's. She said it would be perfect for Italy next year...and it was half price. It had a halter top and a long skirt. She slipped on sandals and a lace bolero jacket. She looked at herself in the mirror. She had never worn anything like this before. NO, she would change into something more subtle.

She turned to see Eugenio in the doorway. "Yes, very nice."

"No, I am going to change. I am being ridiculous."

"No," he said a bit too loud. Molly turned to face him. "Please, Molly," his voice softened. "I do not like the man who has made you feel like this, who made you not see how beautiful you are on the outside and missed seeing how beautiful you are inside. And if you do not choose me, you need to find someone who will look at you as I do."

"Not choose you? Seriously? Look at me. I am happy, as I have never been. I am in Rome and in love, and it is because of you. I know you are not free and I know that all we have is here and now but it is enough for me."

"Then wear the dress and let the world see my Molly."

"Then I guess I am ready to go."

As they boarded the tram, an older man put his hand out in a gesture to help Molly step up. Molly smiled and accepted his hand, "Grazie."

"See?" Eugenio smiled.

It was late afternoon when they finally arrived at San Pietro. They walked into the church and Molly was surprised that there were almost no people there. It was one of the less visited attractions in Rome and near closing time but Molly liked the idea of having the next few minutes without a crowd. Eugenio took her camera from her hand and stepped back. Molly began to walk toward the statue, her eyes scanning the massive figure before her. She had only seen pictures but now she was feeling that sense of awe she had felt so many times since she arrived in Rome. Eugenio watched as she held her necklace, silently taking in every inch of the masterpiece before her.

After a few minutes, Eugenio touched her arm, bringing her back to the present. "Molly, this is Nino. He is a guard here."

"It is very nice to meet you," she extended her hand.

"Nino is going to help us but it must be very brief."

"I do not understand."

Nino looked around to make sure no one else was near. "Come," he said quietly. He took Molly's hand and led her to the railing that kept visitors at a safe distance. He unhooked the maroon velvet rope and stepped back. Molly stepped into that forbidden space. She pictured Michelangelo standing on this exact spot, and she reached out and let her fingers glide gently over the marble. She felt like her soul was touching the greatness of the master himself.

Eugenio watched her through the lens of the camera, her face was beautiful and he never grew tired of looking at her. He watched her touch the statue, treating it like a fragile piece of glass.

Not wanting to disturb the majesty of the time and place, Molly let her hand rest for just another second on the curve of the foot and then stepped back.

"Thank you, Nino." She leaned over and kissed his cheek. Eugenio spoke to him in Italian and shook his hand. Nino nodded.

They walked across the room toward the exit and suddenly Molly turned and took one more look at MOSES. Then, like a small child over-come with the moment, she put out her hands, "MICHELANGELO! WOW!" Eugenio laughed and took one more picture before they walked out into the bright sunshine. He took her hand, now feeling very comfortable holding her hand in public, enjoying the warmth of her hand in his own.

"I do not know what you said to Nino, but thank you. That was extraordinary!"

"He understands passion....and love. AND NOW WE EAT!" He felt Molly's fingers tighten. "Molly, is okay. My cousins will like you and the food is excellent. And being together makes it perfetto!"

"Then, lead on. I am starving."

They walked past the Colosseum and along via dei Fori Imperiali. Men dressed as gladiators were having their pictures taken with tourists on the sidewalk and people were hawking their wares in front of the small carts of souvenirs. They stopped in front of the Altare della Patria.

"Was completed in 1925 to honor Victor Emmanuel, the first king of unified Italy. It is also Italy's Tomb of the Unknown Soldier." He pointed to the honor guard and the Eternal Flame. "In 1921, our soldier was chosen by a mother whose child had been killed during WWI. His body

159

was never recovered. She chose our soldier from the remains of eleven unknown soldiers. There was a state funeral on November 21, 1921 and he was laid to rest."

This time Molly took the camera. "This picture should be of you."

They caught the tram just around the corner and headed back toward Trastevere. When they crossed the bridge, Eugenio took her arm. "This is our stop." He pointed to a tall apartment building across the river. "This is where my grandparents lived. And this is their bridge."

They walked along the river for a block and then turned down a narrow street that opened into a small piazza with a fountain. The restaurant spread out before them. *IL FRATELLI MARINO* was the sign across the front. They walked between the two patios adorned with flowering plants and lights to the entrance. They were greeted by a very handsome man and he and Eugenio exchanged words and hugs. Then he turned to Molly and kissed her lightly on each cheek. "I am Carmine, Eugenio's cousin. Maybe he already tells you of me. My cousin, he tells me of you and I see the happiness in his eyes I no see for a long time. Welcome. Now, come, come! I have a nice table for you on the patio. Away from others for now so you can talk. I tell Nick you are here and we do special dinner for you."

They were barely seated when an older man joined them. He spoke to Eugenio in Italian and then added, "Ciao, Molly. I apologize." He kissed each cheek. "We are soon to be very busy but I prepare a special dish for you. Penne Carbonara and a nice wine. Eugenio, you look like your papa more each time I see you. Is good."

When they were alone, Molly took a sip of her wine. "Tell me about your father."

Over the prosciutto and melon, Eugenio began to tell Molly about his father and Molly noticed he spoke with great respect.

"When I was young, my father did not take the car out very much, we were lucky to own a vehicle back then so it was for special occasions. But sometimes he would take me for drives in the country and we would talk of things men speak of. He was not an affectionate man but I always know he loves me. When I chose to go into the military, I knew he did not want this for me but he said that I was a man and I should choose what was best for me. And years later, shortly before he died, we took a drive and we talked of many things. Then he suddenly said he was sorry I was never a papa because I would have given a child much love and guidance. And he hoped that I knew he loved me. I never told anyone that Alessia was the one who never wanted children but I think he knew. Alessia said if I had to be in the military, she would not be stuck home with the children. But I know now that she did not want to be tied down to a home....and me."

Molly listened and saw the sadness in his eyes when he spoke of his marriage that she had seen so often in the past. But then he took Molly's hand and smiled. "But now I have Molly." As they ate, it was clear to Molly that he would have definitely passed on that father-to-child love if he had been given the chance, just as a father passes on the gold watch that came down from generation to generation, father to son or daughter, especially a daughter.

At the end of their meal, Molly looked at her empty plate and wondered what Eugenio must think when he saw that she had once again eaten every bite. Not one of those "Oh, I will just have a salad" girls to begin with but everything here was so amazing! She took the last sip of her wine and was about to announce she could not eat another bite when Carmine set a plate down before her. Tiramisu! She started to protest but she decided on maybe just one bite...or two. It was perfection! She pushed it to the middle of the table and handed Eugenio the spoon. Together, they ate every bite!

It was almost 11:00 p.m. before Nick came out of the kitchen carrying a tray with three coffees. "Very busy, always, but is good," he exclaimed as he sat down, leaned back, and sighed.

They walked back to the bridge but instead of waiting for the tram, Eugenio led her up on the bridge. In the middle, they stopped and Eugenio pointed to the view of St. Peter's in the distance. There were still many people out but they did not seem to notice. Eugenio leaned over and without even looking at her, he whispered, "Do not be angry with me but I need to say...I love you." Molly's fingers found his and he turned his head just enough to see that she was smiling.

That night when they went to bed, Eugenio lay quietly and Molly did not know what to do. Finally, she leaned over and kissed him, feeling a tear as her lips brushed his cheek. Molly put her head on his chest and closed her eyes. There was no love-making, no passion that night, just two people perfectly content to just be together. Molly fell asleep listening to the beating of his heart.

Chapter 9

Molly was up early Saturday morning. She slipped out and walked over to the bakery and bought lovely warm pastries and orange juice. When she came back Eugenio had made coffee and was sitting at the table.

"I woke and you were gone. I was hoping you did not leave me." He smiled.

"Never! Just to the bakery." She held up the bag. "Fresh croissants. I am going to be so fat by the time I go home."

"You are perfect and please do not talk of going home. I do not want to think about it."

Eugenio started to tell her a story about when he was young and then he stopped. "What about you, Molly. You speak of Adam and Amanda and Sarah but you never speak of Molly."

"There really isn't much to tell. My dad was a truck driver so he was gone so much. Dad was like a visitor who came to stay every now and then. We always fixed a huge meal the first night he was home because he said he got so tired of food on the road and he missed Mom's cooking almost as much as he missed Mom and me. And we crowded lifetimes into just a few days and then he would be gone and it would be just Mom and I again. Once we flew to Florida and met him and we went to Disney World. It was the best trip I have ever taken, well, until now, even though I threw up after the Magic Mountain ride." She took a sip of her coffee. "Mom died when I was 16. She had cancer. Dad would try and come home more than last year but he wasn't there when she died. He felt guilty but I just think he couldn't be there to watch her die so he left that to his teenage daughter. At the end it was just Mom and I and then one day it was just me. Mom said I shouldn't be mad at him but I was so angry. He always said I reminded him so much of Mom and I think after she died, it was hard for him to even look at me and not think of her. So, I went to live with my aunt and uncle for a while. When I graduated from high school, I went back to live at the house. It was comforting to be home and I felt close to Mom. Anyway, here I was, 18 and living alone...and all I did was work part-time at a small insurance company and I started college. I could have been the wildest child ever but I just studied, worked, and waited for Dad to come home. But he came less and less over the next couple years. I always had money and school was paid for. I had Mom's car and all the freedom and I did nothing with it. Silly me! When I was a junior in college, Dad remarried and "home" became my step-mom's house in Arizona. When Dad sold the house, he put even more money in the bank for me and packed his things and was gone. I would visit from time to time and I was always welcome, but I think Dad felt guilty about leaving me to grow up on my own. And the older I got, the more I looked like Mom. I would see him just watching me sometimes and then he would walk away without a word. Eventually I just stopped going because it was just too hard for both of us. I wrote and sent pictures of the kids but he only saw them twice when they were little. And he passed away when they were in high school. Anyway, when he sold our home, I found a nice two-bedroom apartment near campus. That is how I met Sarah.

One afternoon there was a knock at the door and there stood this very classy girl with long hair pulled back in a ponytail.

She introduced herself and said she heard I had an extra bedroom and she really needed a place to live. She said she was from Atlanta, she was quiet, and she made the world's best scones. I was painting the living room and she took off her jacket and grabbed a brush. By the time we finished and were cleaning up, we had decided she should move in. She moved in that night and we have been best friends ever since.

Sarah met Matthew our second year of graduate school and after graduation, they were married and moved to Atlanta. Sarah was happy she was going home and they bought a house and she was offered her first teaching position. It seemed like everything was going great for her but Matthew was offered a job in Chicago so Sarah packed up her life again and moved to Chicago. Matthew took a job with a good law firm and Sarah started teaching at a small junior college but she loved it."

Eugenio leaned over and took her hand. "Molly, what of you?"

"Well, I stayed in Iowa and took a job teaching. I felt like I had been in school forever so I was anxious to start a real life. Then at Thanksgiving, I went to Chicago to visit Sarah and Matthew. And I met David. He worked with Matthew and he was charming and witty and educated. I used to drive into the city once or twice a month because David would go to Iowa once in a great while, but he said he really hated Iowa. It was only the second time in my life I had been in a serious relationship but eight months into being in the love stage, I drove in to surprise him and caught him cheating. The thing is, I wasn't as devastated as I should have been. I think that if that particular event hadn't

165

happened, we would have broken up soon. I had already begun to realize he was not the man of my dreams. I quietly packed up my things from his apartment while David sat quietly on the couch, saying nothing. So, I went back to Iowa and decided to forget about men for a while. I threw myself into decorating my home and getting on with my life, refusing to return his calls.

About a month later, David showed up at my door late one Friday night. He begged me to let him in so we could talk. He said he had stopped for a drink with the guys after work and he suddenly decided he needed to see me. SO, he got in his car and four hours later, there he was, standing at my door. He said he had made a mistake but this woman worked in his office and she had come on to him. It had been a brief fling and it was over before it had actually begun. It was late and he was in no shape to drive so when I went to the kitchen and he fell asleep on the couch, I let him sleep and went to bed.

Sometime in the night, David came in and got into bed with me. I told him no but he cried and said he needed me and that he loved me so much. I don't know, I guess I missed him, and we ended up making love. The next morning, he said he had to get back to Chicago and he left early. It was the next week-end before I heard from him again. He suddenly appeared with flowers and an apology. He said he was just so afraid that he was going lose me.

This time I didn't let him in but he said he understood and he would give me some time. He called over the next month, saying he wasn't giving up on me, but I knew it was over. Then one morning I woke up about 5:00 a.m. and felt ill and I ran for the bathroom. I remember sitting in the middle of the bathroom crying when, suddenly, it hit me that I was in some serious trouble." Molly took a long drink of her tea and was silent for a minute, as if she was re-living that moment in time, before beginning again. "I called Sarah and that afternoon she appeared at my door with an EPT test, a bottle of wine, and scones. She said "test first" and then we would see who got to drink the wine. And as I sat and sipped tea and ate scones and watched Sarah sip wine, I told her I was going to keep the baby but David was not an option. I certainly hadn't given any thought to motherhood at that point in my life but I knew I could do it. I just wished my mom was still alive so I wouldn't have to do it all alone. Sarah said I wasn't going through it alone, in fact, she had been waiting to tell me in person, she was pregnant as well and we were going to go through it together and we were going to make fabulous mothers and aunts. But if the kids ever asked, she was the younger sister. I made her promise not to tell David but she did tell Matthew. I knew I would have to tell him eventually but just not for a while. I wanted to let the idea settle in and I wanted to tell him when I wasn't so over-whelmed. Unfortunately, Matthew told David and suddenly there he was again. He said he wasn't ready for a family but he loved me and he wanted to marry me so he would try to be a good father. I guess in the end, I felt like I should try, for the baby. So, we got married and I moved to Chicago. I started to substitute teach and when Amanda was a year old, I got a teaching position at Illini Community College with Sarah.

David fell in love with Amanda the minute he saw her and she has been 'Daddy's Little Girl' her whole life. Two years later, Adam was born. David would have been content with one child but I wanted at least two. I had been an only child and I guess I always felt like I was missing something. It

167

certainly would have been easier after Mom died and Dad moved on without me. David was a good daddy to Adam but there was never the connection that he had with Amanda. When the kids were older, we were looking at a house in the suburbs, the one David always promised me. Then one night he took me out for dinner, said he had a surprise for me. Over dinner, he told me he had a chance to buy into this great brownstone that was going condo. He said he had made an offer. SO, we bought a three-bedroom condo. At that time, our children were at an age when their years at home were limited." Molly looked over at Eugenio and smiled, "Bored yet?"

"No, I like knowing all of this of you."

"One day Sarah called and asked if I could come, she needed me. I asked what was wrong and she said she would tell me when I got there...and to bring wine. When I arrived, I could smell scones baking and she was holding two wine glasses. She took a long drink of Moscato and announced 'Matthew is having an affair.' Sarah was not a drama queen and she was never one to fly off the handle so I knew it was true. 'This morning there was a knock at the door and this woman was standing there. She said I needed to just give up and let him go. He wants this divorce and I should stop fighting it. He loves her now. And I said I thought she had the wrong address but she said she had been to my home many times. I left her standing in the doorway and called Matthew. I asked him straight out if he was having an affair and he said he had no idea what I was talking about, and why would I even ask him such a question. I told him there was a woman standing in the doorway telling me you are in love with her and you want a divorce. And then he said...' Sarah started to make this noise and I wasn't sure if she was

168

going to laugh or cry...'he said that he was not having an affair...what was wrong with me? But then he said, 'Just put Lynn on the damn phone.' The instant it came out of his mouth he knew what he had done. He quietly added, 'Shit.' and Sarah said she had just hung up the phone, took a deep breath, and turned to the woman and told her to get the fuck out of her house. The woman started to say something but Sarah is a class act. She told her she was sure Matthew would be calling her to fill her in and to have a nice day. She heard her cell ringing as she walked away.'

I poured us more wine and asked where do we go from here? She started to cry, which made me cry, and we spent the rest of the afternoon getting drunk, eating scones and chocolate and packing Matthew's clothes. I spent the night, and early the next morning Matthew came in looking forlorn and needing a shave. Sarah sat in the kitchen, refusing to speak to him, while he carried his things to the car. At one point, he took my arm and whispered, 'Molly, please talk to her.' I said I wasn't there to talk, only listen. He asked me to look at his side but I took his hand and led him to the kitchen door and pointed to Sarah. I told him he did that. And did he honestly think there was anything that either of us could say that was going to take that hurt and sadness away? He picked up the last box and walked out.

When he was gone, Sarah walked into the bedroom and started re-arranging the closet. I made coffee and Sarah tried to make a joke about needing the extra space anyway. Finally, we pulled the mattress off the bed and dragged it down to the curb and left it. I was making a sign when Sarah came out carrying every sheet and pillowcase in the linen closet. She threw them down on the mattress and told me to grab my purse. We were going shopping. Sarah ordered a new mattress to be delivered and we carried home the bags of new linens from Macy's. While we waited for the new mattress to arrive, we sat on the steps sipping more wine. Suddenly Sarah smiled, 'I wonder if she took a shower while she was here. I could use new towels too.' We laughed and then I put my arm around her shoulder and we sat quietly until the truck arrived."

Molly looked at Eugenio, "Good Lord, it sounds like I spent a lot of time drinking wine, doesn't it? I really don't, at least not very often. Since Sarah died, it isn't the same."

"What of you, Molly? Was Sarah there for you?"

"Yes, Sarah was there when it was my turn AGAIN. I refused to talk about Matthew to David. He sided with Matthew, of course, and I just did not want to hear it. I know marriages have their problems but I knew both of them. And the tension just added to all the other problems David and I were having. There was no talking about anything because David was either gone all the time or he refused to talk, saying we were fine. Then just two months later I showed up at Sarah's door with a deep dish pizza, a bottle of wine, Ben and Jerry's, and P.S. I LOVE YOU. When she opened the door, I held them up and said 'David is having an affair.'

We had gone out for dinner one night and we took a seat near the window. David seemed intent on looking out the window while I studied the menu. The food was okay at best but this was the third time in two weeks David wanted to eat there. In Chicago, small restaurants come and go very quickly and I said I was sure that this one would have a limited run. And I said I would have a hamburger and

French fries, hard to mess up, but when the waitress came over to take our order, David asked me what I was going to have. While we waited, I asked David about his day but he continued to stare out the window. Then I realized he was watching the young waitress in the reflection in the glass. She was having an animated conversation with a young man at the counter. When the girl laughed and touched his arm, David seemed upset. I saw it in his eyes. And the waitress looked over the young man's shoulder and was looking straight at David. She was trying to make him jealous! I tried not to react but I just felt ill. I told David I wasn't feeling well and we needed to go. He said we hadn't gotten our order yet so why didn't I just go home since it was only a couple blocks and he would get our food to go and maybe some soup for me and then he would be right behind me.

I looked over at the girl and suddenly I knew how Sarah had felt that day. I picked up my purse and walked out. It wasn't cold but I remember shivering as I stood across the street, away from the street light and watched my husband talk with this girl. How long? Was this just a flirtation of an older man or were they actually having an affair? I wanted to call Sarah but I hate those people who walk down the street ranting and raving into their cell phones for the world to hear. I went home and sat on the steps of the brownstone and waited. It was almost an hour before David appeared with two bags smelling of grease.

'Feel better?' he asked, trying to sound concerned. No, he was genuine in his question. He held out his hand to help me. 'I brought chicken soup.'

We sat at the kitchen table and I sipped from the big mug he had handed me. I let the still hot broth run down my throat and wash away the lump that had been hanging there, ready to choke any words I tried to speak. Finally, I just blurted out. 'Tell me about the waitress.'

'The waitress? Why? What about her?'

'Because you are sleeping with her.' David turned and faced me.

'WHAT? Don't be ridiculous. Wait, did she call you?''

Molly laughed, "Good Lord! Are all men that stupid?" But the minute she said it, she saw the look on Eugenio's face and her heart sank. She reached out and took his hand. "Oh God, I am so sorry. I didn't mean that. I..."

"Not just men, Molly" was all he said. He got up and walked into the living room. Molly followed him. She stood behind the couch and leaned over buried her face in the curve of his neck and wrapped her arms around his shoulders.

"Forgive me, I am so sorry. If there is one exception to that statement, it is you." He could feel the heat of her tears against his neck.

"Come and sit, Molly." She walked around and sat a few feet away from him. She could sense that they needed a bit of distance while they talked.

"I do things that are not right. I know this, but..."

Molly stopped him, "You mean me." she said softly.

"What your David did was wrong. He hurt a woman who spent many years trying to make him happy and give him a good home and family. He had no right and it breaks my heart to see in you the results of some of those things. I know I am still married but no, I do not mean you. You are the one thing that is right in my life for a very long time except for my work. I wanted to know of you and I am sorry I made you think of such things and spoil your time here...with me."

Molly scooted closer to him and put her hands on his face. "You have not spoiled one moment for me. I am here with you, right or wrong. I don't care. We will talk of all these things but not today."

"Finish your story, please."

"SO, it was just Sarah and I again. One night while we were taking a walk, Sarah said she just did not understand how two hot chicks such as ourselves could end up alone. She laughed, but then she stopped and added that she loved Matthew and all this just broke her heart. A couple months later Matthew called me and asked me to meet him for a drink. He said he really needed to talk to me so I went. He admitted he had really screwed up and he wanted Sarah back. He had a brief affair with a girl from the office but it was already about to end when Sarah found out. And would I ask Sarah to have dinner with him and at least to let him explain before things went too far and the divorce was final. He didn't get any sympathy from me because if it was just a fling and almost over, who was it who kept telling this woman that he had asked for a divorce and Sarah had refused? Who was it who told this woman he loved her? And how did he define "almost over" if he was still sleeping with her? But I remembered what Sarah had said and I wanted her to be happy. I agreed but when I asked Sarah, she said to tell him to go to hell. She had plans for the rest of her life and none of them had Matthew's name on them. She was much stronger than I ever was."

"Sarah never got a call like that from David. He moved in with Tiffany and now they are going to have a baby. All I can think is "that poor innocent child." Anyway, I started taking my writing seriously and Sarah was my editor. We had a publishing company interested in a series of educational books and we made all these fabulous vacation plans in Italy. She was going to retire at the end of the school year and after our trip, she was moving back to Atlanta. I was going to sit in my expensive condo and work until I was dead. But I would have one glorious month in Italy to remember and then I would wait and hope someday my grandbabies would come to visit once in a while." Molly stopped and leaned back and closed her eyes, "And now Sarah is gone and I have surgery waiting for me at home. But I am here now and Sarah is happy I made it. And because of you, I will have enough memories to last the rest of my life, however long that may be."

"Molly, please, do not speak of such things and no more talk of sad memories, only of good times with your Sarah. We will make new memories together, for a very long time." Molly felt him relax and she lay down and put her head in his lap and closed her eyes. She was almost asleep when she heard the TV click on. "Is a guy thing." She looked up to see him smiling down at her. Just before she fell asleep, she said quietly, "It is your turn when you are

174

ready." Later that night, curled up together in bed, he finally decided it was time and he told her of his marriage and of his last trip home. Finally, he had shared with someone who truly understood.

Chapter 10

Molly had slipped out of bed as quietly as she could and closed the door behind her. She would have loved to have stayed in bed, perfectly happy to enjoy the morning breeze and listen to Eugenio's deep sleep. But, she knew he would stay with her as long as he could tonight and then after the long drive back, he would have to go to work first thing in the morning.

She went into the kitchen and worked quietly, almost finishing when she heard the bedroom door open and Eugenio walked over and put his arms around her.

"I am sorry; did I wake you? I was trying to be quiet."

"No, not noise...smell. What did you make? I smell cinnamon."

"I baked cookies. Gina said they would be returning early from Sorrento and I wanted to have something made because I am sure her children will come over to visit. I did make a few extras." She pointed to the plate on the counter. "And I made coffee."

"What shall we do today? What do you want to see?"

"You. I want to just stay home today and then I want to take you out to dinner tonight. I found a place near-by that I really like. Maybe not Marino Brothers, but very good."

They were just finishing coffee when little Alex came running through the gate. "Molly!" He ran and crawled up on her lap. "Ciao, Molly," and he gave her a big hug.

"Molly, should you let him sit on your lap? Is he too heavy for you?"

"Yes, Mother Hen, I am fine." She smiled.

Just then a tall man came through the gate. "I am sorry. I am afraid that Alex has learned how to open the gate." He extended his hand to Molly. "I'm Marco, Gina's husband. Please call me Marc. My family speaks often of you. It is very nice to finally meet you. I hope you are enjoying your stay in Rome."

"Yes, very much. And this is my friend, Eugenio Marino. He is Carabinieri."

Marc shook Eugenio's hand. "Yes, my wife tells me."

"Please, come and join us for coffee. Molly made cookies."

"I do not want to intrude, although my son does not seem to have a problem."

Alex saw the cookies on the table and then he looked at Molly and smiled. Molly handed him one and he took a bite. "Buon, Molly."

Marc took him off Molly's lap. "It was nice to meet you. Perhaps before we leave next week you both can join Gina and I for a drink."

"Yes, that would be lovely. Thank you. And tell Gina I will see her next week."

"Ciao." Marc shook Eugenio's hand once more and started for the gate.

"Ciao, Molly," Alex was still waving when they disappeared through the gate.

Eugenio refilled their coffee cups and sat down next to her. "Molly, we talked of many things yesterday and I think, I worry that we....."

Molly took his hand. "No, we are not broken. How are we going to get to know each other better if we do not talk? We are not young and foolish and we both know we have lived our lives with others. And we will continue to have differences about things. That is just life but at the end of each day, we will be just as we are right now, right here, together, whether we are in this apartment or thousands of miles apart."

Eugenio reached over and took a cookie. "Cinnamon, my favorite." Molly smiled, happy she had remembered that.

It had cooled off by the time they left the apartment and walked down to The New Station. Alex greeted them at the door. "Molly, is good to see you again." He turned and put out his hand to Eugenio. "I am happy to meet you. Molly speaks of you and I do not like to see her eat alone. Now, come, I show you a good table."

They took a seat by the window and picked up the menus. "Everything I have had here has been very good." Eugenio smiled but it upset him that he had to leave her again soon and she would have another four days when other men shared her company and worried about her being alone.

Alex stopped by their table as they ate to make sure everything was to their liking and when he finally cleared away their plates, he leaned over, too close for Eugenio's liking, and asked, "Tiramisu, Molly?"

"Yes, please."

When he returned, he set a plate in the middle of the table and handed Molly two spoons. Molly smiled.

"Thank you, you remembered." Eugenio felt a little less resentment toward this handsome waiter, thinking Molly must have spoken of him to Alex. He decided it was good that Molly had people to talk with so she would not be alone while he was away. But why could she not find just women for friends?

After dinner, they took a walk along the river. Molly put her arm through his as they walked. It seemed natural for them now, so easy. A small car shot past them.

"Do you ever think you could drive in Rome?"

"I drive in Chicago but I think it best if I stick to public transportation here. Much safer for all concerned." She laughed. "I don't know how you do it."

"I do not drive here much anymore. When I come, I leave my car and take the train into the city. Is too hard to even find a place to park anymore."

"I would be so lost all the time, I think. I like the trams. Why are there not more underground lines? This is such a big city. It would be easier to move underground like London and Paris."

"We are an ancient city and there is an entire city of ruins under the modern city. But it is acceptable. We appreciate how lucky we are to live here. So many people and the heat and the rushing is difficult but here we are surrounded by all of this and the world comes to us to be able to see it. Chicago is new and wonderful, I am sure, but Roma was the beginning."

"I think Chicago is a great city but I know I have never really appreciated it like I should. Rome is more than I could have ever hoped for."

"Yes, but someday I hope to move out of the barracks and find a home again maybe near the water. Being near a beach is always better, especially in the summer when is very hot. But come to Rome to visit family. When I bought a home, my wife, she wanted to live near the beach instead of being near the barracks. So, for many years it was difficult for me to spend much time at home."

"I am so sorry, I probably would have gotten a big mobile home and just parked outside the gate so I could see you every day."

Eugenio smiled. "Yes, I am sure you would have." But then he looked at his watch and the smile left his face. "Is time I prepare to go."

On the walk home, Eugenio said, "Dinner was very good. So, you have eaten there before. How do you know of this restaurant?" He didn't want to sound like he was questioning but he could not help but wonder how often she had gone that the waiter would know of her love for tiramisu and her wanting two spoons.

"I just found it when I was out walking, looking for some place to have dinner." Eugenio wanted to ask more but he did not want her to think he did not trust her.

Molly sat on the bed and watched while he packed his duffle bag and carried it out and set it on the sofa. When he went into the bathroom, Molly took the three containers she had in the cupboard and unzipped the bag and slipped them inside. There was a small note attached to the top of each of them with a thumbprint in the corner.

"Is time, Molly." He hated having to leave Molly but he also hated to leave the peace and happiness he felt. It was good here.

Molly tried to smile because she did not want to make it worse but when he set his bag by the door and turned to her, he could see the sadness in her eyes. "I will be back soon." He put his arms around her and held her close.

Finally, she stepped back and took his face in her hands. "Do not worry about me. You work and sleep and I will be waiting for you when you come home."

Molly stood in the doorway and watched, as she did last time, until he was lost in the crowd waiting for the tram before closing the door. Suddenly, she felt very tired. She went in and curled up on the bed and closed her eyes. "It would be nice," she thought, "if I could just sleep until he returns." It was almost dark when she woke up and she could not believe that she felt hungry. She wondered what Eugenio would think if he knew that he had just taken second place to a plate of pasta. "Well, we won't tell him, will we?" she said out-loud.

***

Back at the barracks, Eugenio began to unpack his bags. He took out the three containers and set them on the table next to his bed. He opened the first note and smiled, "Yes," he thought, "I miss you too." He started to open the second note but stopped. No, one a day! He looked at the clock. He had four hours to sleep before he went on duty. He lay down on the bed and still holding her note, he fell asleep.

Molly had walked through the tunnel and into the piazza in hopes of finding one of the little neighbor cafes still open. She was hungry but she also just needed to get out and walk a bit. The apartment seemed so still and lonely with Eugenio gone. The air was warm and the streets were quiet. One tiny shop had sandwiches so she went in and ordered and took a seat outside under the awning. The waiter came out and set down her plate and latte and left without saying a word. Not the pleasant conversations she had with Marcello but it was late and he was probably tired of being pleasant all night and just wanted to go home.

She ate in silence, thinking about what she was going to do the next four days on her own. "There is all of Rome to explore," she thought, "pretty sure I won't be bored."

Just then a little girl and her father walked by. The little girl stopped by the wicker pots over-flowing with flowers near Molly's table. She carefully touched one of the flowers.

"Rosa." Her father nodded. She touched another. "Rosso," and he nodded. "Giallo, azzuro, bianco." Then she touched the leaves, "Verde." He smiled and took her hand. When they walked away the waiter, who had been standing in the doorway, came over. "May I get you anything else?" His English was better than Marcello's.

"No, thank you. Everything is fine and I think I just got a lesson in colors."

He smiled. "Which do you prefer? Pink, red, yellow, blue, or white?"

"Yellow."

"Giallo. Yes, is a good color." He reached over and picked the small flower and handed it to Molly. "Is a happy color."

When she paid her bill, she handed him his tip and added, "Buona notte," with a question in her voice.

He smiled, "Yes, good night."

Molly carefully laid the little flower on the table when she got back to the apartment. How many young girls had taken home flowers given to them by young men and carefully pressed them in books, thinking they would cherish them forever, only to open the book years later and see the dried petals and try to remember why they were there. Or worse yet, remember, and gather them up and throw them into the trash with regret she had even bothered.

She went out and sat on the patio. She was thinking about the little girl and her father. She thought about the walks she and her own father used to take when he was home. On warm summer nights they would walk down to the Tastee-Freeze and have ice cream sodas. And they would talk, Molly trying to tell him all the things that happened while he was away, trying to keep him part of the family. He would call when he was on the road but it wasn't the same.

Sometimes he would swing her up on his shoulders and carry her the last block. She remembered how grand she felt, like they were the only two people in the world. And here was another little girl with her own daddy, strolling together in the big city. Molly hoped she felt it was a special time for just the two of them. Molly opened her computer and began to write.

When she finally stopped, it was almost 4:00 a.m.! She had been writing for four hours. She stood up and stretched, feeling a sense of satisfaction at what she had written. This could be the beginning of a whole new project! She closed her computer and went in and got ready for bed. That familiar scent wafted through the air as she slipped into bed. "It's good, Sarah! This is going to be really good," she whispered. "God, I miss you." She turned on her side and closed her eyes. Instinctively, she reached out but felt the cool vacant pillow next to her. She pulled it close and fell asleep wondering where Eugenio was and what he was doing....and wondering if he was thinking of her.

It was 4:00 a.m. when Eugenio got up and started to put on his uniform. He thought of Molly, of course asleep, and he wondered if her dreams were of him.

Chapter 11

When she had gone to bed a few hours earlier, she had been very pleased with what she had written. She wondered if she would feel the same way in the light of day. But first, she needed to check her email. She hoped to hear from Eugenio but she also felt a little guilty that he would take the time to write when he should be sleeping.

"Ciao, Bella. I shortly return to duty. If I could come to you tonight, I would. I do not like waking without you now. I think of what we have talked and I think you are right. Is not easy for me but I think it is good to talk of all things. I cannot wait until Thursday when I come to you. Your Eugenio"

And there was a letter from Adam wanting to know if Italy was all she had hoped for. He said that there were actually openings in Naples...maybe he should just check out Italy for himself. Being stationed in Italy for a few years....how bad could that be? He also reminded her to relax and take lots of naps. Nothing from Amanda but then she knew how upset she had been about her even leaving and then not offering to take her and Eddie along.

She took a drink of her coffee. For some reason, it tasted especially good this morning. She opened her documents and read what she had written so diligently a few hours ago. "Ya know, Sarah, this is really good."

She took another long drink and began to type. She had never written so much before that came together so effortlessly, but the words had just flowed. She only found three small grammatical errors in all she had written.

A title? Molly leaned back and closed her eyes. She thought about the little girl's face last night as she had touched each flower. Molly went back to the first page and typed "Sarah's Flowers" across the top. Yes, perfect!

Molly heard the church bells and she looked at the clock. It was already noon. She decided she would take a walk and maybe treat herself to a nice lunch. "Again with the food, Molly!" she thought to herself. She had just closed her laptop when she heard the gate open behind her. She turned to see Alex running toward her.

"Molly!" But, before he could reach her, Gina appeared behind him.

"I am sorry we have disturbed you. Our nanny is ill and I am trying to work at home today but now that Alex can open the gate, we have a problem."

"No, please, do not worry. We will figure something out. I was just going out for a walk and have some lunch. I would be happy to take Alex with me. You could get some work done in peace. I would love the company."

"I could not impose."

"It would be my pleasure. And maybe a walk will wear him down a bit and he will nap when we return."

"I would not agree but I have reports that I must finish today. If you are sure, I will take him home and put some shoes and socks on him. I will bring him back in a few minutes. If you are sure?"

"I will change and be ready."

"Bye, Molly," Alex happily waved over Gina's shoulder as they disappeared through the gate.

Molly was just running a comb through her hair when there was a knock. She opened the door to find a young man standing on the step. "You are Molly, yes?"

"I am Molly, yes."

"I am Giovanni, Eugenio's nephew. My father, he remembers where Eugenio says you are staying and my father says to come and bring this to you. My father is Carmine; you dined with him at our restaurant."

"Please, come in." She led him into the kitchen and poured him a glass of ice tea and then opened the envelope.

"Dear Molly,

It was good to meet you when you come with our cousin. We know you are alone with Eugenio on duty. We would like to invite you to come for lunch. Would Tuesday at 2 p.m. be convenient? My son, Giovanni, will return with your reply. We hope you do not have previous plan but would be alright to do another time. Carmine"

Molly read it twice, trying to read between the lines. Was this a sincere invitation or would this be a pleasant warning to go away? Or just maybe she was going to end up "sleeping with the fishes"? "I watch too much TV," she smiled to herself. Eugenio says his family are good people but maybe very protective as well. Only one way to find out. She wrote on the back of the letter that she thanked him for the invitation and Tuesday at 2:00 p.m. would be just fine.

Giovanni read it when Molly handed it back to him. "Papa will be pleased you come. Grazie! I must go now. We are very busy at this time. I will see you tomorrow. Ciao, Molly." He smiled and Molly couldn't help but think he was yet another generation of handsome and charming Marino men.

Gina knelt in front of Alex and told him to be a good boy and to give Molly the envelope. Alex handed it to her and smiled. "Alex would like to buy you lunch today if you think you are prepared to take a small boy to a restaurant. It is the least we can do for your help."

"It really isn't necessary."

"Please, I insist."

"Well, then come, Little Man. Looks like I have a date for lunch." She put her hand out and Alex took it. Gina leaned over and took his face in her hands and spoke to him in Italian. He nodded and gave her a kiss, "Ciao, Mama."

Molly and Alex walked along the streets, stopping to enjoy the flowers that hung heavily from the stone walls. Alex chatted away, half in Italian, half in broken English and sign language, but Molly understood. They walked to the church and sat on the steps by the fountain for a bit and then window shopped as they headed for The New Station. Molly decided that she would be able to get some help in translating what Alex wanted to eat. Her "other Alex" greeted her and extended his hand to Alex. "I see you have a luncheon companion today, Molly."

Little Alex shook his hand and Molly introduced them. When they were seated, Molly opened the menu and handed it to him but he didn't even look at it. "Pizza," he said and smiled. Alex took their order and asked what they would like for toppings. Little Alex replied in Italian "lots of cheese and pepperoni if Molly says it is good." Alex looked at Molly, who understood and she nodded. Molly was surprised how well-behaved and polite her date was. She had grown very tired of trying to eat a nice meal out in Chicago with small children running wild while their parents chatted away as if they had no idea their kids were ruining the meals of everyone around them. Molly remembered taking her own children out to eat and if they were not behaving, she took them aside and had a quiet talk with them, which usually resulted in Adam sitting quietly for the rest of the meal and Amanda pouting and refusing to eat anything else.

Alex stopped by the table as often as he could to chat with them and when he cleared the table, he asked Molly if they were having tiramisu but Molly said she thought gelato would be the order of the day. Alex walked them to the door when they were ready to leave and when he gave Molly a kiss on each cheek, adding, "We are friends now."

Little Alex gave him a disapproving look. "No, mio Molly."

"I think you have a jealous suitor, Molly. But I understand wanting to have you all to himself." She smiled but she felt the heat rise in her cheeks.

189

It was getting warm by the time they walked up the hill, turned at the train station and headed for the apartment. Alex had slowed a bit by the time they were home and when Molly went in to use the bathroom, Alex curled up on the sofa and was almost asleep by the time she came back. Molly sat down and Alex moved over and snuggled up against her and closed his eyes. That is how Gina found them when she came over an hour later. Molly had picked up a book and was quietly reading with Alex tucked under her arm.

Gina tapped on the patio door and slid the door open as quietly as she could. She sat down and leaned back, as if it was the first time she had relaxed all afternoon. "I cannot thank you enough, Molly. To take away from your vacation to help me but this is such a busy time at work for me." She reached in her pocket and tried to hand Molly a 20 euro note, but Molly shook her head. "No, please. I enjoyed the afternoon and we had a lovely lunch. Alex had pizza; it seems to be his favorite. And he was so good."

Gina picked up her sleeping son and as they left, Alex looked sleepily at Molly and waved.

Molly went out and sat on the patio and turned on her computer, hoping for a message from Eugenio but there was nothing. She knew he was still on duty and she was hoping he had gotten some rest before his long day. She sat in the chaise lounge and put her feet up. The sun was hot but it felt good on her face. Maybe Alex had the right idea. She fell asleep wondering what she was going to wear for her lunch tomorrow with Eugenio's family.

When Molly woke up, she tried to stand up but she felt a twinge that stopped her. She sat back down and rubbed her shoulder a bit. At first she thought she might have slept on it wrong, but then she felt a wave of panic move through her.

"Oh no! Not now. Not here!" This was the first time she had felt even the slightest discomfort since her heart attack. She went to her purse and took out the bottle of nitro and put one of the tiny white pills inside her lip as the nurse had instructed her.

Instantly, she felt it dissolve and she sat down on the sofa as she felt her pulse quicken. She waited for the head-ache she was warned would follow. She closed her eyes and felt tears stream down her face. "Why now, when I am so happy?" She leaned back and closed her eyes and tried to relax. Almost as quickly as the pain had come, she felt it subside. She went in and lay down on the bed. She pulled Eugenio's pillow close to her and she thought of Alex curled up next to her. She wished she had Eugenio there with her so she could have that same secure warm feeling. She took a deep breath.....the pain was gone and the air was filled with that sweet scent that had become so familiar to her and she felt calm. "Still here when I need you," she whispered. She closed her eyes and fell asleep.

She made tea and toast when she finally woke up. She went out and sat down on the patio and turned on her computer. How she would have loved to have had a cozy space like this in Chicago instead of three feet of balcony surrounded by a heavy wrought iron railing. Here, with the high walls and plants and lemon trees, it was like a private world in the middle of a huge city.

She wrote Adam a long letter, trying to sound trite but wanted to remind him of where he could find a few things he might need "later." She had tried to talk to him about some of these things while he was home but he kept telling her they would talk later, as if not talking about it would make it go away. But here and now, halfway around the world, he couldn't just dismiss the subject. She assured him that she was fine, conveniently forgot to mention having to take a nitro, and said she just wanted to tell him while they were fresh in her mind. She ended by telling him how lucky she was to have such a great kid and she hoped someday he is lucky enough to have a son just like him.

When she finished, she wrote Amanda a light cheerful letter, ending with how much she loved her. And she thought to herself, she hoped one day Amanda would have her own daughter, and God forbid, not with Eddie. A daughter with her sweet smile but a little less selfish and a little less dependent on the rest of the world than Amanda. But mostly, she wanted Amanda to find herself and her own happiness.

And then she wrote Eugenio. She wanted him to understand that if anything should happen to her while she was in Italy, it was not his fault. It had been her choice to come and if she died tomorrow, she hoped he knew that he had given her more happiness than she had ever known. And if it were possible to love through Eternity, he would forever feel her love for him.

And finally, she wrote one last letter: "Dear Sarah, Well, Kiddo, here I am in Rome, but you know that because I have felt you here with me so many times. It isn't the same without you, but Sarah, it is everything we thought it would be and so much more. The food is unbelievable and the history just engulfs you and its presence takes your breath away. Our wine is so good and so cheap here. I am writing every day and I think it is pretty good. And then there is Eugenio...OMG! Sarah, these last two weeks with this man have been the best of my life. I am so happy but sometimes I feel guilty being here without you. I miss you so damn much. Everyone should have a best friend like you....it would make the world a much better place! You make my world a much better place. I love you. Molly."

Molly wiped the tears from her face and hit YouTube. She decided the rest of the night could use a little wine and Vittorio Grigolo.

***

When the tram reached Lungotevere Raffello Sanzio, Molly stepped off and crossed the busy street. At night, this area along the river is full of locals and an equal amount of tourists, strolling and talking; restaurants are full of laughter and music; smells of flowers and wonderful foods fill the air. But in the light of day, it returns to the hustle and bustle of a big city. Molly turned and walked down the street toward the piazza in front of the restaurant. Carmine was standing near the fountain smoking. When he saw her, he put out his cigarette and walked toward her, leaning forward for the traditional kiss on each cheek.

"Ciao, Molly. I am very happy to see you again. Come, we have a good meal together."

He led her to a small table on the patio. The restaurant was still crowded with people enjoying a leisurely lunch. The waiter brought over a carafe and filled the wine glasses. "I remember Moscato, was I correct?"

"Yes, thank you for remembering."

"I want to thank you, Molly. My cousin, he is very important to me, to all of us, and Alessia, she hurts him. We say nothing because of his love for her but there are many things he does not know. It would only hurt him more. But he is happy now with you."

"He is a good man. I know this has been troubling for him but I only want him to be happy. I do not want to complicate his life."

"It is sad, being Catholic and an honorable man, is difficult. He tells his cousins of his Molly and we think this is a good thing."

Molly took a sip of her wine. She felt relieved that this was not a "sleep with the fishes" intervention.

"I am very relieved you approve."

"My great aunt, you may have to win over. She is very Old World but then again, she more than many in our family understands true love. In time, she will see. Just be patient with her. She is here today and I am sure she will find a way to stop by our table to say hello."

"And check me out?"

He laughed, "Yes, to check you out. But may I ask you an honest question?"

"Yes, of course, and I promise to give you an honest answer."

"Do you love my cousin?"

"Eugenio has become a very important part of my life. And to answer your question, I love your cousin. I know we have a rather strange relationship but I do love him. And I know things are difficult, but please know that I will only do what is best for him, even if that would mean never seeing him again." Molly was surprised at her own words. The thought of never seeing Eugenio again made her heart hurt more than any heart attack.

"Molly, his wife, she sees another man. Giovanni has seen her with other men but this one I think is serious. He sees them when he goes to the beach on holiday. Every day they are there and my son watches how she seduces him. Eugenio never says but I am sure that he knows when we talk. But now I see happiness and a peace he will need when his time in the military is finished. It will not be easy to divorce in Italy but is possible. This would be good. I know my cousin, he has made a good choice in Molly but I worry this is not what you want. I know you have a life in the USA. Divorce will take time but he will be happy again and he would make you happy as well. If this is what you want as well."

Molly took a drink of wine and then leaned over and said quietly, "I have not admitted this to anyone else; I have thought about this but it can only be the fantasy of a silly old woman. There are just too many things standing in the way."

"No, Molly, all things are possible. You just need to have faith." He studied her face for a moment and then added, "Molly, please, I do not mean to upset you and you are in Roma. Paris claims to be the city of love but Roma, the city of eternal love, is better!"

The waiter brought over prosciutto and melon and re-filled their glasses. Carmine raised his glass and tipped it toward Molly before taking a sip. "We Marino men love beautiful women with beautiful souls. You will fit into our family very well. Now, we eat!"

Before they finished their first course, Giovanni joined them. He kissed Molly's cheeks and sat down. "Ciao, Molly. Is good to see you again. I make a perfect tiramisu. You have some for dessert later."

Carmine nodded, "My son is 'pasticcere,' ah, pastry chef. He is the reason why his papa needs to exercise so much. He is very good."

The main course was Fettuccine Ragu di Pollo. Molly took her first bite as Carmine watched, and then he smiled. "Oh my! This is extraordinary. I have only had Fettuccine Alfredo before. Such a thin pasta!"

"I am glad you like. Fettuccine means "little ribbons" and pollo is chicken. But maybe you already know this?"

"No, I didn't. I am learning so much while I am here but I am afraid I will be spoiled for all pasta when I return to Chicago."

"Alfredo is not true Italian. If a restaurant has Fettuccine Alfredo, it is to please the tourists. And since we spoil you, maybe you should just stay and not go back to Chicago and be disappointed."

As they continued to eat, two more young cousins stopped by to say hello. Obviously, she had been a topic of conversation since she and Eugenio had dined there. Just as they were finishing, an older lady came over, her hand resting on the arm of a very handsome man, a subtle way of offering a bit of support.

Carmine stood and pulled out a chair for her. She spoke in Italian and then looked over at Molly. "My aunt just wanted to stop by and tell me we are paying too much for tomatoes." He smiled, "And since she is here...Molly, this is my aunt. And this is Molly."

Molly reached out and took the woman's frail hand. "It is very nice to meet you."

Molly looked down and saw a gold band on her thin finger, a plain gold band with an amethyst stone. Molly smiled, "You are AnnaMaria, Antonio's Anna. It is lovely to meet you."

The older woman's gaze softened and she held Molly's hand a little tighter. "Yes, Antonio's," she turned to Carmine and spoke in Italian once more, "She has honest eyes."

She took her hand from Molly's and rested it lightly on her arm. In broken English, she asked, "You love my Eugenio and are good to him?"

"Yes, I love Eugenio and I try to be very good to him."

"Then I like you."

The man came back and put his hand on the woman's shoulder, "Mother, it is time to go."

She smiled up at him and turned to Molly. "My son, Antonio."

"It is nice to meet you, Antonio." He reached out and took her hand. "Yes, ciao, Molly. It is very nice to meet you."

After they left, Molly let out a deep breath and Carmine laughed, "Were you nervous?"

"Yes, a little. It is important that your family approves. I know it isn't easy for all of you, being Catholic and with Eugenio being married."

"Have faith, Molly."

By the end of their meal, it was just Carmine and Molly enjoying coffee and when she was ready to leave, Carmine walked out to the fountain with her. "Thank you for coming. I am happy now for my cousin, he is lucky to find you. I do not worry now." He gave her "the kisses" and Molly turned and headed for the tram. At the corner, she turned and looked back to see Carmine leaning against the edge of the fountain talking on his cell phone. She wondered if he was talking to Eugenio, or did Eugenio even have any idea she had been invited to lunch. Her question was answered when she got back to the apartment and turned on her computer.

"Thank you for your afternoon with my cousins. Please do not be angry with me, I did not know until Carmine left me a message. He means no harm. He has been more like a brother to me and he knows of my feelings for you. I hope it was a good time for you. Just a short break from work now but I will be online to see you when I return to the barracks later tonight. Missing you. E."

At 8:00 p.m., Molly ran a comb through her hair and put on some lip gloss before turning on her computer. She noticed that her arms and face were tanning nicely and it looked pretty good! She couldn't remember the last time she had a good tan.

It was almost 9:00 p.m. before Eugenio came on line. He looked tired but he leaned back in his chair and smiled when he saw her. "Ciao, Bella! I miss you."

"You look very tired."

"Yes, there has been some trouble and we have been working long hours but I will get some dinner and sleep soon. But I worry you are upset with me for my cousins' invitation."

"No, it was lovely. ...you don't have to worry."

"When I come to Rome, you will tell me what you talked about."

"Yes. And I met AnnaMaria and Anthony. He is very handsome, I am sure like his papa."

"Yes, we Marino men are very handsome, just some of us not so tall." He smiled.

Molly smiled but then she suddenly looked very sad. "I miss you. I wish you were here."

"I know. But at least now it will only be two more days, not like when you were in Chicago."

"I wish we could talk longer but I want you to get something to eat and get some sleep. I don't want you too tired when you get here."

"No, will not be a problem. I will come to you as soon as I get off duty on Thursday."

Molly kissed her fingers and pressed them to the screen. "Be safe. I miss you."

He gave a small wave and blew her a kiss and was gone. Molly closed her computer and leaned back in her chair. Two more days....she would just stay busy until he came home. She opened her folder and looked at her list. There were still many things she wanted to see tomorrow so she would get an early start. Tonight, she just wanted to curl up in bed and read a while. She hadn't even bothered to fix any dinner; she was still full from that wonderful lunch!

***

Molly had set the alarm for 7:00 a.m. because she wanted to get an early start but by 6:00 a.m. she was wide awake and decided to get up and make coffee. She was going to take the train out to Ostia Antica before it got too hot. Most people want to visit Pompeii, destroyed by Mt. Vesuvius, but Molly had read an article about Ostia and she had researched all she could on it. Unlike Pompeii, Ostia had just been deserted and left to ruin. It had been the harbor city of ancient Rome, founded at the mouth of the Tiber River. In fact, its name means "mouth" in Latin. With the demise of the Roman Empire, Ostia fell to ruin and was abandoned after the 9th century when it was constantly being raided by Arab pirates. Molly felt being left to one's own decay to be quite sad. Most recently, she felt the same about Detroit but here and now, she was excited about a day to wander and ponder this piece of Italian history.

She took the bus over to the train station and was happy when she was greeted with smiles by two women she had seen on various other occasions. It made her feel like she was becoming a tiny part of the neighborhood. She got on the train and was lucky enough to get a seat. The train was already full of people, obvious by their attire that they were headed, one stop more than her, to the beach. She stepped off the train, and being not quite sure where she was going, she followed a group of tourists guided by a small man waving a yellow umbrella. It wasn't long before she realized she would be just fine on her own so when the man stopped to give instructions, she walked past them and through the archway that led into the city.

Molly bought a map but she had seen so many pictures, she felt she knew where she was going and what she wanted to see. She wondered where all these people had gone; what happened to all the children who had once lived and played in these homes. When she finally reached the amphitheater, she sat down on the stone steps at the top. It is not the Colosseum but then nothing else in the world is. She took out the lunch she had brought. She laid out a napkin and opened her fresh melon and pear and cheese. And of course, some chocolate and a couple bottles of water. She looked down at the stage below and thought of the events that had taken place there. Plays, lots of plays, but no mention of gladiators, so it did not hold the brutal history of the Colosseum.

"Do you ever wonder what life was like back then?" The voice behind her made her jump. Molly turned to see a tall obviously English man standing there peering down at her.

"May I?"

"Yes, of course."

"Are you on holiday?"

"Yes, and you?"

"Yes, I am with a group but they bore me so I decided to strike out on my own. 'In search of intelligent life.' He laughed at his own joke, a rather loud laugh, more like a braying jackass, than a human laugh. He took a leather tobacco pouch and pipe out of his backpack.

"I don't think you are allowed to smoke even out here. I saw signs."

He tapped his pipe on the edge of one of the stones and the ashes fell and the breeze blew them away. "Then I shall just play dumb tourist if I get caught." And he laughed again as if no one would ever consider him dumb.

Molly had met many men like him over the years so she knew the answer even before she asked the question. "Are you a teacher?" Molly knew he taught in higher education but she decided to make him work for the opportunity to toot his own horn.

"Professor of Economics at London University. I am Professor Nigel Bournesworth." He extended his hand.

Politely, Molly accepted it but felt a little uncomfortable when he held it longer than was acceptable. "Molly McMillian." She would have added a "nice to meet you," but her mother always taught her not to lie. She almost smiled at her own bit of unspoken humor.

Then his lecture mode kicked in. He lit his pipe and leaned back. "Ostica was founded back in the 4th century, BC. Lovely bit of ruin, obviously another example of the fall of the Roman Empire. Much like the Colonies these days."

"Actually, we are the United States of America....we won that one!" Molly took a drink of her water and turned and smiled at this pompous ass. "And," she began again, "it was founded by Aucus Marcius in the 7th century, BC."

"Ah, an American with a love for Italian history. I fear I offended. There is a small café at the entrance. I would love to buy you a cup of coffee or something cool to drink. I know Americans prefer everything with ice." He leaned over and smiled, one of those leering looks she was sure he used regularly on his young female college students. "I think you could be a pleasant diversion from what has become a very tedious trip."

"No, but thank you. I have water here and it's cold. I just want to sit here a while...enjoy my own thoughts. I am thinking I might like to include Ostica Antica in one of my own college lectures." She smiled.

"Well," he said, getting up rather abruptly, brushing himself off, "I won't continue to bother then." He turned and without another word, he walked away.

"What an ass!" she thought, "I noticed he didn't bother to ask what I teach." She took a bite of the pear, so sweet, and let her thoughts wander back to ancient Ostica.

With few trees and no breeze to speak of, Molly decided it was time to head back before the heat began to take its toll. The train into the city was not air-conditioned and Molly had to stand so she was relieved when they pulled into the station and she could step out into the hot, but at least, fresh air. Back at the apartment, she took off her shoes and sat down on the couch. It had been a good day, despite the intrusion. She felt pretty sure that while he felt the group he was traveling with was beneath him, they were glad when he walked away and let their vacations proceed nicely without his presence.

Despite the nice lunch she had eaten "amongst the ruins," Molly felt hungry but first she wanted to bathe. There had been so much dust all day and she felt like she was bringing a bit of the ancient city back with her. She was more than ready to wash it away. She stood under the shower and saw a steady stream of dirt wash down the drain. When she finally decided she was close to using up all the warm water, she stepped out and wrapped a towel around her. She made a sandwich and poured a glass of iced tea and went into the bedroom. She propped the pillows up and opened her notebook to make a few notes before they slipped her mind. She ate as she wrote and then suddenly felt tired. Maybe she would close her eyes for just a few minutes and then get up and do some writing. She turned the fan on and lay across the end of the bed, letting the cool breeze dry her hair. Sometime later, she kicked off the towel and pulled the sheet up around her and fell back to sleep.

It was much cooler when Molly finally woke up. Her thick hair, which took forever to dry, held only the faintest hint of dampness when she ran her fingers through it. How long had she been asleep?

She looked at the clock. It was almost 9:00 p.m. She had been asleep almost three hours. It had cooled and the air had a hint of rain. She checked her mail but there was nothing from Eugenio. She consoled herself with the hope that he was getting some much needed sleep.

Molly worked at her computer into the wee hours of the morning. She could not believe how much she managed to get done every time she sat down to work.

As she closed the patio doors, she noticed drops of water on the glass. She slipped under the covers with a twinge of excitement, knowing that in just a few hours Eugenio would be there with her again. And with the gentle sound of the beginning rain, she fell asleep.

Chapter 12

"Somewhere in this TV is a music channel," Molly thought, flipping through the channels. Then suddenly something caught her eye. It was pictures of what looked like an explosion and she could see so many police on the scene. She recognized some of the uniforms from some of the pictures Eugenio had sent her when his unit had special duty and had to wear their bomb removal gear. He had been telling her how much they hated it because of the stifling hot gear they had to wear for sometimes hours at a time. There was a reporter interviewing a member of the Carbinieri, but her focus was on what was behind them. It was what was left of a car. She went to her computer and searched through the pictures until she found the one she wanted. She stared at the picture; Eugenio was standing in front of his vehicle and the license was CC1347. She ran back to look at the TV. Half of the plate was blown away but she could still see CC1. Why hadn't she learned Italian so she knew what was happening? The interview ended but she sat motionless, scanning the continued footage of the explosion, for exactly what, she wasn't sure.

Suddenly it dawned on her and she ran through the back gate and knocked on the door, not waiting for an answer. She opened the door and shouted, "Gina!"

Gina came into the kitchen, "Molly, what is it? Are you alright?"

"No, please, could you turn on your TV and tell me what is happening? There was an explosion and I don't know what is happening. The license plates...." She began to cry.

"Come and we will turn on the telly and we will see what is happening."

Molly followed her into the living room. Any other time Molly would have taken in the gorgeous surroundings but right now she only focused on the television mounted over the fireplace. Gina turned on the news and silently they watched a few moments before she spoke. "Two policemen were taken to the hospital, one has died. Several people near-by have been injured as well. They do not know the reason for the bombing but there have been many protests in recent weeks. Students are protesting financial programs being dropped and older people are protesting because they have raised the age for retirement to 68 now. I am afraid the government has made some bad choices and the common people are paying for it. But there has been no violence, only demonstrations, until now. But in this heat, people are becoming more difficult. Is it possible to call Eugenio?"

"Yes, I could at least send him a text." Gina handed Molly her own cell phone and Molly smiled and took it in her shaking hands. Gina left the room and came back shortly with two cups of coffee. They continued to watch and Gina explained what was happening, holding the phone tightly, hoping for it to ring. When the news moved on to another story, Gina took the phone and set it on the table. She took Molly's hands in her own.

"Molly, please stay here until we hear something. We can wait together and we will pray to hear soon."

"Thank you," she said, wiping her cheeks with the back of her hand. "But I told him if he could not message right back, to call on my phone or send me an email when he could. I need to be home to wait."

She gave Gina a hug and hurried back to the apartment. She sat on the couch with the computer and phone on the table, continuing to watch the news, hoping for a glimpse of Eugenio, waiting for any word. A few minutes later there was a tap at the patio door. Gina came in, carrying Alex.

Alex ran over and climbed onto Molly's lap and gave her a big hug. He saw the tears welling in her eyes and he put his little hand on her cheeks and gently wiped away the tears that began to stream down her face. "No sad, Molly." He put his head on her chest and hugged her again. "See, is good now!"

He smiled at her and Molly looked into his innocent little face and smiled back. "Yes, Alex, good now."

"I told my husband we will stay with you until we know of Eugenio."

"I will be fine, Gina."

"Yes, you are a strong woman but we will stay. It is not good to worry alone."

They talked and Alex sat quietly and colored with his markers, sensing that something was wrong and that he needed to be on his best behavior.

"Shouldn't you be getting ready to leave for Sorrento soon?"

I spoke to Marc and he said not to worry. We will leave in the morning when we know things are alright. He insisted we stay, Molly."

Molly fought back the tears again, knowing in her heart why they were staying with her. But she smiled and thanked Gina.

About 4:00 p.m., Marco and Beatrice knocked on the patio door and walked in holding two large pizzas. He set the pizzas on the table and leaned over and gave Gina a kiss. "I think we should have some food. Has there been any news?"

"Nothing but a repeat of the earlier reports. And no word from Eugenio."

"Molly, please, do not worry. He has been in the military for many years. He knows to be careful."

"Yes, I keep telling myself that he is alright. It is just not knowing. I know this sounds selfish because there was a policeman who has been killed, but please, not Eugenio."

"Come eat something. I am not a cook but I order pizza very well."

"My husband is a typical man, Molly." Gina gave her husband an adoring smile.

Beatrice took Molly's hand. "Please, Molly, come and eat with us."

They all sat around the little kitchen table and Gina and Beatrice reached out and took Molly's hands. Alex and Marco joined the circle and Marco bowed his head and said a prayer in Italian and then added in English, "and bring our new friend, Eugenio, back to our Molly safe and sound. Amen."

Molly looked around the table and smiled. What a lovely family! "Thank you."

For a while, Molly relaxed and they chatted and had a nice meal. While Gina and Molly cleaned up the table, Marco and the children took a walk and came back shortly with gelato. "Beatrice said you like our Italian gelato."

"I am afraid that is putting it mildly." They each took a dish and carried it out to the patio. Alex sat next to Molly and he offered her a bite of his own several times, each time, smiling up at her. Finally, Marco said, "I will take the babies home, Gina, you stay with Molly."

"No, please, Gina, go with your family. I am fine and I know I will hear very soon. Your family needs you."

"You will let us know if you hear anything?"

"Yes, of course." She accepted a hug from Marco and Beatrice, and Alex climbed up on a chair and gave her a big hug."

Gina took her hand, "You come over any time if you need me, Molly. It doesn't matter what time."

Molly leaned against the doorway and watched as they picked up their children and carried them back through the gate.

She walked into the kitchen and started to do up the dishes but suddenly she thought, what if something had happened to Eugenio? She was an outsider; she would not even be able to go to him. He has a wife and how would she explain her presence? As comforting as the apartment had been since the day she first walked in, she suddenly needed to get out and get some fresh air. She needed to just take a short walk and clear her head from all those negative scenarios that kept running through her mind. She threw the strap of her purse over her shoulder, and grasping her phone, she went out and slammed the door.

She took a deep breath and started to walk. She walked down to the corner and started across the street when she stopped and turned to look behind her. She had walked by this church so many times and barely noticed. SS Francis and Catherine Church. It was a more modern plain white building set back from the street, unimposing. Not one that tourists would flock to, but more of a neighborhood church. She suddenly wanted to go in but she could tell by the sign that they were holding MASS. She walked up and sat on a step and closed her eyes. She didn't know how long she had been there when she opened her eyes to see a young priest standing nearby, not wanting to disturb her. He walked over and sat down next to her. He reached out and took Molly's hand and together they sat without speaking for a few minutes. Then he stood and helped Molly to her feet. He looked up and then blessed himself and smiled. Molly felt tears and he touched her cheek and said quietly,

"Answered." He turned and walked up the steps and disappeared in a side door.

Molly wiped her cheeks with the back of her hand and took a deep breath. She turned and walked back toward the apartment. She had never walked west from the apartment so she continued on past her door and Gina and Marc's house. It was larger than she realized and the front had large stone urns adorned with flowers along the short sidewalk to their door. On the next block she found a small fruit market and she stopped and bought some melon and oranges and strawberries. She would fix Eugenio a nice fruit platter for breakfast in the morning. Yes, positive thoughts!

Just before she walked into the apartment, she looked up. Through the trees, she caught a few rays of sunshine making their way through the thick leaves to the sidewalk. "Well, Eugenio, at least you have the big guy looking after you now," she said out-loud. And in her heart, she honestly believed her words.

She set her phone and her computer back on the table and turned the TV on. She leaned back against the cushions of the sofa and closed her eyes. It had only been a few minutes when she suddenly woke up. She grabbed her phone although she knew she would have heard it. She looked at her computer, nothing there as well.

She went into the kitchen and did up the dishes she had left earlier. "Have to get this place cleaned up before he gets here," she thought. She was going to have faith....right now it was all she had.

She carried her phone and computer in and set them on the bed next to her. It was getting dark but Molly stared at them....wishing a message to pop up on her screen. She felt so alone and then in the quiet of the evening, the air grew heavy with that warm comforting scent. "Oh Sarah! I am so worried about Eugenio. I lost you. I am not sure I could stand to lose him too. I would rather die myself than lose both of you. My heart would rather just stop than to have to go on like this." She reached up and closed her fingers around her necklace and closed her eyes and fell asleep from sheer exhaustion.

It was not daylight yet when she woke. She grabbed her phone. Nothing! She hit the key on her computer and the screen came to life. There was an offline message! "Ciao, I am Mario. I am Carabinieri with Eugenio. He asked I send you a message to say he is ok but had a problem at work and will be late to caserma. He say he will come as soon as he is off duty. No worry." Molly jumped up, knocking her phone on the floor. She carried her computer out and plugged it in and sat at the table. She read the message over and over. She went in to wash her face and looked in the mirror. "Good Lord! You look like crap, Molly!" She washed her face and pulled her hair back. Her eyes looked dark from smudges of make-up from her tears. She was still wearing her clothes from yesterday. She stripped down and wrapped a towel around her hair and stepped into the shower. The warm water felt good as it washed over her. She slipped into a robe and walked into the kitchen. She was just making coffee when she heard the key in the door. The cup fell from her hand and shattered on the tile floor but she didn't care. She ran to the door just as he walked in..... still wearing his uniform and looking very tired but nothing ever looked better to her.

She put her arms around him and held him close.

"I am sorry I could not call you but I send a message with a friend still at the barracks. I was worried about you."

Molly laughed, "You were worried about me? Good Lord! You could have been blown up."

"I worry because you would be sad without me anymore." He laughed.

"Stop, it's not funny," but she smiled. She knew he was trying to make light of the situation. "I saw the CC on the license plate of that car and I thought it was your car. I remembered pictures of it you sent. "

"Molly, all Carabinieri cars have CC on the plates. I am so sorry to frighten you. I had to tell my family and then I come to you. I want only to see you."

"And your wife?" Molly could not believe she had just let that fall out of her mouth but there it was.

"Yes, I call but she did not pick up. I leave a message. But I hoped you would not hear and worry. Then I see your message on my phone but I could not call. I come into Rome with my unit when we finish. I just want now to be home with you."

He kissed her. "Do not be angry but I need a shower and coffee first and then I just want to hold you."

Molly hated to let go of him but she reluctantly released him. He set his backpack down and after giving her one more, quick kiss, he headed for the bathroom. While he showered, Molly cleaned up the broken glass. She poured a cup of coffee and picked up a clean towel and opened the bathroom door. Eugenio had picked up her clothes off the floor and folded them and laid them on the counter. When he stepped out of the shower, Molly held out the cup and the towel. He wrapped the towel around his waist, took a long drink of coffee, and then took Molly by the hand and led her into the bedroom.

Gina wanted to check on Molly before they left for Sorrento. They wanted to get an early start to beat the traffic, if that was even possible in Rome. She walked over and was about to knock on the patio door when she saw the military backpack sitting on the floor. She let out a sigh of relief and whispered "Grazie." She turned and walked back to her house, closing the gate quietly behind her, knowing her friend's heart was once again at peace.

Molly slipped out of bed and went to the kitchen. She wanted to just reach out and touch the man sleeping next to her but she knew he needed rest. Her time would come later. She quietly made coffee and cut up the fruit she had purchased. She wanted to have a good breakfast ready for him when he woke up. When she had asked him, when he first arrived, if he was hungry, he said he was just too tired to eat. She hoped when he got up that she wouldn't see the stress and fatigue she had seen in his eyes last night.

They hadn't made love, instead, they kissed quietly in the dark, and then he had turned on his side and slipped her arm around his waist. Molly pressed tight against his back and

216

they had fallen asleep. There was so much Molly wanted to ask, to know, but she knew they would talk in the morning but for now, knowing he was safe and unharmed was enough. She looked out through the patio doors at the vast clear sky. "Grazie," she whispered and closed her eyes.

It was almost 10:00 a.m. before Eugenio emerged from the bedroom. He looked out on the patio. "Molly?" Not wanting to wake him, Molly had curled up on the sofa and had fallen back to sleep. Eugenio knelt down next to her. "Why did you leave me? Are you alright?"

She opened her eyes and smiled, "No, I just didn't want to wake you. You needed your rest."

"No, Molly, even if I sleep, I want you near me. Ok?"

Eugenio walked out to the patio with his coffee and sat down. After wearing that heavy gear for so long, it felt good to just sit and let the cool breeze blow over his chest. Molly brought out the plate of fruit and set it down. She reached over and took a bite of the melon, sweet and ripened to perfection as always. She was going to miss that when she went back to Chicago. Then she looked around and sighed. She was going to miss all of this.

"I am not very religious, you know that," she began quietly, "but last night I prayed for you." She told him about walking over to SS Francis and Catherine Church and how the young priest had sat with her.

Eugenio smiled, "Thank you. I am Catholic and we pray a lot. We keep God very busy. He was probably very happy to hear from someone else."

"The thing is, I have tried to be a good Christian and do what was right and fair but I was never comfortable with such formal religion. When I was little, I went to Sunday school, but I figured if you want to talk to God, it didn't matter where you are. He would listen."

"Catholics just think it is more polite to go to His house." He smiled and took her hand, "I joke."

"My grandmother used to talk about those "Front Row Christians" who were such horrible people all the rest of the week but made a big production of sitting in the front pew every Sunday. Gram had neighbors, Mary Jo and Bruce Bushman, who complained about everything, never volunteered or contributed, or made any effort to even be pleasant, but Sundays they were at the church an hour early to get that front pew. Gram used to say they were the type who sowed their wild oats all week and then showed up at church on Sunday to pray for crop failure. After I grew up and stopped going to church, Gram wrote me and said that Bushmans had left town. Mr. Bushman had been having an affair with the high school principal and they had a child. It all came out when the child started school and the boy's father's name was on his medical records when he was registered for school. In a small town, things like that tend to come to light very quickly. And Mrs. Bushman was heard using a barrage of very unladylike language....'not very Christian of her', Gram had added."

"The church is changing but very slowly after hundreds of years. Catholics were not to eat meat on Fridays but now...is okay. Still, I remember our nonna and my mother would make sometimes light soups and breads and pasta with marinara sauce but mostly we had fish. And I did my Catechism and I went to MASS and then the family would gather to eat. When my grandmother was no longer with us to make us feel guilty, it became less religious and more about family tradition. But Molly, I still go to Confession and I talk to God and I believe He listens to my prayers. I just know that sometimes He says no. And later, I see many times He is right."

"I am just very happy that He granted my prayer last night."

Eugenio went into the kitchen to refill their coffee cups but he came back without them. Instead, he was holding the tiny brown bottle Molly had left sitting on the shelf. "Molly, why did you have this out? Have you been ill? Is it because of yesterday? Am I the cause of this?"

Molly turned and saw the bottle. She had forgotten to put it back in her purse. Damn! "No, I am fine. I just had a little pain a few days ago and I wanted them handy. Of course you are not the cause. You are better for my heart than any medicine I could ever take."

"Did you call a doctor? Why did you not tell me?"

"Honestly, it was nothing. I would tell you," she lied.

Eugenio went into the bedroom and came out dressed. "I will be back." He gave her a quick kiss and left.

"He is angry," she thought. "Why didn't I put that damn bottle back in my purse?" She went into the kitchen and began to make pancakes. She thought he would just walk a bit and come back and she would make him see that she was alright. By the time she had set the table and the batter as ready, she heard him unlock the door.

"Here," he said, taking a small box out of a plastic bag.

Molly opened the box. It was a necklace with a small capsule on a silver chain. "You put your nitro inside and always wear so you will have it with you." He took it and carefully inserted the tiny pills inside and sealed the capsule. He slipped the chain over her head and sighed, "Better now."

It was almost noon when they finally cleared the patio table and went in and sat on the sofa. Molly reached out to hand him the remote but Eugenio set it back on the coffee table.

"Molly," he said quietly. "It is time we talk."

Chapter 13

We need to talk! So many times she had heard that expression in her life and it was always followed by the very words no one ever wants to hear.

"These last twenty-four hours have been very difficult for both of us. It made me understand there is much for us to talk about, there are things we need to decide and things we need to do. Molly, you are leaving Rome soon. There is little time for us."

"And there they were.....those words.....I will be leaving Rome soon. Our time is almost over," Molly thought. Molly wasn't quite sure where he was heading with all this but his tone was so serious.

Just then they heard Eugenio's cell phone and he went into the bedroom to grab it from the nightstand.

She could hear his voice rise but with Italians, that means nothing. Again, she wished she had learned more Italian than the fifty words and phrases Sarah had taught her.

After what seemed forever, Eugenio came out and sat down. He took Molly's hand. "Please do not be angry with me, and please understand. My wife, she has come to Rome. She says important that she sees me as soon as possible and will I come to her. I ask her to tell me but she say no, only in person. I tell her I will come to her in one hour at my uncle's home. First, I say the restaurant and she say, "No, private.""

"Of course you have to go. She is your wife, Eugenio. She probably wants to see for herself that you are alright. I will be here waiting when you get back and we will talk then. But now, you must go." She tried to make her voice sound light and unconcerned but the words seem to catch in her throat.

As times before, Molly stood in the doorway and kissed him good-bye, and watched until he stepped onto the tram, but this time it was different. She wondered if things would be the same for them when he returned. What if he will only come back to pack his things and tell her he is sorry. Just before he had gone, he had kissed her and held her close, whispering against her cheek. "I love you, Bella. I will return soon." He leaned back and looked into her face and smiled, "No worry, no bombs this time."

"No," she thought, as he walked away, "this could be worse."

Molly decided she needed some fresh air; maybe a walk would make the time pass more quickly. She walked through the tunnel and into the sunshine of the plaza. She walked along the busy street, trying not to look at her watch every five minutes. She was looking at a display in the window of a small bookstore and decided to browse a while. She started to open the door and then stopped. Good Lord! How many books did she think they would have written using the only 50 words she actually knew? She turned and walked on.

She did go into the little shop where she had purchased so many things for the tea party. She found a shelf of toys and games that were familiar to her. She bought a small puzzle and a Battleship game she thought would be fun when Beatrice and Alex came over. And then she headed back to the apartment, once again to wait for Eugenio's return.

She saw Marcello standing in the doorway of the coffee shop as she approached. He smiled and waved when he saw her. "Molly, you must be enjoying Roma very much. I have not seen you for many days." He walked over to meet her and gave her a kiss on each cheek. "Tell me everything you see."

She took a seat under the awning. "Marcello, could you bring me something cold to drink, please, with ice?"

He returned with a bottled tea and a glass with four small ice cubes in the bottom. Molly smiled as Marcello twisted the cap and poured the tea. "Now, Molly, tell me all about what you see."

Molly tried to sound light and chatty. He laughed when she told him of the pompous professor from England. Then he stopped and studied her for a moment. "I see sadness, Molly. Are you no happy in Rome now?"

"I am very happy," she lied, "It is just that I go back to Chicago next week. It makes me sad to think of it."

"Then you should stay. Come and live in Rome and be happy. Chicago is very big and very cold."

"Ah, Rome is huge and goes on forever."

"But we have cozy places we find of our own, it makes it seem smaller."

Molly thought about her neighborhood back home, the fire station, the Chinese restaurant, etc. Yes, we make our own cozy places in a big city as a way of surviving. She saw Marcello watching her. "Yes," she continued, "Chicago is very cold."

"See, is settled. You stay."

"If only it was that simple," she thought. When she left, Marcello said, "Next time bring me your pictures."

Molly unlocked the door and stepped inside. "Lucy! I'm......oh the hell with it." She kicked off her shoes and walked out onto the patio. When she checked her mail, there was a long letter from Adam waiting. Just what she needed!

Adam was full of news. First of all, Nick is getting married. He has been dating this girl for only a few months but he knows she is the one. And of course, he wants Adam to be his best man. Nick and Adam have been friends since grade school. Adam had gotten a new coat for Christmas but right after the holidays he started wearing his old coat again, giving one excuse and then another. David demanded to know where the coat was and Adam said he had given it away. David had been furious and told him he was grounded until he got it back. Adam had refused. And he would not say to whom he had given the coat. Finally, one day after school, Molly and Adam had walked to the corner market and Adam confessed that he had given the coat to Nick and he would not ask for it back. He said he had been bullied by a couple boys on the way home from school and Nick had stepped in to help. Together they had taken on the two boys and they never bothered Adam again. Nick liked a girl at school and he wanted to ask her to go ice skating but he was embarrassed because his winter coat was a hand-me-down and was too small and torn. Adam insisted Nick take his coat. The next day after work, Molly went to Marshall Fields and bought Adam an identical coat. It had been their secret and over the years it was common to hear "I've got your back" passed back and forth between the two boys in a variety of situations. And Molly would just smile to herself, knowing of their special bond.

Adam also mentioned that just out of curiosity, he had looked into a transfer to the US Embassy in Naples after his tour in Afghanistan. He said it would be part of the diplomatic corps but it would be nice to only see sand when he went to the beach and he would like a job where it was unlikely too many people would be shooting at him. He had added, and maybe he would be close enough to visit his mom more often if she decided to stay in Italy.

Twice in one day! Why would anyone think moving to Rome was even an option for her? She wasn't even sure what the next few hours would bring.

***

Eugenio had stopped to smoke a cigarette before he knocked on his uncle's door. He wondered why Alessia had come to Rome to see him. It certainly couldn't be out of concern because of the bombing. Had she somehow found out about Molly? He took a long last drag of his cigarette and smashed the butt onto the pavement with his boot. He walked across the street and pushed the bell.

225

His uncle answered the door and said quietly, "She came about an hour ago. She said she was to meet you here. She seems very happy and she and your aunt have been sitting in the kitchen drinking coffee and talking since she arrived." He stepped aside and followed Eugenio through to the kitchen at the back of the house.

In the afternoon sun, Alessia was a beauty in a short pale yellow dress, in her late 40's, and still had the legs to carry off the shorter hemline. She was beautifully tanned. "Must be all those hours at the beach with Carlos," Eugenio thought. The deep V-neck of the dress revealed an elaborate multi-stone necklace that he knew was not in their military budget. Nor were the matching earrings.

She turned when she saw him come in and she did something that bordered on theatrics. She stood and rushed to him and gave him a big hug. "I am so relieved that you are unharmed. I was busy and did not hear my phone when you called." Still clinging to his arm, she asked, "Is there someplace we can talk?"

Eugenio's aunt started to get up but Eugenio stopped her. "No, we will not inconvenience you. We will go for a walk in the park along the river."

Alessia picked up her handbag, thanked her hostess for a lovely chat, said good-bye to Carmine, and followed Eugenio out the door. They didn't talk until they had crossed the street and followed along the river until they got to the small park. They sat on a bench away from the young mother reading and rocking a stroller with her foot.

"Why have you come, Alessia? When you do not want to see me in our own home?"

She opened her mouth but they both knew what she would say would only be a lie. "Eugenio," she began quietly, "Things have changed. I want to talk to you and please do not be angry with me. I do not want to hurt you. I know you love me so very much but I think because of this love, you want me to be happy. This will be very difficult for you but I have fallen in love with someone else. It just happened. He has asked me to go away with him and I know he will ask me to marry him. Of this I am sure." She paused and waited for Eugenio to speak but he only sat and looked at her.

"Just happened?" he thought. "No, it did not just happen." But he remained silent.

Alessia reached out and took his hand. "Eugenio, I want a divorce. It will be difficult but I want only my things. If you will make this easy for me, I will give you the house, my car…. everything. I know you retire soon and you can have our house when you leave the barracks."

"Yes," he said without emotion. "Yes, we will divorce."

Alessia looked surprised. "Yes, just like that?"

"Yes, just like that. A divorce will take time but is possible. I do not hate you, Alessia. I want you to be happy."

Although a bit set back, Alessia, none-the-less, was relieved. When she had checked herself in the mirror this morning before leaving home, she had smiled and thought how hard it was going to be on her husband to see her go off with a wealthy man who would shower her with gifts worthy of her beauty.

"I have already been to an avvocato. He has drawn up the papers and it will be easy if I do not ask for any of your retirement and you will just sign. He will also take care of papers for the church. Is this going to be alright with you? I need this done very soon, Eugenio."

"Yes, I will look at the papers and if they are agreeable, I will sign. Whatever it takes."

Alessia looked at Eugenio, studying his face for a clue. She had been ready for a fight, for a plea for counseling, for more time to work out their problems. Why was he so forgiving? Her vanity could not resist asking, "Why do you not want to fight for me? Are you not angry that this man has stolen my heart?"

He turned and looked at her and said quietly, "One cannot steal a heart, it has to be given willingly. I think you offered it to him. We had many years together but we have no children, no family to worry about. If this man gives you a happiness you did not have with me, you should go. I am glad you will walk away because I have known of your affair and it would be very difficult for you if you wanted to take too much from me. My religion is important to me but I know you do not care. If these papers reflect this, then I will sign."

Alessia was disappointed at the lack of drama, the ease with which he was willing to let her go but she needed to be free so she could have Carlos. He would not want to be involved in a scandal. Eugenio was highly respected in the military. This was the easiest way. She had set her sights on this older wealthy man and she was confident that this was the best way.

"Thank you, Eugenio. My avvocato will contact you very soon." She stood, expecting him to give her a kiss and a hug but when he did not stand, she turned and walked away, adding a bit more to her walk, certain that he would be watching her leave. When she reached the sidewalk, she turned, intending to blow him a kiss but he had lit a cigarette and was looking out at the water, seemingly unaffected by the situation.

Eugenio walked toward his uncle's house, sure they would be concerned about Alessia's sudden appearance, knowing that things had not been well between the couple for some time.

***

Molly had gone in to take a shower and did not hear her phone. She sat on the patio with a towel wrapped around her damp hair and went into the kitchen. It was almost 5:00 p.m. She was a little hungry and she wondered if she should have a little snack, or if she would be dining alone tonight. She took the towel into the bathroom and carefully folded the towel over the rack and raked her fingers through her hair. She went to the kitchen and noticed her phone on the counter. A simple message was waiting for her: "On my way home. I love you."

It had been sent almost 50 minutes ago!

It was a silly thing she did....her kids called it her happy dance......often used to entertain them when they were little and later as part of a duo with Sarah to entertain themselves and embarrass their now older children. She had even done it once for her college class, which she said she would do if they all passed their Macbeth finals.

It had been a while but she suddenly felt the urge. It was a bit of the Teaberry Shuffle, a bit of Michael Jackson Thriller, and a couple of Richard Simmons' exercise moves, ending with a well-executed pirouette. But she stopped mid-turn when she saw Eugenio step through the door. "Good Lord! The man is going to think I am a total idiot!" She pulled her hair back from her face and tried to look composed. She grabbed a pamphlet from the counter and tried to look at ease although she knew her face was flushed and her heart was beating wildly.

Eugenio walked across the room and stood behind her and wrapped his arms around here. He pressed his face into her damp hair and without a word, just held her. Molly waited. Finally, she turned to face him, her eyes questioning what she was afraid to ask out-loud.

"I am to be divorced," he said quietly. There was no emotion in his voice and Molly tried not to react but mentally her happy dance had taken on Broadway proportions.

She held him close. "I am so sorry."

He stepped back and looked at her. "No, Molly, do not be sorry. It is what I want. Things are very different now and we need to talk."

"We need to talk," she thought. "Here we go again." But this time she was pretty sure she was going to like what was coming next.

Chapter 14

"I want to make a list."

"You mean like a bucket list?"

"No, I am very organized and I have to be very precise at work. Is important to get things done. We have many things to talk about so I want to make a list and then we will talk of each thing. And then we will make a plan. It will be a good plan."

"And maybe a Plan B just to be safe."

"Yes, and a Plan B." Eugenio took a tablet of paper Molly had left on the table and took her hand. They walked over to the sofa and sat down. Molly had to smile because he had such a serious look on his face.

"First, we need to speak of your heart. I know you have taken nitro and that means you are going to have surgery when you go back to Chicago. I cannot be with you, Molly."

"I never expected that you would be there. I know you are married and I know that you could not possibly take leave to be with me."

"No, Molly, I would be with you. I would not let you go through that alone but I will be deployed soon. My unit is, as Americans say, 'in the bucket.' We are next to go."

"When?"

"Soon. A peace-keeping mission for six months. I have done it before and it will be okay and it will be my last before I retire. I want to do once more with these men in my unit. But we will talk of that later. I hate that I will not be there for you when you need me the most. It is natural that you are scared but the doctors today, they are very good. These people are going to open your chest and cut into your heart. A person who has had that happen to her will be changed forever. Well again, but will appreciate life much more. I know you do not want to speak of it, but you need to talk to me and let me help."

"It is not the surgery. It is the idea that if I die, I will be alone with strangers huddled over me. I will be there, full of drugs and tubes, and the last thing I am going to see is the look of panic on the faces I don't know, and the last thing I will hear is "CLEAR!" Or worse yet, in a stark white sterilized hospital bed all alone."

Eugenio squeezed her hand and walked out of the room. Molly was surprised that he hadn't said anything, something comforting. Maybe he thought she was being silly or maybe he thought of his own possible demise, in some foreign country, fighting a war not his own. What would his last thoughts be? Suddenly her heart truly ached at the very thought of it. She really hated this idea of a list!

She wanted to go to him but instead she walked out on the patio. She remembered sitting outside working and hearing Gina and the children out in their yard. Alex was laughing, one of those wonderful innocent child laughs. Wouldn't that be the perfect way to leave this world, listening to the sound of a child's laughter!

"Molly," Eugenio held out his hand. "Come with me, please."

He led her into the bedroom. "Do this for me," He began to undress her. He did not say a word as he gently untied the ties on her shoulders and let her dress slip to the floor. He reached behind her and unhooked her bra. Usually there were kisses and caresses but instead he only put his fingers to her lips when she tried to speak. He knelt and slid her panties down over her hips and held her hand while she stepped out of them. He pulled back the covers and helped her lie down on the cool sheets. He pulled the top sheet up across her back.

"Lie on your side and close your eyes." She did as she was asked, waiting for him to join her but then she heard him leave the room. The drapes had been drawn and the room was warm from the afternoon sun. The only sound she heard was the whir of the fan on the table. She didn't know what he wanted but she would do as he asked.

Then she heard him come back and undress and she felt him slide under the sheet next to her. She started to turn to him but he stopped her. "Molly, close your eyes and listen to my words." He slipped one arm under her pillow and the other one around her waist. He let his leg move slowly between hers and he pressed his chest so tightly against his back that she could feel his heartbeat. She felt his manhood press against her lower back, not the usual hard perfection, but still, it felt hot against her skin.

"Know this time, Molly, the two of us together. Feel our hearts beating together. There is no war and no illness. There is only now. Feel this, Bella, and remember. Feel me

234

next to you and feel my heart giving strength to your own. The doctors will make you well again and send you back to me. I pray of this. But if God takes you from me, you will not be alone. If you take your last breath, do not think of strangers and sterile white rooms. Only of this perfect warm evening in this soft green room in Roma with me and know you are surrounded with my whole being. You will be encircled by my love. And I will be there with you when God lifts you, making your heart well again and freeing your soul. It is only then you will let go and feel my touch fade from your skin, as you take God's hand. I will know, no matter where I am, because my heart will stop for a moment and I will feel a hole in my own soul until we are together again, for eternity. When I am deployed and I am alone and start to worry that I may not come home to you, I will feel you with me and know the touch of your skin and the scent of your hair. I know these things and they will be real to me. And our love will surround me and make me safe. But if I die, you will be with me and I will feel you next to me, holding me as I breathe my last."

He brushed her hair back and pressed his face against her cheek. "You will never feel alone again." And then in what seemed more like a breath than actual words, "I love you, Molly."

Molly felt her tears flow down her face and onto his cheek. She let her hand slide over his, entwining her fingers with his. And they fell asleep.

When Molly woke, Eugenio was still next to her but she knew he was awake. "They are going to stop my heart," she said quietly. "What if it doesn't remember you?"

"Your heart will never forget me, as mine will never forget you. Is impossible now." He kissed her shoulder, his fingertips brushing her nipples slightly and the peace that Molly had felt was quickly replaced with a desire to make love with this man. She felt him hardened against the small of her back. She turned to face him and smiled, "No, my heart will never forget you and neither will the rest of my body."

Eugenio reached over and opened the computer he had set on the nightstand. Vittori Grigolo! My Heart Will Go On! He smiled down at her, "But only make love to me."

***

Some time later, Eugenio gave her a quick kiss and stood up and stretched. "Come, Bella, put on your beautiful white dress and we will go out for a nice dinner. We need food!"

Molly laughed and swung her feet off the bed and threw her robe over her shoulders. From the bathroom she shouted, "Pasta....and tiramisu, lots of tiramisu."

"Sometimes," Molly thought as she stood in front of the mirror, "a woman really needs to give herself a little credit." She turned to one side and then the other. She had a lovely tan, something she had not had in so many years of living in Chicago. One has to really make an effort to take in the sunshine living in Chicago, either enduring a long drive or fighting the crowds who gathered on Lake Shore Drive when weather allowed. Her hair was having a good day as well, falling across her shoulders, not smooth, never smooth, but in soft waves. Years ago, she had been shopping and an older lady with an Irish brogue and that wonderful ginger hair to accompany it had just walked up to her in Marshall Fields and said, "It is not easy to have our hair, is it, Dear? But I will tell you a secret. Style your hair, then, run an ice cube over it. I made a large one I keep in the freezer. Then a touch of hairspray and no frizz from the humidity." She put her fingers to her lips and walked away. Silly idea but amazingly, it has worked.

When she walked into the living room, Eugenio was watching TV but when he saw her, he picked up the remote and turned it off. "Bella," he smiled. She sat down next to him. It had taken time after David had left for her to realize that she was actually an attractive woman but she always felt beautiful when she saw her own reflection in Eugenio's eyes.

"Shall we just walk and find someplace new to eat tonight?" As much as he liked The New Station, he wanted Molly all to himself just in case Alex was working.

They left the apartment and turned right instead of heading down toward the train station. She slipped her arm through his and they walked along the tree-lined street. They walked along in silence, Eugenio waiting for her to say something about the afternoon, and Molly wanting to tell him how much it had meant to her. Had he been foolish to think that his words would help her? And how could she even begin to tell him what a wonderful thing he had done for her.

They found a small restaurant with a covered patio. Since it was still pretty early for dining in Rome, they had the place to themselves and they were seated along the back wall, wanting to be as far away from anyone else who might

237

come in. Molly took a sip of her wine. "You have never really told me about the bombing."

Eugenio tried to explain the unrest in Italy. "Financial and political problems and the government making bad decisions. So many illegals coming into the country that it is impossible to take care of them without Italian citizens suffering even more."

"Sounds like the USA." Funny, Molly thought later that she hadn't said "home".

Molly looked around them the pleasant surroundings, the sweet scent of flowers and lemon trees along the wall. She reached over and took Eugenio's hand, "And yet, here we are....happy."

"I want this for you, Molly, for us, for a very long time."

Just then the waiter appeared with two of the biggest portions of pasta Molly had ever seen put before her.

"Do Italians give doggy bags?"

"Doggy bags? Why? We do not have a dog."

"No, no," she explained, "to take home when people cannot eat all their food."

"Ah, yes, take away. But I never need ask."

Molly tasted her ravioli and a small "Oh my!" escaped from her lips.

Eugenio told Molly of how his grandmother had rolled out great sheets of pasta to make her ravioli and how her recipe was one used at the restaurant today. "This is very good, Molly, please do not tell my family I say this." He laughed.

When the waiter came to clear the table, he asked about dessert but Molly waved her hand. "Please, no, it was wonderful but I cannot eat one more bite." In fact, she had not been able to finish and Eugenio had finished the last on her plate. When they left, Molly said it was good that they could walk for a while.

Molly stopped to smell some of the flowers that were hanging in planters along a wrought iron fence. She looked peaceful as her fingertips cupped the tiny yellow flowers.

"Ok," she said. "My heart. What is next on our list? I don't want to ask the questions, much less expect answers. I want it to be like this, right here and right now, the two of us. But it isn't that simple, is it?"

"It is never just the two of us. I too, have questions and need answers. Come, I know what we do."

They walked past the apartment and headed toward the train station but at the corner, Eugenio stopped in front of the steps of SS Francis and Catherine. It was late and MASS was over. He squeezed her hand and walked up the steps. He knocked on the side door and when it opened, he stepped aside. Moments later, the double doors at the front opened. The young priest who had prayed with her motioned for her to come in. He stepped aside and Molly walked in. "I am not Catholic," Molly said, questioning if she should be there.

"Scoperta pace," he said quietly and turned and left them.

"Find peace," Eugenio translated. He took her arm and led her to the first pew, directly in front of the marble altar, a simple elegance in pale grey stone. It was plain, adorned only by a single arrangement of white flowers.

"He will listen, Molly. And then He will help us."

Molly sat back and looked around and then closed her eyes. She could feel Eugenio close to her. She could hear his slow and steady breathing but he remained silent. So many things began to run through her mind. She remembered Sarah's funeral and she thought about her visits to other churches in Rome. And of Eugenio. Then, little by little, she began to focus. She took a deep breath and began her silent conversation with God.

Eugenio watched her, he saw the uneasiness and tightness begin to leave her face. He saw her shoulders start to relax and he watched as tears rolled down her cheeks. He wanted to hold her but he knew he was not part of this. He was only a by-stander. His time would come soon. He closed his eyes and silently began, "So many things, God, and we cannot do this on our own."

Molly opened her eyes and without speaking, she quietly walked out. She sat on the steps and waited and a few minutes later, Eugenio came out and sat down next to her. "Come, I will buy you a coffee," he said. He stood and put out his hand. It was a warm gentle strength that helped her to her feet.

Behind them, the young priest was standing in the doorway. He crossed himself and looked up into the darkening evening sky. "Grazie." He bolted the doors and left the silence of the great room to God.

Eugenio drank his shot of strong coffee and bought a bottle of peach tea for Molly. "Tomorrow we will talk again."

Molly suddenly felt very tired and just nodded.

They did not make love that night. Instead, Molly kissed his shoulder and closed her eyes. She felt him gently touching her hair and in minutes she was asleep.

Eugenio lay awake in the dark. It felt good to have Molly wanting to touch him and kiss him and just be close to him. He had missed that. He remembered all the times he had lain next to his wife, feeling as much alone as he had all those nights in the barracks or worse, on a cot in some foreign country, and knowing all the while that she had been unfaithful to him. She had never apologized, never mentioned separating, but instead put up an invisible wall between them. It had been eighteen months now since he had thought of the barracks as home, coming back to the house less and less, feeling like a guest in his own bed. But that was over. Although they had just agreed to end the marriage, Alessia had done that long ago. Now there was only to make it legal.

Shouldn't he feel more distraught? He used to fall asleep at night wondering how his own wife had given him a quick good-night kiss and had fallen asleep thinking of other men. And yet, the last time he had been home, hadn't he fallen asleep thinking of Molly? He felt guilty, guilty of the very

241

thing he has accused her of. There were so many things to sort out where everyone was concerned. When Molly rolled over on her side, he moved over next to her and put his arm around her. For the second time in just a few hours, he pressed himself against her back and fell asleep with his breathing in sync with hers.

Some time before daylight Molly found herself unsure how long she had been dreaming and how long her dreams had slipped into reality. Eugenio was lying on his back next to her. Molly let her fingers brush against the soft hair on his chest and stomach. She was amazed at the shape he was in for a man his age. She felt an involuntary movement, a response to her touch even before he was awake.

Chapter 15

Saturday morning in Rome with Eugenio and absolutely no plans except to be together....oh, well, that and making few life-changing decisions...there is that! Was there even the smallest possibility that Molly would ever end up living the rest of her life in Italy? Up until yesterday, it had only been a fantasy but suddenly.......

She took a sip of her coffee. How would her waistline ever survive living in a country that had fabulous food down to a fine art? Living in a world of pastas and rich sauces and cannoli. Cannoli! She had forgotten about cannoli.....she had let her mind and palate be controlled by gelato and tiramisu and that wonderful tartufo. And Eugenio's family owned a restaurant, and there was The New Station, and that little place where they had dined last night, and the restaurant near the Colosseum, and so many more places to try. Of course if she lived there she would be doing a lot of cooking at home but still.....a small groan escaped from her lips.

It was cool and sometime in the night it must have rained because drops still glistened on the plants and the air smelled fresh and clean, with the gentle scent from the lemon trees. She had slept so well last night. Eugenio had made her face her fear of surgery and she had talked about it for the first time. She had actually said the words out-loud and with someone there for strength and comfort.

And today they would talk of other things. She sipped her coffee and her mind wandered back to food! "A little ADHD, Molly?" she thought. But in Italy, how could one not think of food?

Centuries of food in Europe that had developed into an art, not just survival, dated back to ancient Greece. However, the Greeks had believed in moderation as the highest virtue in eating.

But along with this moderation came the idea of dining as a relaxing, pleasurable restoration of both body and soul. Music and entertainment were added and people would recline on couches and just talk. Conversation became an art in itself. And from all of this came the Epicurean philosophy that pleasure was the main objective in life. Epicurus taught a balance of enjoying life's pleasures within the boundaries of self-restraint.

By the time the concept of fine dining reached the Roman Empire, it had taken on a grander scale. Of course the poor still subsisted on grains and vegetables and little poultry and meat, but the rich and aristocracy took dining to a whole new level. Nothing was "too exotic" or "too much" or "too extreme." Fish, cheeses, seafood, and every edible bird was prepared and served, including peacocks, ostriches, and cranes. Meats, from wild boar to venison to dormice were served in elaborate fashion. Emissaries were sent to search the world for hard-to-acquire foods.

And it wasn't that these foods had a unique and tantalizing taste, well, other than chocolate, but they were, instead, desired because of their rarity. In fact, some of these things just plainly did not taste good but the Romans found ways around that. They cooked "heavy" with herbs and spices and with heavy sauces. They presented to their guests the food by name and then hid the actual flavors of the "exotic."

The wealthy became obsessed with the unique and bizarre. It must have driven the cooks half insane to one-up everyone else and themselves to stay in good favors with their hosts, who expected to be offered up something worthy of a surprise of exclamation at each and every meal.

By the rule of the Caesars, gluttony was mixed with the bizarre and the extreme. Caligula stuffed himself to excess while watching a floor show consisting of slaves being tortured while he dined. Kind of like a week-end buffet with a really badly staged performance at Las Vegas' Caesar's Palace.

With the Italian Renaissance leading the rest of Europe out of the Middle Ages, the Roman cuisine was given a make-over, losing the excess and taking on an air of elegance. Long tables piled high to the point of collapse with food were replaced with small tables, set with the finest linens and crystal, and silverware. Guests did not display the gluttony of the Middle Ages. Instead, Italians began with fresh fruits and light wines. Meats were served in small portions. And desserts were born in the form of flaky pastries and sugared fruits. Manners were followed and guests washed their hands several times during the meals with perfumed waters set in small bowls at each setting.

Just then Eugenio brought her back to the present when his coffee cup clicked lightly on the marble table. He leaned over and kissed her cheek. "What were you thinking about?" he asked lightly.

"Cannoli," she said, smiling. She took the last sip of her coffee. "How about a nice big American breakfast? And then maybe later we can find a really good cannoli."

The whole time Molly was making breakfast, she kept looking over at the notebook on the coffee table. So many things, so much of their future was in the notebook, carefully listed in 1-2-3 order. It all looks so simple on paper. Her heart had been number one on Eugenio's list. It easily could have been all about him, but he chose to put her first. And he had given her peace of mind and she knew she would have that peace of mind no matter what the outcome. She picked up the two plates she had prepared and walked onto the patio.

When they had finished, Molly went in and picked up the notebook. She re-filled their cups and laid the book down in front of Eugenio. "What is Number Two on our list?"

He took a drink of his coffee and opened the notebook. "My marriage," he said quietly. "Is over, only need to be legal now." He put a check mark next to the Number Two.

"Wait, please, you can't just say that and move on. We need to talk about this. Remember, we are talking about everything."

"Molly, I tell you of my marriage and our problems. Now, she wants to marry another man, to take him from his wife. To do this, she must be free. She will give me the house. She will walk away if I will sign the papers very soon. This is good, no fighting. There is much paperwork to deal with for the church but this can be done. Not like it used to be, almost impossible. But we have no children and is much easier today than years ago."

"Talk to me....honestly. It can't be that easy."

246

Eugenio reached over and took her hand. "No, Molly, it is not easy. I have had many months to think of this. I know she has been unfaithful but I loved her. It has been some time since I know of this new man and I have felt guilty many times when I have thought of you during my marriage. But now it can end so quickly and we can both be happy again. And my retirement will be better. I will have my home now. Alessia is still a beautiful woman, Molly, but only on the outside. With you, there is beauty on the inside and on the outside. When we were sitting in the park talking, I was only thinking of coming here to you. It is sad to end many years of marriage but, if it does not end, I could not expect you to continue to want me." He finished his coffee. "So, Bella, you see, we have completed Number Two." He was quiet for a minute and then he said, "Ciuri Ciuri."

Molly looked at him. "I don't understand."

"My cousin, he makes cannoli at the restaurant and is very good, but Ciuri Ciuri is a bakery near the Colosseum that has very good cannoli." He put his finger to his lips. "Shh, is another secret from my family."

"Our secret."

"Did you bring a bathing suit?"

"Ah, yes, but I don't think that I could..."

"Molly, is going to be very hot today. I think we should go to the beach. It will be cool and there is a nice place to have lunch right there. Please, we go?"

"Well," she thought, "He has already seen me naked. How bad could it be?"

Molly remembered the day she and Sarah had gone bathing suit shopping and then decided the hell with it. Later, after a great lunch with a couple of rum punches under their belts, they had gone back and took a realistic look at the situation. Sarah had shouted over from the dressing room next to hers, 'Ya know, Molly, if I could suck in my thighs like I do my stomach, this one isn't half bad.' Molly had chosen a black one piece but she also had purchased a cover-up that hit just below her knee. Now she slipped it on and stood in front of the mirror.

"You are right, Sarah," she said out-loud, "not bad if I could only suck in my thighs." She packed some towels into a small travel bag. Eugenio was packing ice and water into a thermal cooler when she walked into the kitchen.

Molly stood in the doorway, the light showing her figure through the light gauze material.

"Yes, very nice." He walked over and kissed her. Eugenio always made her feel beautiful.

They took the bus over to the train station and took the same train Molly had taken out to Ostia Antica. It seemed like everyone was going to the beach, an escape from the heat of the city.

They had to stand, but the train wasn't that crowded and Molly held onto the pole and watched the scenery sail by. At Ostica Lido, they stepped off the train and the air was

248

warm but much cooler. They followed the crowd as they headed for the water. It was only about a ten-minute walk and Molly could smell the sea air so she knew they were close. They turned a corner and there was the water before them, as far as the eye could see in both directions. They went to a small private beach and Eugenio got a ticket for two deck chairs and an umbrella. The beach was packed and children were running and playing at the water's edge, but side by side on their lounge chairs, Molly reached out and took his hand and they both just laid back and relaxed, blocking out of the sounds around them.

Finally, Eugenio stood up. "Let's get wet!"

The water was cool and clear and Molly wasn't a swimmer but she waded out about waist deep and then plunged into the water. "You can save people, right?" she yelled over her shoulder.

Eugenio stood knee deep in the water and watched her as a wave caught her and drew her back toward him. She sputtered and laughed as she stood up again, trying to catch her balance but falling over and letting the next wave take her close to him again. He reached out his hand and helped her to her feet. She hugged him.

Eugenio was used to his wife sitting near the water, drink in hand, never thinking of getting even her feet wet. But this woman, so uninhibited and free!

Molly wondered if she was embarrassing Eugenio with her childlike behavior but she couldn't help it. With this man, she did not feel all the restrictions she had always felt with David. She reached down and splashed him and took off to run away but he grabbed her and together they both went into the water head first. Later, they walked ankle deep in the cool water and Molly picked up rocks, smoothed by the rough waters. When they finally went back to their deck chairs, Molly closed her eyes and fell asleep, listening to the children's laughter and the waves.

When she woke, she laid quietly enjoying the illumination that danced in her eyes as the sun touched her face.

She could feel Eugenio watching her. "I am starving," she said, not even opening her eyes. They walked up to the small café set up on a wooden floor built over the edge of the sand. They ordered bruschetta and a fruit platter to share before walking back toward the train station.

The train back to the city was full even though the beach was still very crowded when they had left. Molly was lucky enough to get a seat but she was feeling gritty even though she had rinsed off in the showers before they had eaten. Now she was anxious to wash the sand and salt and sea water out of her hair and put a nice conditioner on it. As it dried in the stuffy train, she felt like she could actually hear her hair frizz but Eugenio looked down at her and only noticed how blue her eyes were and how happy she looked.

In the shower, Molly put her head back and let the warm water stream through her hair. She could never in a million years, picture herself frolicking on the beach. Frolicking, hmm, unusual word, not one she could ever remember using before in her life. She and Eugenio were just not the "frolicking sort of people," but today they had been straight out of a Coppertone commercial.

It was almost dark when they left the apartment for dinner. They caught the tram and went down to have dinner at a little restaurant they had seen when they had first visited the Pantheon. They had both commented on what a nice place it was and that it was even air-conditioned. Ristorante da Donato on Via del Seminario had a curved stone ceiling and soft lights. It reminded Molly of a cave. It was still crowded but a lively waiter, who introduced himself as Nick, seated them in the back and joked that they could kiss without anyone seeing. He handed them menus and warned Molly that she should not drink too much wine after such a long day in the sun; that it could make her quite ill. Molly looked up from her menu, her look questioning.

Nick gently touched her shoulder. "Rosa."

"Yes," Molly nodded, "Very pink."

Eugenio smiled at the fact that she knew the word. Molly had been tanning quite nicely since she had arrived in Rome but even with lotion on, the glaring sun today had turned her light brown tan to a rather intense pink. But she knew the discomfort that was coming was worth every minute of their day together.

Dinner was wonderful, Molly had ravioli and she ate slowly, wanting to savor every bite of the soft little pillows of pasta as they melted in her mouth. When Nick came to clear the plates away, he asked if they would like dessert and Eugenio spoke to him in Italian and he nodded and walked away.

When they headed back to catch the tram, Eugenio took her hand and led her in the opposite direction. In the middle of the block, Eugenio pointed up. "Ciuri Ciuri."

It was a small shop but even at that late hour, it was full. He ordered four cannoli that the lady placed in a box and tied up with a thin ribbon. And then Eugenio ordered a peach gelato and handed the cone to Molly. "This is their best. And will be cool for you."

Molly took a tiny bite; it was rich and creamy and the bits of fresh peach made it even more refreshing. When they walked outside, she said "Oh yes, very nice."

She held it out to offer him a lick and then suddenly jerked it back. "No, it's too good, I changed my mind." But he grabbed her hand, leaned over and took a bite.

"Did your mother no teach you to share?"

Molly turned and held out the cone "Everything I have is yours if you want it," she said quietly. As they walked back to the tram platform Molly asked, "Do you know what scones are? Sarah made the best scones in the world."

"Yes, very British and smell wonderful fresh from the oven."

"How do you say scone in Italian?"

"Focaccino. Do you think now of your Sarah?"

Molly nodded and held out the cone for him to take another bite.

Chapter 16

Sunday morning! Molly had mixed feelings about Sunday mornings in Rome. Saturday nights were always more than she ever imagined and she loved waking with the comfortable feeling that Eugenio was next to her but they also began the countdown to his having to leave......so little time left until he had to go.

Yesterday had been wonderful. They had made love, very slowly, very gently, taking their time and savoring every minute together. Before they fell asleep, Eugenio had put a cool sweet smelling lotion on her back and shoulders. Just before she had fallen asleep, she had leaned over and kissed him "Grazie, Eugenio. You made me feel young again today."

Molly woke wondering how close she would resemble a boiled lobster when she looked in the mirror. Her skin still felt warm but she saw that a lot of the pink had turned to a lovely tan and her face had a healthy glow she hadn't seen in years. Her hair, however, had taken on a lot of volume and she raked through it and pulled it back from her face with a barrette. She slipped on her robe and headed for the kitchen to start the coffee.

The weather had taken a turn because when Molly walked into the patio, the day was grey, not one of those "just before it rained" grays, but as if the sky had been draped with a fine gossamer web that gave the world a calm soft feeling, like God's way of saying all was right with the world.

Molly made coffee while Eugenio showered. She picked up their notebook from the table and opened it and started to laugh. Penciled into their life plan between Eugenio's divorce and deployment, he had added "buy Molly cannoli."

He walked out and sat down on the patio and set two cups on the table. His coffee drinking had been Americanized. Instead of grabbing that one shot of espresso on the run, he had come to enjoy sitting with Molly and having a relaxing cup or two, taking his morning intake of caffeine in a more enjoyable and leisurely manner. "I will make breakfast this morning," he had said, from the kitchen. He carried out two plates with some sliced melon and the cannoli they had brought home last night.

"Perfect." She took a bite of the cannoli, the nice crunch to the shell and the sweet filling. "Yes, very nice. So, Mr. Marino, what is our plan for today? Or are we just staying home?"

"My nonna had a saying, 'Se si desidera fare di Dio sorriso, dirgli il votro piano peroggi. Se si desidera farlo ridere, lui il piano per la vostra vita.' It means, 'If you want to make God smile, tell Him your plan for today. If you want to make Him laugh, tell him your plan for your life.'"

"Your grandmother was a wise woman."

"When we were young, religion was a very big part of our lives. Every day we prayed, and Sundays and holidays were very special but were centered on our religion. Now that we are older, we still have our religion but is different. What I do every day, I know God watches over me. I could not do the things I do or have even survived many times without

Him. And I pray but not as devoutly as I should, but I pray and He answers. He may not always say yes, but He listens. Religion is not in my head, Molly, He is part of my soul."

"I wish I had your faith."

"I believe we are a born with faith but there are things that make us doubt. I believe some day you will have it again. But for today, I think you must have things to take back to Chicago with you, for friends and for you. If you aren't too sore, maybe we can do the street market. You can find many things there and is very close. But you wear, ah," he touched her shoulders, "something to cover."

Molly took another bite of her cannoli, "Mother Hen."

Eugenio smiled and went into the kitchen to refill their cups.

When they left the apartment, they walked passed SS Francis and Catherine Church and across the street. As far as the eye could see, stalls, three deep, lined Via Portuense.

"How often do they do this?"

"Every Domenica."

"Sunday?"

"Yes."

"Why did I not know this before?"

"Because," he smiled, "We do not leave the apartment on Sundays until later. The market is from 8:00 a.m. to 2:00 p.m. By 4:00 p.m., is gone. The stalls are packed and taken away and they come and clean the street.

"Are there food stands, like vegetables and fruits?"

"No, not market food but stands to eat snacks, but everything else, I think."

Stall after stall, Molly looked at purses and clothing and sunglasses and key chains and shoes, hundreds of sellers hawking their wares. Molly bought the boys at the fire station all t-shirts and a coin purse for Mrs. Cooper and a necklace for Amanda. She would get some nicer gifts this week as well but they had fun and Eugenio held her hand and guided her through the crowd. By noon, they had headed back when Molly suggested they go to The New Station for lunch. She forgot that Italians eat a big meal at noon and soon, they were being served huge plates of pasta.

"What is our Number Three?" Molly asked, between bites of a pasta that she could only describe as luscious.

"I will leave soon, Molly. My unit is, as American troops say, in the bucket. We will leave soon either to go to Iraq for a peace-keeping or my unit goes on duty for a removal of illegal immigrants. Italy does not treat illegal persons as the United States does. We cannot afford to take care of them at the expense of our own people. Each year over 300,000 come. We keep them for a month and give them medical care and food and clothing but then we take them to a ship in Sicily and the ship returns them to their own countries. We have so much coastline, so it is easy for them to come but they cannot stay when we find them. If not, we go to Iraq again, there is still much trouble there and is difficult for citizens. I have nine months' duty left and then I retire, but about six months I will be gone."

"What will you do then?"

"Plant a garden, enjoy my home, and maybe work part-time doing security, but no stress. And what will you do when you retire, Molly?"

"Probably sit in my condo and wait until I have grandbabies to come and visit. And I hope I will have my books on the market so I can stay busy," the light left her eyes. "What is next on the list?"

"Not yet, Molly, we have not finished yet. I want to talk more of this but not here. When we are home. But for now, dessert?"

"I think coffee and the last two cannoli sounds good."

"Yes, I would like that."

The afternoon still had that grey sky and the air was light. There was just enough breeze to carry the scent of the flowers and trees along the street as they walked. People seemed to have slowed their busy pace and walked along chatting. Young parents passed with strollers or holding the hands of their small children. Molly recognized the father and young daughter from the café. She wished she could thank them for giving her the idea for a book. Instead, she smiled and the father nodded as they passed. Teen-agers, of course, whether alone or with others chatted on their cell phones or texted as they walked, oblivious to the world around them. Some things must be universal, she thought.

Molly tried not to notice Eugenio checking his watch. It remained unspoken but they knew the time was drawing near again.

Eugenio took Molly's hand and led her to the sofa. He took a deep breath and turned to her. "When I tell you my thoughts to retire, Molly, what if I ask to come to Chicago and be with you? Do you want me to come to Chicago for us to be together?"

Molly thought many times about them being together but she never once thought about him coming to her. It was always her coming to Rome. She knew she would be happy anywhere with Eugenio but she knew that it would be very hard for him to move and she wondered if he would come to resent her because of their decision.

"No," she said quietly, but before she could continue, Eugenio got up and walked into the bedroom. Molly followed him but when she walked in, he was standing with his back to her, looking out the patio doors.

"I am a foolish man. You say love to me and we talk of being together and I believe you, but you don't want me when is finally possible."

"Eugenio, please." She started to walk across the room when that all too familiar pain engulfed her chest and she pressed her hand against her heart and sat down on the edge of the bed.

Eugenio turned and put out his hand to stop her but his face turned ashen when he saw her and knelt beside her.

"Where are your tablets, Molly?"

She pulled the two necklaces, chains now entwined, from under her blouse. Eugenio unscrewed the small tube and let the bottle fall. He carefully opened the brown bottle and let two tiny pills slip into her hand. She put them inside her lower lip and pressed, feeling them instantly dissipate. Eugenio helped her scoot back and lie on the bed. He took his pillow and propped it under her feet. He lay down next to her and held her hand "Molly, I am so sorry to upset you."

She squeezed his hand, "It's not what you think."

"Shh, do not need to talk right now. Just relax."

She took a breath, the pain had subsided and she turned to him. "You are indeed, a foolish man if you think for one minute that I do not want us to be together. But you have such a wonderful family here and they have waited such a long time for you to be close again. And you love Italy and you have served your country and deserve to stay and enjoy your retirement. I do not think you would be happy in Chicago with no garden and yard to work in." She took another breath and decided it was now or never. "What if I would come to Italy and live? Would you want me to come?"

"As long as we are together but in Italy, yes. Would be good for us." He brushed her hair from her face and kissed her.

"It is almost time for you to go so what is left on our list?"

"No more, Bella, is finished."

Molly rested her head on his shoulder and closed her eyes. "Could it possibly be that simple after all this time?"

Molly felt a little weak when she tried to stand up a few minutes later but the pain was gone and she went into the bathroom and splashed some cold water on her face. When she came back, Eugenio had started to pack. "Time for that last cannoli before you leave?" She tried to make her voice sound light.

"I do not like to leave you when you are having pain. I worry that you are alone."

"It isn't like I have a lot of people who can drop by but I promise I will be very careful and call Gina if I need help. I will be fine. I will text you often so you won't worry."

Eugenio made coffee and brought out the last two cannoli. He took a bite and leaned back in his chair. Molly waited for him to say something but he only smiled.

"What?"

"The list was good and now we are organized."

"Yes, it was good. And soon you won't have to leave me on Sundays anymore."

Just then Molly heard the gate open and Gina leaned around the corner. "Do you mind? The children just wanted to say hello to Molly?" She saw the backpack on the table. "We will just stay a moment."

Alex ran in and was going to get on Molly's lap but Eugenio stood up and spoke to him in Italian. Alex stopped and glared at Eugenio but Eugenio spoke to Gina who came over and took Alex's hand. She knelt in front of him and spoke very softly. He turned and nodded at Eugenio. He walked over and took Molly's hand and kissed it and hugged her arm. Molly kissed the top of his head. She looked up at Gina, "He worries too much."

When they left, Eugenio walked them to the gate, talking quietly to Gina. "Good Lord!" she said when he returned, "Mother Hen."

At the door, Molly held him tightly. "Stop worrying about me. Just hurry back to me."

"Yes, Thursday I will come back. You relax and call if you need me." He looked into her eyes, "Promise me."

"I promise. And I will be here waiting."

He threw his backpack over his shoulder. "Mio caro, Molly," and he kissed her one more time before opening the door. She watched until he disappeared into the crowd waiting for the tram, blew a kiss in case he could see her, and closed the door.

"Wow!" Molly said out-loud. So many things had happened in the last four days, amazing things. She looked out at the

261

patio, pretty sure Eugenio had left a couple bites of cannoli on his plate. "No sense letting it go to waste...but it's going to end up on mine." she thought.

Just as she sat down, Beatrice came running back through the gate. "Molly, Mama say this is to hear Alex when he takes a nap. She say for you to plug in when you go to bed and you can push button if you need her and Papa. Then she will no worry." She handed Molly a small box and smiled, "Feel better, Molly. Bye." Molly opened the box......a baby monitor. She wondered if this was Gina's idea or Eugenio's, but she decided she would honor the request because it was nice they were concerned. Later that night, she plugged it in next to the bed. "Good Lord!" she thought before she fell asleep, "I hope I don't snore."

Chapter 17

Molly woke early Monday morning, thinking this is her last week in Rome and suddenly had so many things she wanted to see and do. Then, she smiled and leaned back on her pillow. BUT, and for a change, this is a good thing, she would be returning...and next time she would stay forever.

She opened the tiny wardrobe and stood perusing her clothes. "What goes with pink?" she said, noticing that her shoulders were still a little more colorful than she liked. She put on a white gauze top and white slacks. She had brought capris with her, but she could not bring herself to wander the fashionable streets of Rome with her cankles on exhibition.

She sat down for a quick cup of coffee and a croissant. She picked up the notebook from the table. Their list, each item carefully checked off and at the bottom Eugenio had signed and dated it. "The man needs to learn to relax. If he was American military, he probably would have done it in triplicate and had me sign it as well," she thought.

Then, she picked up the pencil and began to jot down some things she wanted to purchase and what she needed to get done over the next four days. She didn't want to leave anything to the last minute because she wanted her last three days with Eugenio to be just the two of them with no rushing around to get things finished and ready for her departure. Three more days and nights together and then...and then a lifetime together.

Who would have thought that two years ago, when Sarah had asked one night over pizza, "Moll, have you ever thought about, well, the idea that we should stop thinking about Rome and just go? Seriously, I mean actually just pack our bags and go for a whole month?"

This was certainly not the trip that Molly had planned but so many times she had felt Sarah with her. And this month with Eugenio and Gina and the kids had been more than she ever imagined. Once she was living in Italy, she hoped she and Gina would remain friends.

Shopping today! Molly wanted to visit Via Condotti, the fashionable shopping area of Rome. She was never one for designer names, but today she wanted to wander. Marconi had lived there many years at Number 11. What would he think, after his invention of the radio was so monumental in his day, if he saw today's vast technology?

"Molly?" Gina came through the gate. "Am I disturbing you?"

"No, please, come and sit. I was just planning my day."

"That is why I have come. I have an appointment today for Beatrice and we were wondering if we might take you to tea this afternoon. I know this is last moment but if you are not busy..."

"I was just going to go over to Via Condotti and walk around and maybe do a little shopping for some things to take home."

"We would be close. Do you know Babington Tea Room near the Spanish Steps?"

"As a matter of fact, I was thinking of stopping there today. Sarah mentioned once she wanted to have tea there and I want to go for her."

"Would you rather go alone?"

"Oh no, I am sure Sarah would love it if you and Beatrice joined me. Should I change?"

"Of course not. It is not as formal as it used to be, although there is still old atmosphere and some of the older ladies like to dress for afternoon tea, but times have changed. Beatrice will no doubt be a bit over-dressed though." She laughed. "It really is a landmark although not as ancient as most. It was opened in 1893 by Isabel Cargil and Anna Marie Babington as a place for English ladies who had been transplanted to Rome for whatever reason. It has managed to survive two world wars, the advent of the fast food craze, and the "grab an espresso and go" life style. And the rule still survives that dogs are permitted as long as they are "well-educated.""

"It sounds lovely."

"Shall we say 3:00 p.m. and we will have afternoon tea?"

"Yes, I should be shopped out by then. And tell Beatrice I said thank you."

Molly went in and pulled her hair back with a gold-braided headband and put on a bit of make-up. She slipped on a pair of heeled sandals. She wouldn't want Beatrice to think she wasn't dressed properly for High Tea.

Via Condotti was already busy by the time she walked from the metro. She looked across the street to make sure she had her directions right. The Spanish Steps were as imposing as ever, the pink Keats House on the right and to the left, a brick building with a small sign over the door "Babington Tea House." She turned and started to walk. Chicago, of course, had its fair share of shopping and designer names, but when the streets are narrower and the shops are more intimate, they just take on a feeling. Dior, Prada, Jimmy Choo, Hermes, and so many others. She tried on a pair of gloves in Giogio Sermoneta. "Oh my God!" she thought, these are the softest things she had ever felt. She had never paid over $100 for a pair of gloves in her life, but she REALLY loved them. She found a shop that sold limoncello and she set two small bottles on the counter to take home. Her plan was to give them as gifts but she was pretty sure she would keep one. She turned and picked up another bottle, just in case! She found a bracelet in Giovannetti Jewelry for Amanda and she bought a small Murano glass turtle for Mrs. Cooper. She looked at her watch…it was already 2:45 p.m. Molly headed back through the crowded street toward the tea room.

She sat on The Steps and raked her fingers through her hair and put her headband back on, wishing she had a mirror to check the volume of her hair since the day was warm and humid. Soon she heard "Molly!" and she saw Beatrice and Gina walking toward her. Gina was wearing a pale green pantsuit, looking very cool and collected as always. Beatrice was wearing a white sundress and sandals and white straw hat. She carried a small white purse.

"You look very elegant."

266

"Yes, I do." Beatrice said, quite confident that she was properly dressed.

The tea room was cool and had that Old World touch. They were seated toward the back, away from the tourists who had come in and wanted to sit near the windows. "Molly, do you have a picture of your friend?"

Molly looked at Beatrice.

"I am sorry, I told Beatrice about Sarah. I hope you don't mind."

"Oh no, of course not." Molly opened her purse and took out a picture of Sarah and handed it to Beatrice.

"She is very pretty." Beatrice slipped out of her chair and walked over to the empty setting on the table. She took the teacup and set it on the plate and propped Sarah's picture against it. She sat down and smiled.

Molly smiled and she felt tears welling in her eyes and she reached up and touched her necklace. "Thank you, Beatrice."

Even though it was warm, they chose to have hot tea instead of one of the various iced teas offered. After all, it was High Tea! The room held a lovely scent. Everyone but Molly had thought it was from the kitchen where all those lovely pastries were prepared but Molly knew Sarah's scent all too well.

Before they had left, they had asked the waitress to take their picture. Back at the apartment, Molly was looking through her pictures of the day. The picture at the tea room was by far the best. Gina was sitting with her arm around her daughter and Molly was clutching her necklace and smiling over at the chair next to her. It may not have been visible to the rest of the world but Molly knew!

She slipped her gloves on once more before she wrapped them in tissue paper and put them back in their box. Gorgeous and so soft. Almost worth cold weather to be able to wear them! She unwrapped the little turtle and held it in the palm of her hand. Mrs. Cooper had an extensive collection of Murano pieces and she often commented that she knew it was an expensive hobby but she loved each and every piece. She wondered if Amanda would enjoy the bracelet itself as much as she would enjoy telling people her mother had gotten it for her when she was living in Rome. She wondered what Amanda was going to say when Molly told her that she was going to actually be living in Italy soon. No sense worrying about it now, next week would be soon enough.

Molly looked at the clock, it was only 4:00 a.m. but she was wide awake. Ideas were running through her head. She knew she might as well get up and write because she knew she would never get back to sleep. She made coffee and went out to the patio.

There was a message from Sarah's daughter hoping Molly was having a great time and that she was anxious to hear all about the trip when she returned home. Molly downloaded the picture at the tearoom and sent it with a long letter. By the time Molly had finished her breakfast and was ready to work, she had received an answer.

"Dear Molly, Thank you so much for the picture. Mom had talked about that tea room and she wanted to take you there for tea the day you would go to visit the Keats Museum. Thank you for making her part of your visit there. It would make her happy to know you were having the trip the two of you had planned together. She told me on more than one occasion that we can make all the plans we want but if it isn't what God has already planned for us, well, you understand. I think of her every day, Molly, and sometimes I feel her so close to me and please don't think I am losing my mind, but I can smell her near me. Just remember that you cannot live someone else's dream and make this trip about you and your dreams. Mom wants you to be happy. Talk soon. Love, Emily"

Molly sent a quick message back: "It's her scones, Em. I always know she is with me.....that lovely comforting smell of those wonderful scones. Emily, this trip is my dream and so much more. I will be home next week. I will call. Love you, M"

God's plan....Sarah and Eugenio's grandmothers were wise women!

There was something Molly wanted to buy and she simply wasn't sure what it was just yet. This gift had to be special. She worked through the morning and then decided to go out and do some more shopping. She wasn't sure where she was going, but she took the tram down near the Colosseum and began to walk, stopping to window shop and occasionally stepping inside to look through the cases. Finally, she saw what she wanted in the window of a tiny shop near Ciuri Ciuri. She went in and asked to see the piece in the window, pointing to it when the man spoke to her in Italian. Yes,

turning it over in her hands, it was just what she wanted.
"Do you speak English?" she asked of the man. The man
held up his finger for her to wait and he walked to the back
of the shop. A young girl came back with him.

"May I help you?" she asked in very good English.

"Yes, I would like to purchase this but I would need it
engraved by tomorrow. Is that possible?"

The girl spoke to the man and he nodded.

"Yes, Papa says is possible. What would you like?"

Molly reached into her purse and handed a slip of paper to
the girl.

She handed it to the man and he asked, "Italiano or
Inglese?"

"Italian."

He nodded, "Mercoledi pomeriggio."

"Wednesday, tomorrow afternoon. You come back then?"
the girl repeated.

"Yes, thank you."

Molly walked out onto the sidewalk, she looked down the
street and the little sign caught her eye. She turned and
walked down to the shop and went in. She looked through
the glass at the variety of gelato. "Peche in a cone, please."
She walked into the sunshine and took a lick of the cold rich

cream. She could look up the avenue and see the Colosseum. She decided to just stroll a while and enjoy the day, despite the heat. This is a good day...no, she was in Rome and Eugenio would be back tomorrow. Today is a great day!"

When she returned home, there was an email from Eugenio waiting. "I am sorry, Bella, that this is the first time I am able to write you. I have made a new list of things now for us to talk of when I return, things that we have to settle before you leave. I am very hot and tired but I could not sleep before writing to you. I think of these things after I leave you. We are so close now, Molly. Time will go quickly and then you will return to me. I will make you happy, Molly. This I promise."

"Ah," thought Molly. "As all good fairy tales should end. 'And they lived happily ever after, Italian style.'" She made a glass of ice tea and kicked off her shoes. She had a few more notes to make and then she would put her writing away until she returned home...no, until she went back to Chicago.

She propped her notebook up on the table with the vocabulary words she wanted to use, five new Italian words. She wondered if she was ever going to learn enough Italian herself to actually live there, but thus far, she had done pretty good and soon she would have Eugenio with her all the time. That's the plan, she decided. She would just never leave the house without him!

It was just getting dark when she stopped and closed her computer. She took off her cheaters and leaned back and closed her eyes. In the distance, she could hear the church

271

bells. There was something comforting in the bells. She wondered how many generations of families had grown up listening to the bells. They were probably like everyone who lives near someplace wonderful...they barely noticed. Molly promised herself she would never forget to appreciate the bells and the glory hidden behind those plain and unadorned doors.

Chapter 18

It was going to be hot today - that much she had surmised from the news. She didn't have to convert to Fahrenheit to know 33 degrees Celsius was going to be hot. She decided she should get to the supermarket before it got too warm. Over a quick glass of orange juice, she began to jot down a few things she would need. "Good Lord! Another list."

Molly slipped on a sleeveless top. Her arms were now a lovely soft brown, no longer that 'you idiot, you spent too much time in the sun' pink. She pulled her hair back with combs. A hot day meant volume.

Marcello smiled and waved as she approached the coffee shop. "Buon giorno, Molly" and he took her hand and made gallant gesture of showing her to a small table shaded from the morning sun. "I hoped you did not leave Roma and not say good-bye to Marcello."

"No, of course not. Something cool today, please, and a croissant."

"Yes, yes, is to be very hot today." When he returned, he asked, "When do you leave us, Molly?"

"Sunday, but," she added with a smile, "I shall be returning."

"Ah, you throw your coin in Trevi Fountain?" He studied her face for a moment. "No, I think you are returning because you are in love. Always in love with Roma, but I think a man has won your heart. I can see." He pointed to her eyes. "Yes, I see in your eyes, there is much love."

"You are too wise to be a waiter, Marcello."

"I know, I know, is true," he shook his head in mock embarrassment, "But this is my life. I will be old with a cane and I still bring coffee to the tourists and listen to them complain. Is too strong! Is too small! Paying for refills? But you, Molly, you come and be happy with our ways. And when you return, we will always talk and you tell me all of this man who has won your heart. He is a good man, yes?"

"He is a very good man. And you and I, Marcello, we will be friends."

As Marcello left to wait on other customers, Molly took a bite of her croissant and leaned back in the wicker chair and looked around. She had come to think of this as her neighborhood and she would miss it. She hoped that even though they would not be living in Rome, that when they came back to visit family, that she would have time to come back, even if it was only to have a cup of coffee and listen to the church bells.

At the supermarket, she bought cheese and melon and some strawberries and then she just wandered up and down the aisles. Would she ever get the hang of shopping in Italy? When she went back to Chicago, the first thing she was going to do was order some language tapes. She was going to be ready when she came back.

In Chicago, she had pretty much stopped shopping for groceries except for bare essentials at the neighborhood grocery or fruits and vegetables at the green grocer. She smiled to herself, thinking how she was going to enjoy

274

cooking for Eugenio. No more take away cartons and pizza boxes instead of dishes.

She was surprised how many familiar items she actually saw when she took the time to look. Barilla pasta, Hershey's, Yoplait, etc. Meat might be a problem. She had been raised on Iowa corn-fed beef and pork. She did love those delicious thick steaks and pork chops on the grill, and BBQ ribs. She did not find these in the butcher's case. Maybe Carmine could help her. "However," she thought, "I have probably already eaten enough red meat to last me a lifetime. And bacon, Corn King bacon." She sighed. "Probably the reason why my heart is in the shape it's in. But almost worth it!"

On her walk back, Molly tried to think if there was anything she needed to buy yet - any gift she may have forgotten. "I wonder if they have a T-shirt for Tiffany. 'Somebody went to Italy and brought me this lovely shirt while I am stuck here in Chicago with David.' Probably not."

Molly put her groceries away and then took the garden hose and began to water the plants and lemon trees across the back wall. The lemons were only tiny hard dark green balls. She wished that she could be there to see them when they became lovely yellow fruit. Suddenly she felt very sad. Three more days and she would have to leave. It hardly seemed possible that she had been there almost a month. Back to her condo that barely caught two hours of direct sunshine on any given day.

She pulled her lounge chair around so it was halfway in the shade of the patio and half in the sunlight. She sat down and kicked off her shoes and pulled her skirt up to expose her thighs. The warm sun felt good on her skin. She leaned back and relaxed. She needed to remember to take a picture of the lemon trees. So many pictures but she wouldn't really need all those pictures she and Eugenio had taken on her camera. She remembered every moment, every place, and every smile. Each was gently etched into her mind...and into her heart.

She heard the bells from Santa Maria and suddenly tears began to flow. Was this all too perfect? Was everything going to work out according to plan? What could go wrong? Oh yeah, Eugenio's wife could change her mind, Eugenio could be deployed soon, and then there was her heart.....minor details! She brushed the tears off her cheeks and closed her eyes. "Have faith, Molly," she reminded herself.

Molly felt something touch her arm and she turned and opened her eyes. Alex was standing next to her. Behind him, she saw Gina coming through the gate.
Alex turned and put his fingers to his lips. "Addornentato."

"Oh, Molly, I am so sorry." She took Alex by the hand and began to scold him.

Molly sat up. "Honestly, Gina. I wasn't asleep. Please have a seat."

"If you are sure. It seems like we are imposing."

"No, let me get us something cold to drink. I wanted to talk to you before you leave for Sorrento tomorrow." She went into the kitchen and poured glasses of tea over ice.

"Is there a problem?"

"Oh no, nothing like that. I just wanted to tell you how much I have loved staying here and getting to know you and your family. It has been more than I ever expected. I leave on Sunday, and I need to let you know....." Her words caught in her throat, "how much I will miss you. I hope when I return, that you and I can remain friends."

"So, things have worked out for you and Eugenio? I am so happy. I prayed that love would win in the end...or now a new beginning. Marc says I am a romantic and that is a good thing, yes?"

"Yes."

"I want to ask you. We will be returning on Saturday because we have to attend a dinner on Sunday night, so I wanted to ask you. If Eugenio is not able to take you to the airport, the children and I would love to take you. You can let us know after you speak to him."

"That is very sweet. Thank you. We haven't really talked about my departure yet; we have kind of avoided the subject but I guess we can't wait any longer."

"Yes, but you will return soon?"

"Yes, I will return but we do not know when. There are so many things to take care of, but we have gotten this far. I am hopeful it will not be long."

Gina took a sip of her tea. "I will be sorry to see you leave. You have been a good neighbor."

Again Molly felt tears. "I am so sorry. I am just feeling so sad at the thought of going."

Alex took her fingertips and touched her tears and turned to his mother. "Molly triste?"

"Yes, Love, Molly is sad."

Alex brushed them away and held out his hands. "Andato." He smiled.

Molly laughed. "Yes, gone. Wouldn't life be so easy if we all looked at life through a child's eyes?"

"We should not always be the teacher, I think. Well, I have many things to do today before Marc comes home so we won't keep you. We will talk before we leave for Sorrento." She leaned over and gave Molly a kiss on each cheek. "No more tears, Molly."

"No more tears."

Molly went into the bedroom and took her suitcase out of the wardrobe and laid it on the bed. She began to pack things that she knew she wouldn't be needing. She didn't want to spend one single minute of her last three days with Eugenio doing anything but being near him. "And that," she thought with a smile," will be tomorrow night!"

Later that afternoon she walked down and caught the tram. She had an appointment and did not want to be late. She walked along the busy avenue, not noticing the heat radiating off the sidewalk. She went into the little jewelry shop and waited while the young girl she had spoken with yesterday finished helping another customer. She nodded at Molly and went into the back room. She came out and opened the box and waited for Molly's approval. Molly carefully lifted the shiny object from the velvet-lined box and turned it over in her hand. "It is bella, grazie!" She smiled. It was perfect!

"Prego! My papa will be pleased that you are pleased."

Molly paid her and tucked the box into her purse When she left the shop she hesitated for a moment, should she? She turned and walked down to the other shop she was acquainted with. She left with a small box and two dishes of peach gelato. She walked back to the jewelry shop and handed one of the cups to the young girl. The girl smiled. "Is very good. Grazie. You are a tourist in Roma?"

"For now. I am going to be moving to Italy soon."

The girl took a bite of the cool rich gelato and smiled. "Good, you come and visit us again." She walked behind the counter and came back with a card and handed it to Molly. "This is our shop," she said and then turned it over to show Molly the back. "And this is me." She had written her name and email address.

"Thank you, I will." She put out her hand, "I am Molly."

"I am Sophie."

Molly finished her gelato and Sophie took her empty cup and spoon and threw it away. "Ciao, Molly." She said as Molly headed for the door.

"Ciao, Sophie."

Molly walked along the street heading back to the tram feeling much better. She stopped and looked in the windows of the little boutiques. Something caught her eye and she went in and picked up a small teal blue purse. She had already gotten her daughter a gift but she knew Amanda would love this and, although Molly hated to admit it, maybe Prada would soften the blow when Molly told her she was leaving Chicago."

When Molly stepped off the tram, she turned to walk to the apartment when she stopped. It was a bit early but one more dinner at The New Station sounded pretty good. She slowly walked down the hill and saw Alex standing outside smoking when she approached. "Am I too early?"

"Molly! Good to see you. Maybe just a bit but we can talk as friends for a few minutes." He brushed off the short stone wall along the drive and waved his hand. "May I offer you a seat?"

Molly smiled, remembering Marcello earlier in the day. "Why, thank you." She sat down while he stood next to her.

"Do you eat alone tonight?"

"Yes, Eugenio will be here tomorrow but tonight I eat alone."

"Will you leave us soon, Molly?"

"Yes, Sunday I go back to Chicago," She smiled, "But I will be coming back soon I hope."

"I think this time to stay, with your Eugenio. Yes?"

"Yes, to stay." Molly was surprised that Alex had remembered Eugenio's name.

"Then we will celebrate tonight and you will come to the restaurant when you return to live. We are friends now, yes?"

"Yes, we are friends."

Alex put out his cigarette and walked over and opened the door. "Come, Molly, have a dinner that you will think about when you return to the USA."

It was almost 8:00 p.m. when Alex opened the door for her and she walked back out onto the street. She turned and gave Alex a hug.

"I will see you again, Friend." She turned and started up the hill. She almost felt guilty feeling so full and still having cannoli to take home.

There was a nice breeze that took the edge off the heat. What a perfect day she thought as she rounded the corner, well, almost perfect. She stopped for a moment by the steps of the church, wishing she could go in but she knew it was time for Mass. Just then the tram pulled up and stopped and a crowd stepped onto the sidewalk. Molly turned and started back to the apartment when she heard her name. She turned and saw Eugenio hurrying across the street.

He put his arms around her. "I work very long hours so I come tonight and not tomorrow. I send you an email but I did not hear from you but I come." He kissed her hair. "I missed you."

"Let's go home," she whispered and linked her arm through his as they walked. "Now," she thought, "it is a perfect day."

As they walked away, a silent figure stood on the steps of the austere church. He watched the couple and then he raised his eyes slightly, nodded, and smiled. "Grazie," he said softly.

Chapter 19

"Did you have plans for this evening? It is good that I come early?"

Molly turned and smiled at him, "Are you serious? I have been out all day and was just coming home to wait for you."

"I worked a very long duty and take hours so a man could take care of a family emergency so I could finish early. I come right to Rome. I think I need a shower but I wanted to come as soon as possible."

"Well, you shower and I will make you something to eat."

"Yes, and then...."

It was almost midnight when Molly woke. Eugenio was sleeping soundly, not snoring but a heavy breath that Molly found comforting. After they had made love, he had turned on his side and gently stroked her hair. "Your heart has been good this week?" He always worried that the strain might be too much.

Molly had taken his face in her hands, "My darling, you are the best medicine for my heart."

Molly started to reach out and touch him but she stopped. Even now, thoughts of the past came back to haunt her feelings. After the last time she had had sex with David, she had reached out in the night to touch him but he had taken her hand and moved it away. "Leave me alone, Molly. You got yours, now let me sleep." And Molly remembered thinking sadly at the time, no, she hadn't. In fact, it had been a very long time since she had really "gotten hers" with David. And for some reason as she laid there next to her husband, she thought about something she had once heard when she attended a lecture about Queen Victoria. Victoria had tried to marry her children into as many of the European countries as possible, thinking of it as a way of keeping peace throughout Europe; family is after all, family. And having married a German prince, one of her daughters had told her mother of her concerns. She knew of royal duties and of running a household but what of herself? What if she found herself with a husband who gave her children but did not make her happy in the bedroom? Victoria's reply to her daughter had been, "Then close your eyes, my dear, and think of England!" Had she stayed for the sake of family, not wanting her children to feel as alone as she had been when her family had broken apart?

As if on cue, Eugenio had reached over and put one arm under her pillow and the other around her waist. "I need to feel you next to me." he whispered.

Molly closed her eyes, feeling very contented AND SATISFIED! Nope, not that problem here!

When Molly woke again, the air had cooled. She grabbed Eugenio's shirt that was neatly folded on the chair, and slipped it on. She walked into the kitchen to see Eugenio making coffee. "Is okay?"

Eugenio smiled. "Now you begin to sound like me. But I already wear. My shirt must be sweaty. I will get you a clean one."

"No, I like this one, it smells like you."

"I like the way you look. My wife, she would never wear. Not fashionable. Only expensive and ......" he stopped.

"And sexy?"

"Yes, and sexy, but not for me for a long time. I only pay the bill."

Molly walked over and put her arms around his neck. "I am sorry. I didn't mean to...."

"It's alright, Molly. But you look very sexy in my shirt; you do not need expensive to be sexy for me. But I will buy you beautiful things if you would like."

"I think I prefer this shirt." she walked over and unbuttoned his shirt, "Fact is, I think I want this one too." She pushed the shirt off his shoulders and began to kiss his neck.

"And I think," he said, responding to her touch, "Coffee will have to wait."

Later that afternoon they were sitting on the patio drinking iced peach tea when they heard "Knock, knock!" and Gina stuck her head through the gate. "I am sorry but if you are not busy, the children would like to see you before we leave for Sorrento."

"Please, of course, come in."

Alex ran in and climbed up on Molly's lap. "Ciao, Nomino Molly." He put his chubby fingers on her cheek. "No lacrima."

"Yes, Alex, no tear."

Beatrice walked over and gave Molly a box, wrapped carefully but showing signs of a young hand. "I have a gift for you. I picked it out myself so you no forget Rome and me."

"Yes," Gina said, almost apologetic, "Beatrice insisted."

Molly opened the blue tissue paper. It was a touristy T-shirt of the Colosseum.

"You like?"

"Beatrice, thank you." She gave her a hug. "It is beautiful and I love it. I was going to buy one just like it but now I have this one. I will think of you every time I wear it."

Beatrice smiled, "See, Mama, I knew it was a good gift."

"I wanted to ask about Sunday before we leave for Sorrento." She turned to Eugenio. "I did not know if there would be time for you to accompany Molly to the airport. The children and I would be very happy to take her if you like. That way you would not have to say good-bye at the airport. I think would be better for you to be alone together as long as possible."

There it was....the very subject neither of them had wanted to be the first to mention all day. "Yes, I would be very grateful if you would do this for us. And I will no worry about Molly taking so much luggage on her own. She must leave by 10:00 a.m. Is good for you?"

286

"Yes, we will be here. And now we must go. Marco wants to leave early, he does not like to drive in the city when it rains and we are to have heavy showers very soon." Gina walked over and gave Eugenio a hug. "In case, we do not have time on Sunday, please know you are always welcome to come and visit us."

Beatrice and Alex both walked over and offered hugs as well. Molly could see it meant a lot to him to be included as a friend.

After they left, Eugenio went in to refill their glasses, making a mental note that once he retired, there would be more tea and less coffee. He was going to learn to relax and take life easier.

"I watch you, Molly, with the children. I see the joy in your face when you are with them."

"Children are unique little creations whose innocence reminds us all of better times before reality becomes such a harsh part of life. They have such wonder in their eyes when they do or learn something new. And their laughter makes the world a better place. When my kids were little....." Molly saw the sadness in his eyes and stopped. "Good Lord! Why can't I just shut up? That was so stupid of me."

"No, is alright. It is not your fault that I was never to have children. But I have cousins with many children and one day you will have grandchildren and maybe you will share them with me."

"I love you and I will be very happy that you will be a grandfather to my own babies." It felt good to be able just tell this man how she felt....so many guarded conversations with her ex-husband just seemed to fade from her memories. Eugenio will be a better grandfather than David, she was sure!

He smiled. "Thank you. I think Papa Eugenio is good name. I am lucky for you."

Molly looked puzzled.

"Is wrong, I think. I am very lucky to have you love me, you understand?"

Molly nodded, "Me too."

Eugenio went into the kitchen and opened the refrigerator, perusing the contents.

"Are you hungry? I can fix something or we can go out. Whatever you like."

"I think a picnic. Would you like to go on a picnic with me, Molly? I have something I want to show you."

Eugenio took bread and cheese and fruit out and put them in the little cooler bag. He added two bottles of water and the last bottle of Moscato. Molly added a knife, corkscrew, paper plates, and napkins. She took the small blanket off the sofa and slipped it into a bag.

"And just where are we going to have this picnic?"

"Is a surprise but I hope you will like."

They walked down and caught the tram over to the river
and then stepped off and cross the busy street to catch the
#115 bus. They passed by Santa Maria Bastillica and
continued up until Molly could see the dome of St. Peter's
Cathedral. Molly had not gotten this far before and as the
bus began to climb, the tall buildings began to fall away and
the lush green of Janiculum Hill surrounded them.

When they stepped off the bus, they walked through the
stone archway and up the stone walk-way until they reached
the top. Rome lay spread out before them, from the Pincio
Gardens of Villa Borghese to the Colosseum. The sun had
started to go down, shading bits and pieces of the city and a
sprinkling of lights were coming on. And as if on cue, from
below, the bells of Santa Maria's began to ring.

"You like?"

"It is amazing." The Colosseum and the Seven Hills and the
dome of the Pantheon loomed in the distance. Without the
rush of people and traffic and the noise, the city once again
took on his ancient look. Molly leaned against the wall and
let her eyes follow the river and finally focused on the
pyramid off to the right. "Who could ever come to Rome
and not fall in love?" she asked.

'I think you are not talking about me, Molly. I fear Roma
has stolen your heart from me."

Molly reached over and took his hand. "Nope, not even
Rome could take my heart from you."

They found a place on the grass and spread their small blanket out and set out their picnic. Eugenio opened the wine and Molly laughed, "I think we have forgotten glasses." She tipped the bottle and took a sip and handed it to Eugenio. "Haven't done that since college."

"We need to talk some more, Molly. Is okay?"

"Yes, of course, am I going to have to get drunk to hear this?"

"What? Oh no, I think you joke."

"I'm not sure. Depends on what we have to talk about."

Eugenio took a drink and set the bottle down and took her hand. "Molly, I have received orders. My unit will deploy in fourteen days. It is what we have talked of but I wanted time to have things more settled. It is too soon."

"But," Molly answered, trying not to let the rush of emotions she was feeling show on her face, "the sooner you go, the sooner you will be home and then I will come to you."

"I want time to go quickly so you have your surgery and I complete my service and we will be back here as we are now. There are so many things we need to do."

"I cannot believe I am saying this....but if it makes you feel better, we will make a list. But right now,.." She took a sip of wine. "It's perfect."

Eugenio leaned back on one elbow and looked at Molly with all of Rome laid out behind her. He reached over and took her camera and although he took pictures, there was really no need. This image he would remember in the lonely nights to come.

Molly scooted over and sat next to him as they ate. "It truly has to be the most beautiful city in the world. I know your house is near the beach but I will love the times when we come back to visit."

"I have so much family here, we will visit often. If we do not return often, I am afraid Carmine will send my nephew for us. Is important the family stays close. They will come to visit now in the summer because we are near the beach.....very good to get out of the city in the heat. They would never come before when...."

Molly nodded, "....when Alessia was there."

The sun was going down and they sat without talking, nibbling on bread and cheese and taking turns sipping wine. Finally, Molly leaned back on the blanket and closed her eyes. The air had cooled and there was not a sound around them. It was like this moment had been created just for the two of them. She felt Eugenio lean closer and she expected him to kiss her, but when he didn't, she opened her eyes and saw him sitting quietly watching her.

"I just...." Eugenio was thinking of all the times he had tried to just reach out and touch his wife and, although she never pushed him away, he knew it had only been tolerated. There would be no return of affection or desire.

"I know." And Molly reached up and put her hand on his cheek. "I wish you were always going to be close enough to reach out and touch." It was like she knew!

It was almost 10:00 p.m. when they finally packed up and started back down to the bus stop. Molly stopped to take one last look. Night had fallen over the city and thousands of lights twinkled in the dark. "I wonder what Caesar would say if he could see his beloved Roma now?"

Molly was looking out the bus window, watching the city come closer again. "How can just being able to touch someone bring such joy in life?" Molly thought, but then she realized that being able to feel the touch of the ones she loves has been the best things in her life. She remembered how many times she and Sarah had walked arm-in-arm, stopping to window shop, but mostly just walking and talking and laughing together. She thought about how safe and happy she felt when she reached up and held her dad's hand when she was little. She remembered waking up in the hospital and feeling Adam holding her hand. And she thought about all those hours she sat with her mother, just holding her hand.

Sometimes, Molly would fall asleep with her head on the edge of her mother's hospital bed and wake to feel her mother gently stroking her hair. For a few brief minutes, she been a little girl again, being cared for by her mother, not a teen-ager who had become the caretaker of her dying mother. What made Molly think of them now? Eugenio had been watching her in the reflection in the window and he suddenly reached out and took her hand and kissed it. Molly leaned back against the seat and smiled. "Damn, he's good!" she thought.

They caught the tram back to Trastevere. Even that late in the evening the cars were crowding the streets. Such a different scene of Rome than from atop Janiculum Hill, a place caught mid-way between the lights of the city below and the clear evening sky. A place between fantasy and reality, where only the two of them had existed.

When they had first stepped off the tram, Eugenio had asked her if she wanted a gelato. She had replied," I only want you....but... I do have to leave soon." She tried a Nutella gelato this time. As she walked back to the apartment, one armed slipped through his and tasting this absolutely wonderful ice cream, she prayed their life together would always be this simple, this perfect!

Molly went into the bathroom and slipped into a nightgown and robe, but when she walked into the bedroom, she found it empty. She walked out onto the patio. Eugenio had taken a blanket and pillows out and laid them on the cool evening grass. She knelt before him and let him slip the straps from her shoulders. He cupped each breast and kissed them gently. Molly laid back and looked up at Eugenio, silhouetted against the Roman sky. And they made love, very slowly, very gently. Molly, lulled by a sense of contentment and the scent of the lemon trees, lay quietly when Eugenio got up and lit a cigarette. When he returned to sit next to her, he leaned over to kiss her and felt a silent stream of tears on her cheek.

"Molly, what is it? Are you are feeling alright?"

She pointed to a single plane as it made its way across the sky. There had been times when the future had been too over-whelming to even think about with her mother and then Sarah, but even facing their own mortality, they had offered strength to Molly. They had both held her close and with almost the same identical words, had told her, "Do not think of the future. Think of us right here, right now....together."

Eugenio brushed away her tears and lay down next to her. "No, no, is all wrong. On that plane is someone who is coming back to Roma to be with her lover. And when the plane lands, he will be waiting with a single red rose and he will take her in his arms and promise they will be together always. See, you were mistaken." Then he put out his cigarette and slipped his arm around her and leaned back to share her pillow. "Don't think about the future, Molly. Think of us together right here, right now.....together."

Molly smiled, "Damn, he's good!"

Sometime later, they picked up the blanket and pillows and had gone into the bedroom and without words, they had cuddled up, "spooning" as people used to say, and had fallen back to sleep, content with the 'right here, right now'.

Friday morning, they both woke with so many things on their minds. Over coffee Eugenio took her hand. "Molly, today we talk of serious things once more and tomorrow with all settled, we will just be together.....no worries."

"Deal."

"When I return from duty, how soon will you come to me?"

"As soon as you want me. Are we going to have a place to live by then?"

"I wish I could show you my house. I want you to like it. My wife, she say she wants nothing so we will have almost everything we need but I want it to be your home, Molly, so whatever you do not like, I will replace. Just please, not me." He laughed but Molly knew what he was thinking.

"Never." She reassured him.

"And I have a car and a motorcycle so you will have a vehicle. The traffic is not so busy as here. You will be able to drive."

"I think on the back of your bike will be good too."

Eugenio took a drink of his coffee. He remembered when he and Alessia were looking for a home. They could have gotten a home near the barracks so Eugenio could be home so much more often but she had wanted a house near the beach and in the end, he gave in and they had purchased a home, hours away. But Molly, she only wanted him and he knew she would be happy anywhere as long as they are together.

"We will come to Rome to visit family and I think, now your friends. The traffic here in the summer is so......." he waved his arms, searching for the right word.

"Hectic, crazy, absolutely insane....."

"Yes, all. With cars and people and heat, is no good. But we will say our prayers and come all the same. And I want

295

you to meet my friend, Mario. He and I have served together for many years. I hope you will become very good friends." Then he laughed, "But he will smell so good that maybe you will prefer him instead of me."

"What? I don't understand."

"I joke. Mario is a single man who has never found a good woman. He is shopping one day for a present for his aunt and he sees this very attractive lady at the perfume counter. She smiles and flirts and sprays a sample of men's perfume on his neck. Then she leans over and tells Mario how wonderful it smells on him. He wants to impress her so he buys a bottle. When he signs the credit card receipt, it is 700 euro. It is Clive Christian's No.1, the world's most expensive men's perfume. He wants to ask this lady out for coffee so he buys it and then she tells him she wishes she could afford to buy it for her husband because it is very sexy. He tells me he is a stupid man, but lucky for him it was on sale."

"Hmmmm, now I am anxious to meet this sexy-smelling friend of yours."

"I hope you joke."

"Yes, joking. I am coming back to Italy only for you. I will sell my condo. It won't be difficult. It is hard to find a nice place in the city and I have to admit, my condo is pretty nice. I am going to be able to make a nice profit on it."

"Will you miss it? It has been your home for many years."

David had promised her a home in the 'burbs' when they decided they needed a bigger home. She had found the perfect place but he purchased the condo and surprised her one night over dinner, saying it was such a great deal he couldn't pass it up. Would she miss it? Well, she did have lots of memories with the kids but, no, she was taking her memories with her. Would she miss the condo? She doubted it very much. Her neighborhood was a different story. She felt it was her little piece of Chicago but that was changing too. But then she turned and saw Eugenio watching her, waiting for the right answer. "No, I am ready for something new. I am ready for a new life....with you."

"And what of your work? I know you are on medical leave but will you return to work at all in the fall semester? You will need your insurance for your surgery and after."

Leaving the college is something Molly really hadn't thought about. She had worked there for so many years and although she could retire, she had never really thought about it. What else would she have done? But now she had a whole new world waiting for her.

"No, I am ready to retire."

"I would like to take you to a late lunch today. I have to talk to Carmine and I think one more dinner at Marino's and you will not change your mind about coming back to Italy."

When he went in to shower, Molly checked her mail. There was a message from Mrs. Cooper letting Molly know that she would be at O'Hare on Sunday to pick her up. Amanda wrote, saying she had been offered a job in San Diego and she really wanted to take it. Eddie was dragging his feet about moving but Molly smiled when Amanda continued that in the end, it would be her decision. There was hope! Adam sent a short note, just checking in and would write more when he had a day off. A confirmation of a doctor's appointment next Tuesday.

There was also a letter from Pearman Publishing. Molly had submitted some of her and Sarah's work and a layout of the learning manuals that would accompany each story. Could she please call and set up an appointment at her earliest convenience? They were very interested in this set and any future work. Molly re-read the letter twice and then leaned back and closed her eyes. That warm sweet aroma filled the air around her. She took a deep breath. "I think we did it, Sarah," she whispered softly.

When she opened her eyes, Eugenio was standing in the doorway. "Did I put that smile on your face or is something else making you happy?"

She looked over at the tiny lawn. The grass still held the traces of the blanket where they had made love last night. "Both actually."

"Good news?"

Molly told him about the publishers and the interest they had shown. If they offered to publish her, their work, she would be able to continue to write after she moved.

"Now we shall have a special lunch today, to celebrate!"

"We have so many things to celebrate. I should be getting ready."

Eugenio sat down and lit a cigarette. He looked around the tiny yard. He, too, noticed the imprint of the blanket from the night before. His house had a small back yard. He could make it look like this one, only better, with their own patio and of course, lemon trees. He would enjoy doing this for Molly. He had always enjoyed gardening but it was impossible to do much, living most of his time in the barracks and Alessia had never cared, so their yard was just that, grass! But he would make it a special place for them.

***

Carmine was standing near the fountain smoking when Eugenio and Molly approached. He gave Molly a kiss on each cheek and then turned and embraced Eugenio. "Was good, your news. I am pleased for both of you."

"And is what I ask taken care of?"

"Yes, yes, I do this for you. Now, come and eat. The busy lunch is over so we prepare special for you, Molly, whatever you like."

"Everything you prepare will be wonderful, Carmine."

"Ah, I see, my cousin, you find a woman who knows perfection." He laughed.

Carmine took them to a garden table away from the other late lunch diners and left them with menus.

"I hope you do not think my cousin is too full of conceit. He makes a joke but yet he is very serious."

"He has every right. The food here is extraordinary. Maybe it is a good thing we will not live so close that I come too often. It would endanger my waistline. But I am afraid that my cooking may be a disappointment to you after this."

"Molly, I live on military food so do not worry." He looked at her over the rim of his glass. He was still afraid he would offend her when he tried to joke and was relieved when Molly laughed.

"Well, then I stand a chance. I am actually a pretty good cook but I am afraid that I am out of the habit. I have lived alone for so long. But I am going to love cooking for you."

"But you know I joke with you? I love American cooking but you do not have to work in the kitchen to make me happy."

"Labor of love. However, we do need a BBQ grill. I make great ribs! The problem is that I haven't found any good steaks or baby back ribs in the supermarket."

"Ah," said Carmine, as he set a carafe of vino on the table, "is good then that you have a new cousin who owns a restaurant. He can help you order the best meats."

Molly blushed when she remembered she had that same thought at the supermarket. Eugenio was afraid Molly had been embarrassed by Carmine's assumption that they would marry. He took her hand, "You look very rossa, Molly, do you feel alright?"

"Yes, I am fine. Just hungry."

"I think Carmine has embarrassed you, calling you 'cousin'. I know we have never spoken about this, Molly, but I think of this often. When we go home this afternoon, we have serious talk....." Then he added, "But no list." He took a sip of the wine. "I like better without glasses alone with you! But I think when I retire, maybe not so much espresso."

"Yes, more American coffee, weaker and bigger cups. No need to keep up all that energy that you need to work the long hours you do. You can relax more."

"But I think, with you, I will still need to keep up my energy."

A thought crossed Molly's mind.....stupid David, he really never did have any idea!

Before they left, Eugenio and Carmine spoke in the doorway and Carmine handed him a small bag. Returning to the table, Eugenio said, "Cannoli for later."

Molly went out and sat on the patio when they got back. The day was warm and she leaned back and closed her eyes. They had never discussed marriage. Eugenio was still married and yet she had come to him, knowing she was technically "the other woman," but she had accepted the situation. Now things would be different and Eugenio would be single. She had never thought about what would happen if they actually got to this point. And yet, here they are. Molly would be happy to come and live with this man, with or without the paperwork. Certainly, she would not love him any more or think any less of him if he did not want to get married again. Whatever decision he would make would be fine with her. She was happy.

When she opened her eyes, Eugenio was standing in the doorway watching her.

"You have to marry me," he said quietly.

"Why, are you pregnant?" She laughed but she stopped, not wanting to offend.

"Yes, and now you must make an honest man of Eugenio."

When he sat down next to her, Molly took his hand. "You know it doesn't matter to me if you do not want to. Please do not feel we have to be married. I will come to you anyway. I just want to be with you."

"I know, but this is something I think about, being with you, living here together, but always as married. If you want me as your husband."

Molly started to speak but he stopped her. "Please, not now. I want to wait until things are taken care of first. I want to do it right, Molly. So, when you come back to Italy and there is a perfect moment, then I ask and you give me your answer."

Molly nodded. Back in her youth, she would have immediately called Sarah to gush the news and then begin to scribble "Mrs. Eugenio Marino" over and over again. But being the mature adult she was, she was content to enjoy this warm feeling of bliss and keep the secret to herself, at least for a while.

"We do need to talk about getting me a VISA to stay in Italy. I can't just come and stay without someone asking questions."

"You must apply to stay for one year on a work VISA ......or, you can apply as my fiancée. The VISA can be renewed if necessary. When we marry, you can apply to stay forever. Is not like other countries. Italians make it easier for people in love to be together. I know I say to wait to give proper answer but I hope you will apply as fiancée. This would make me very happy to think of."

"If it will make you happy, fiancée it is."

"I promise, Molly, I will do properly with a ring one day."

Molly suddenly had the urge to pick up her notebook and write Mrs. Eugenio Marino just once. Just to see how it looked. Instead, she gave him a quick kiss and went to the kitchen to make some ice tea. So much to think about! She set the glasses on the table and picked up her notebook. "I really need to make another list!"

They went to bed early that night, not to make love, but just content to lie next to each other for one last Italian night. They had talked about so many things all day but the mood had been light and the urgency of each situation had fallen into not "if" but "when" things would happen. They talked of a future and they were happy.

Now in the darken bedroom, there were no words. There would be sadness soon but for now, together here and now was enough!

More than once, Molly felt Eugenio reach out and gently stroke her hair, and before falling asleep, he felt her body move closer, until he could feel her heart beat as she pressed against his back.

Sometime in the night, the rains came and Molly felt Eugenio pull the duvet up around her. He kissed her bare shoulder and tucked the soft material up around her neck. Molly smiled. Life with this man was going to be good!

Chapter 20

Rain did not come often to Rome in the summer, but when it did, it came with the anger of the ancient gods. A boom of thunder woke Molly. Eugenio had not even stirred, so she slipped out of bed and walked into the living room. Although the back yard was protected from the strong winds by the stone walls, the rain was coming down in waves that pounded against the patio doors.

Molly stood silently remembering the day she had stood near the airport windows in Atlanta, and how she had wished she was on the other side, finally being able to let go, letting the rain mix with her tears so no one would see her cry. And then it was almost like someone or something had come to her rescue. She had been given an opportunity for a quiet diversion that began as a simple act of kindness for a man in uniform. She could offer a cup of coffee or lunch, the very least she could do. And yet, when they had parted two hours later, Molly would have willingly accepted if he had offered a good-bye kiss. The kiss she had wondered about for so long and when it finally came, it was not good-bye, but hello. And it was everything she thought it would be....and so much more.

Eugenio stood in the doorway of the bedroom watching Molly and he remembered the first time he had seen her, that day in Atlanta. He had been lost in his own thoughts but he found himself watching the beautiful woman standing across the aisle. She had her back to him but he could see her reflection in the glass and he watched as she struggled with tears, wiping them away with the back of her hand. He had started to get up once to go over and see if she was alright but tears are common at an airport and he did

305

not want to embarrass her by invading her privacy. He had walked over and stood staring out at the dismal gray day that matched his own mood. And then he heard someone speaking to him and he turned and saw her standing there, offering to buy him lunch, reaching out to a total stranger as appreciation for the uniform and as a simple gesture of kindness. He remembered thinking later that he wished it had been himself who had offered the first bit of kindness, so grateful that Molly had been strong enough to make the effort. How close they had come to just walking away, never knowing it would lead to, well, this.

And now here they were again, watching it rain, waiting for another eminent departure. But this time it would be different. And right now, he was not going to miss an opportunity to kiss this beautiful woman. He walked over and wrapped his arms around her waist and felt her lean back against him. He brushed her hair off her neck and pressed his lips against her neck. Molly turned and smiled. "I was just thinking..."

"I know." He cupped her face in his hands as he had that day at the airport but this time he leaned in and brushed his lips across her cheek until they found her mouth. If it had been their first kiss ever, he thought later, it would have been worth the wait!

When people think they have a lifetime together, they tend to take things for granted but when the clock is ticking, it is like the sound of the clock inside the crocodile, warning Captain Hook of that which he feared the most. For Eugenio and Molly, it was a reminder that their time together had been reduced to a mere twenty-four hours. And with the reality that their lives were now in the hands of fate and faith, every look, every touch, every kiss held special meaning.

Over breakfast, Molly had seen that look in Eugenio's eyes and she had only to reach out and put her hand over his to offer the comfort he needed. "I know," she said softly.

There was an intensity that surrounded them like the moisture that hung heavy in the air. And when they made love, it was almost like two people driven, seeking every ounce, every inch of the other, seeking not demanding, a closeness like never before. And afterward, they lie quietly, not speaking for fear of giving away the flood of emotion that permeated the air around them. Suddenly Molly started to laugh and she leaned over and playfully kissed Eugenio's cheek. "Damn, Darlin' ."

Eugenio leaned deep into the pillow and let out a deep sigh. "I know!"

Later, Molly had fallen asleep on the sofa and Eugenio had covered her up with a light blanket. He had been watching a movie but found himself watching her instead. He walked into the kitchen to get a cup of coffee and noticed her camera sitting on the counter. He sat down and began to look through her pictures. The Colosseum, The Spanish Steps, Moses, the pictures she had taken of him with the Colosseum behind him at the restaurant, ones he knew she had taken when he was on duty......He loved the one of Molly on The Hill, sipping wine straight from the bottle but his favorite was the one Carmine had taken yesterday.....Carmine had told them "Sorriso" and they had turned to look at each other instead of the camera. Yes, this was his favorite! A whole month of memories that Molly

307

would be taking home with her. No, not home, just back to Chicago. Italy is her home now! All they had to do was.... why did he think of all this now but as soon as Molly left, he would be busy getting ready to deploy and he had a court date, only to have someone declare his marriage over, although it was only the formality of making it legal. His last tour of duty, the end of what he could look back on as a satisfying and successful military career. One he could be proud of! He would miss it but with Molly to return home to, his days and nights would be full and happy. Yes, he would be ready to retire!

He looked over at Molly. There was so much she would have to do as well. Maybe he expected her to do too much on her own. It was bad enough that he could not be there for her surgery and be there to care for her afterwards but there would be her retirement to deal with, the paperwork involved in moving to Italy, packing, and selling her condo. She would have to pack up her old life on her own without anyone there to make it a happy occasion instead of a chore. He had definitely asked too much of her to do alone. He walked out and opened Molly's computer and began to type. Maybe there was something he could do ....at least he could try. With Adam's help, he just might be able to pull it all off. He had just finished when he heard her begin to stir. He went in and sat on the floor next to the couch. Molly leaned over and wrapped her arms around him. "I am sorry, why did you let me sleep so long? I want to spend every minute with you today."

"You are, just asleep." He laughed and stroked her hair. "Molly, I have an errand to run but will you do something for me?"

"Of course."

"Put on your white dress for me. I want to see you in your white dress one more time before tomorrow."

A wave of sadness washed over her but she took a breath and smiled. "I am going to take a shower and then, the white dress it is."

Eugenio kissed her and headed for the door. "Take your time. I won't be long."

Molly walked into the bedroom and sat down on the bed. "I am not going to cry, I am not.....damn!"

Despite the heat of the day, the hot water that poured over her felt good. Molly really didn't want to go out. She would have preferred to stay at the apartment eating whatever food they had left. But Eugenio wanted her to wear her white dress so he planned on them going out to dinner. He probably would not be full on bread and cheese and coffee.

She ran a brush through her hair and pulled it back with combs. She slipped on her white dress and sat down on the edge of the bed.

So, we have finally come to our last night together.

Eugenio had literally run down to the restaurant where they had eaten before. He hoped he had remembered everything she had eaten that night. He grabbed the packaged food and hurried back to the apartment. Molly was still in the bedroom so he hurried and set the table on the patio and set out the food.

The rain had stopped hours ago and the sun had come out to dry away most of the water. The evening shadows had cast a calm over the tiny back yard.

Molly looked over at herself in the mirror. She remembered Roy Schneider in "ALL THAT JAZZ" when he would drag himself into the bathroom in the morning, and no matter how awful the night before, he would take a couple pills, wash his face, and then put a big smile on his face and say, "It's show time!"

Molly stood up and smoothed her skirt and put a touch of Escada along her neckline. She turned and faced the mirror, took a deep breath, and smiled. "It's show time!" she said out-loud and opened the bedroom door.

Eugenio was standing at the counter making the last of the peach tea. He turned and smiled. "You look beautiful. Molly, I know you wanted to eat out but I find myself being very selfish so I do this." He led her to the open patio door. "Are you disappointed?"

"No," she said. "It is just what I want." She turned and this time the smile was genuine, "It's perfect!"

Molly remembered the huge bowl of pasta she had eaten that night at the restaurant and how she had not been able to finish it. Tonight she looked at the food but her heart just wasn't in it.

"Please, Molly. We are not to be sad. This is our celebration. Tomorrow we are leaving to end our old lives apart, but tonight we celebrate our first month together. I think it was a very good month. Now, eat!"

Over dinner, Eugenio talked about his home and all the things he wanted to do when he retired. He would no longer be just the occasional handyman.

"I always wanted a nice back yard and patio." She looked around. "I love this place but maybe a little bigger. And we can have lemon trees." She stopped. It was his house and she was already making plans.

As if he could read her mind, Eugenio said, "Yes, lemon trees. We will make it very special for us. And we will do it together and have many good times there."

"And your family, Eugenio. We will have family come for picnics and parties."

Eugenio remembered all the times he had wanted to have family come but Alessia had never wanted company, well, his company. "The children come and they are loud and messy. Why can't they leave the children home?" But now with Molly, their home would be filled with family and the sound of children's laughter. He took a bite of his pasta. Yes, life would be very different with Molly.

As they made plans, Molly began to eat. Eugenio brought out the last 1/2 bottle of Moscato and started to pour it into glasses and then stopped. He wiped the top with his sleeve and handed it to her and Molly tipped the bottle and took a sip. "Only when we are alone. I think your country would not forgive me if we did this in front of anyone else."

"Yes, just us."

The food, the wine, Eugenio - is this what her life would be from now on? Is it possible that it could be so simple and yet so perfect? Yes, with Eugenio, life would be just like this.

Eugenio took the last sip of wine and leaned back and closed his eyes. Molly watched him, seeing the stress and tension she had seen in him so many times, gone now. She got up and walked over and kissed his forehead. He opened his eyes.

"You relax. I will clean up."

Eugenio did not argue. He did not expect Molly to wait on him but at this moment, it felt good to just sit and enjoy the moment. Molly cleared the dishes away. She was amazed that there were no leftovers. She had eaten every bite of pasta and the prosciutto and melon they had shared. She washed the dishes and set them on the drain board and walked out to wipe off the table. Eugenio had fallen asleep in the chair. He stirred when she brushed against him. "I am sorry. I did not mean...."

"No, I am finished."

"I am just so full and so...." he searched for the right word.

"Content?"

"Yes, is a good word. Content."

"I would like to take a walk one last time before I leave tomorrow. I won't be long."

"Do you not want me to join you?"

"I just thought..."

"No, I want to come."

They were just leaving the apartment when they heard the distant bells of Santa Maria. Eugenio nodded and took her hand. As they walked down the narrow streets, Molly slipped her arm through his. Molly looked up at the now familiar wall with the single window with the flower box. In the last month, the ivy had grown and was now hanging several feet below the box. The piazza was full of people, some heading for the church for MASS, but others were just enjoying the evening air. Children ran and played under the watchful eye of parents and grandparents. When they left, they decided to walk one block over and started back to the apartment. Change of scenery, they decided.

Two blocks from the apartment, they saw a tall brick wall that was covered with flowers. Shelves and hooks were embedded into the brick and mortar and wall was alive with color...vines and flowers in every color. "I would love something like this," Molly thought. Just then Eugenio stopped and took out his phone and snapped a picture. "Maybe we could do something like this, if you like?"

"Perfect."

They walked back to the apartment but Eugenio stopped. "One more gelato?" Molly nodded. She wanted one more of everything she had come to love. While she made her decision, Eugenio stood at the window and then turned and ordered a scoop of peche gelato in a cup. When they left, Eugenio carried the cup and when they crossed the street, he stopped and started up the church steps. The young priest had been standing there alone. Eugenio spoke to him and handed him the cup. The young man took the cup and smiled. He waved at Molly. "Vai con Dio."

Molly nodded back. "Grazie."

Eugenio joined her. "You understood?"

"Yes, Go With God."

He smiled. His Molly was going to do just fine here!

When they got back to the apartment, Molly walked into the bedroom and took off her shoes. She put them neatly by the door and started to take her dress off. Eugenio took her hands. He reached up and untied the straps and kissed each bare shoulder as the soft material fell away. "Molly, I hope you know......" he started, but Molly turned and stopped him with a kiss.

 She nodded and kissed him again and then looked deep into his eyes. "Make love to me."

Chapter 21

Is it possible to hit both ends of the emotional spectrum at the same time? Molly woke before dawn and felt a sense of contentment she had never known with, with....David. His name had almost slipped her mind and she smiled in the darkness. Sarah would have loved this moment, but she also knew that in just a few hours she would be saying good-bye to Eugenio. Even a few months would seem like forever but then they would have the rest of their lives together. People say "for the rest of our lives" but no one ever has as much time as he or she wishes. But if she only had a short time left, she wanted to spend it just like this, quiet times with this man.

What she didn't know was that an hour earlier, as she slept, Eugenio had turned on his side and lay watching her sleep, watching as the moonlight found its way through the trees and sent shadows dancing across her face. He reached over very gently and touched her face and even asleep, she smiled, He had always been a devout Catholic and tried to follow his belief in the Lord. As he watched Molly sleep, he had thanked God for finally giving him someone he would be happy with for the rest of his life. "For the rest of his life"....leaving soon on his last tour of duty. His friend, Mario, with whom he has served so many years, asked once if maybe they weren't pressing their luck. How many tours had they almost not made it home....were they pushing the odds? Mario said it was different for him; he was single and no children, no family at all to speak of. But Eugenio, he has this whole new life waiting for him with this woman he talks of non-stop. Eugenio told him that once he and Molly were married, they would find Mario the perfect mate and the four of them would be great friends even after they retired. But if his time left on this earth was to be brief, he would choose times like this, with this woman, to live out his days....and nights. He leaned back on his pillow and fell back asleep.

When the alarm went off at 6:00 a.m., Eugenio rolled over, gave her a quick kiss, and got out of bed. "Good morning, Bella. I will make coffee." He knew he would make love to Molly once more before they had to leave but he needed to take a few deep breaths to stifle his feelings. In just a few hours, he would stand at the door and kiss her one last time when all he wanted to do was to lock the door and keep out the world that was so intent on keeping them apart.

Molly slipped on her robe and walked out onto the patio. It was going to be a warm day but she would be gone before the heat over-took the city. She sat at the table and looked around. This tiny yard, the family next door, times with Eugenio, and the days and nights she had been alone. How could a whole month have gone so quickly? When Eugenio appeared with two cups of coffee and a plate with one piece of toast, four cookies, and some cheese, Molly laughed. She knew that was the end of their food!

"Eugenio," Molly began quietly, "About that afternoon when we talked about my surgery. I will remember every word and I will know you are with me. I am sorry we didn't meet years ago; my life would have been so different. I cannot promise that I will be here to love you every day for the rest of your life but I promise you that I will love you every day for the rest of mine. And if it is possible, I will love you for Eternity."

"Molly, this is Roma, Eternity is possible."

Gina knocked on the gate. "Molly, may we come in?"

"Yes, yes, of course."

"I just wanted to tell you that I will be here at 10:00 a.m. to take you to the airport. That will give you plenty of time. My car is parked in the back. Perhaps Eugenio could bring your bags back and we can load them there."

Alex was tugging at his mother's arm. "And Alex has been practicing this."

Alex walked over and stood in front of Eugenio, stood tall, and saluted. Eugenio stood and smartly returned the salute. Alex smiled and then stepped forward and gave him a hug. Beatrice walked over and gave him a hug as well.

"Come, my babies, we go now and see you both in a little while." And they slipped through the gate and Molly heard the chain being slipped on. Gina wanted to make sure they were given time to say good-bye.

She picked up the dishes and carried them to the sink. Eugenio took her hand, "Leave them, Molly, I will do them later."

It was 9:30 a.m. when Molly headed for the bathroom. Eugenio waited until he heard her close the door and then he slipped the small box from his duffle into the side of her travel bag. He hoped she wouldn't find it until she was back in Chicago. Molly finished dressing and pulled her hair back with combs and took a deep breath. She looked in the mirror and forced a smile. "It's show time!"

Eugenio had set his backpack and duffle bag in the living room. He walked out onto the patio and lit a cigarette. Molly opened her purse and slipped the small box into the side of his bag. She hoped he wouldn't find it until he was back in the barracks. Molly walked out to the patio and slipped her arms around his waist. "I wish I could tell you....."

He turned and kissed her. "I know."

Promptly at 10:00 a.m., Gina and Alex came to the back door. "I have the car ready." Eugenio picked up Molly's bags and carried them out and put them in the trunk. "Take your time. I will pull around in front." Gina smiled.

Molly was just finishing up the dishes when Eugenio came back. "I did the dishes. Can't have your men seeing you with dishpan hands." She tried to smile but it was just too much for her. Tears streamed down her face. Molly used to joke that her heart had been broken and put back together so many times over the years with David that it must look like a Picasso painting but at that moment she felt it was about to shatter.

"Listen to the doctors, Molly, and come back to me."

Molly nodded. "Eugenio, I ..." she tried to speak between sobs.

Eugenio smile. "I love you too. Now, come, is time."

Eugenio put on his backpack and picked up his duffle bag. Molly took her purse and closed the front door behind them.

Eugenio opened the car door. Molly slipped in and when Eugenio leaned over and kissed her, Alex and Beatrice giggled in the back seat. He closed the door and Molly took his hands through the open window and kissed his fingers and tried to smile.

"Soon."

"Ciao, Bella. Yes, soon."

As Gina pulled into the turning lane, Molly turned to see Eugenio standing quietly watching the car as it disappeared around the corner.

Molly watched as Gina and the children waved one more time and then turned, disappearing into the crowd. Molly picked up her purse and travel bag and walked toward the security check-in. She reached into her bag for her small bag of "liquids" to put in the tray and she saw the light blue wrapping. She stepped out of line and pulled the ribbon loose and opened the tiny box and took out the small locket. She opened it and read: "You gave me your heart and for this, I will be eternally grateful. I love you." She held it to her heart and took a deep breath. "I am not going to cry, I am not ....damn!"

Molly closed her eyes as she felt the plane lift and thrust itself skyward. When she opened her eyes again, she looked out at the vast city below her. Aqueducts, the Colosseum, the dome of St. Paul's, the Pantheon, now all 3,000 feet below her. She could not have written a greater love story than the one she had just lived. The food, the wine, the people, all set in such a magnificent city! And of course, Eugenio. She did not find herself sobbing hopelessly as she

319

expected, but wiping a single tear from her cheek with the back of her hand. She took the locket out of her purse and fastened it around her neck with the other two.

When she looked out the window again, she saw that the city had fallen away to open spaces. She looked down and saw a single car as it headed away from the madness of the city. It couldn't be Eugenio, he was on a train heading east but she thought of him traveling alone back to his barracks to pack his life into a duffle bag and backpack to head for God knows where. Too much to bear, Molly closed her eyes again.

Eugenio was barely out of the city when he looked out the train window and saw a plane barely visible. He walked to the club car and lit a cigarette and took a long drag. He thought about that night they had laid out in the yard and he had tried to comfort Molly. A lover returning to Italy, not someone leaving behind the one she loves. He took another drag of his cigarette and looked out the window. The plane was out of sight now, leaving only a white trail that had almost disappeared into the mist, but he continued to stare out the window, playing over their last few hours together in his mind.

When he finally went back to his seat, he decided to read a while to occupy his time. He opened his backpack and saw the box wrapped in blue paper with a note attached. "You came to me when I needed you the most. You gave me a world I never knew existed and you gave me a lifetime of happiness in one short month. 'My heart will go on' - as long as you love me." He opened the box and slid the silver lighter out of the velvet pouch. It felt smooth and cool in his hand and he turned it over. On the front was engraved:

"Open my heart and you will see engraved inside: Italy"
(Robert Browning) On the back "MIA EROE… Love,
Molly"

Holding it tightly in his hand, he leaned back and closed his
eyes. Molly's hero, what more could he ever ask for in life.

***

When she arrived at O'Hare, Molly found the Coopers
waiting for her with a welcome home sign! She smiled and
waved. Mr. Copper took Molly's travel bag and Mrs.
Cooper gave Molly a hug! "It is so good to have you home.
You look gorgeous, so tan." Then she stepped back and
eyed Molly for a moment and added, "And so happy."

At the condo, Molly found Nick waiting on the steps. He
carried her suitcase up the steps and waited while
she opened the door to her condo. Fresh flowers were on the
table with a card. "Welcome home, Mom. Love, Adam."
Nick carried her bags into the bedroom. "Can't stay,
Molly, on duty but I will be back tomorrow if you aren't too
tired. I would like to talk to you."

"Of course, come for coffee when you have time."

Nick walked over and gave her a hug. "You look
wonderful! I assume it was a good trip."

"Yes, very nice." She smiled and thought if he only knew!

Molly kicked off her shoes and walked over and smelled the
flowers. She made a glass of peach tea and sat quietly,
looking around. It was just as she left it but something was
321

very different. She sipped her tea and looked out the window at the imposing building across the street. Then it hit her...this condo wasn't HOME anymore!

She went to her computer. Adam sent her a brief message. "On duty and busy but I spoke to Eugenio and we have hooked you up with people who will be there to help you. Please, let them do their jobs! Talk soon. Love you, Adam."

And then she opened her letter from Eugenio she knew would be waiting. "Hope you had a good trip home. Please let me know what the doctors say. It is not your heart I think of now. You are going to be well and come back to me. Instead, it is my own heart. It breaks to think I cannot be there for you. We leave in 10 days, Molly, but starting today I count the days until March 15th, when we are together again. Until then, know I think of you every moment. Then he added a smiley face and added, "Is perfetto, Molly, you and I."

Molly went in and lay down on the bed. She wished she could just sleep until March 15th; the time was going to pass so slowly.

Early the next morning, Molly walked to the market for milk and eggs and bread. Back in the real world there were no warm croissants or sweet melon. Coffee and toast would have to do. When she got back she put her suitcases on the bed and began to unpack. She laid the gifts on the table, remembering how much she had enjoyed shopping for everyone. She was just finishing when she heard a knock at the door. Mrs. Cooper was there with some muffins.

"I hope it isn't too early. I knew you would be exhausted. I want to hear everything."

"Oh, Molly," she cried when she opened her gift. "He is so sweet. You shouldn't have but I love it. Sooo," she added, waiting for Molly to tell her all the details.

"It was more than I could have ever hoped for. And Eugenio..." She stopped.

"From your letters, I know it is serious. What happens now that you are home?"

"Well, this really isn't home anymore. I am going back to Italy as soon as we can work out the details."

"Oh Molly, we will miss you but I am so happy for you. Things must have gone REALLY well. I guess you won't be telling me everything." She smiled and took a bite of her muffin.

The next ten days went by so quickly. The doctor had scheduled Molly's surgery and Molly was to rest and take short walks and not to worry. Andy and Nick came every day, bringing her small gifts with notes from Adam attached. They brought food and offered to do "whatever needed to be done."

One afternoon when it was just Nick and Molly having tea, Nick asked her what her plans were for the condo. She told him she was going to sell it because she was leaving, but added that she was sure Adam and Eugenio had already told him that.

323

"I would like to make you an offer, Molly. I am getting married and how cool would it be to live so close to the station! If we can swing it, I would like to buy it."

After he left, Molly sat by the window...yes, she could see the station from her window. And now that it was paid for, she could offer it to Nick for a reasonable price and still make a decent profit. She really wouldn't have to work when she moved to Italy. With money in the bank and her retirement to add to Eugenio's retirement, they could live very comfortably. However, now that she had an offer on her children's books, she really wanted to complete the project. It would be great to still be productive for a while longer to help her through the transition because she really did love teaching. It would be something of Sarah and herself to pass on to their grandchildren. And she did have a few months before she would be leaving...this final project would keep her busy when those cold winter winds blew through the Windy City.

Molly was awake most of the night, not worried about her surgery, but about Eugenio starting his last tour of duty. There had been so many others. Was he tempting fate and luck this one last time? Molly had faith in his ability but it was his devout loyalty she was concerned about. He was a commander and she knew he would do anything to protect the men in his unit. What if one of them screwed up and caused...no, she was not going to let herself think about it. All they had standing between them and happiness was Eugenio's last tour, her heart surgery, her retirement, his retirement, an endless stack of paperwork, selling and packing up her condo, and moving halfway around the world. Molly smiled and closed her eyes. "Is no problem." In the darkness, Molly took a deep breath and instantly felt the comfort. "I knew you would here. I knew I wouldn't be alone."

They had talked the night before but Molly found a letter waiting when she turned on her computer. Eugenio would have left by now, being seven hours ahead, he told her he knows his prayers will be answered so please don't worry. She wrote back a simple "I love you" and switched off her computer.

Mrs. Cooper said she would pick her up at 7:00 a.m. but Molly said no, she did not want her to have to fight early morning traffic to get her to the hospital. She did agree to let her call a taxi to pick her up. At 6:30 a.m., Molly picked up her bag. It was going to be a nice day and she decided to sit out on the stoop and wait but when she opened the door, Andy was sitting there waiting for her. He stood up and waved and an ambulance pulled out and made its way to her doorstep.

"Your chariot, Madame." He took her bag and helped her into the front seat next to him. "Better view than in the back!"

As he swung around and headed north, they passed the fire station. All the men were lined up across the front.

"Hurry home, Molly!"

"Love you!"

"God speed!"

Molly smiled and waved but could not stop the tears. Andy reached out and took her hand. "It's okay, Molly, we told Eugenio and Adam we would take good care of you."

"But how...?"

"We are all just a click away these days. Adam forwarded me a letter from Eugenio and I told him I had his back. Adam did want me to lock his sister in a closet until you felt better and added an LOL, but I think he was serious."

Molly laughed. She had accepted the fact that Amanda was her father's daughter but after all these years, she had made peace with that.

Andy swung into the hospital parking lot and up to the front entrance. "I would stay but I have to get back in case someone else needs this." He set Molly's bag on the sidewalk and helped Molly out of the ambulance. He gave her a kiss on the left cheek. "From Eugenio." He kissed her on the right cheek. "This is from Adam." and then he kissed her forehead. "And this is from all of us at the station."

Molly watched as Andy waved one last time and pulled out into traffic. She picked up her bag and started through the automatic door when she heard that all too familiar voice, "Mother!"

Chapter 22

Eugenio was lying on his bed. The barracks was stripped of any sign that this tiny room had been his home for over eighteen months. His bags were packed and by the door. Soon they would be boarding the bus to take them to the airport. He looked at his watch. Molly would be going into surgery any time now. How he wished he could be there, holding her hand to assure her everything would be alright; to tell her he loves her and that he will be there waiting when she wakes up.

Just then there was a knock at the door. Mario stuck his head in. "Eugenio, Alessia is here. She says she needs to see you. She says it is important. If you don't want to deal with it right now I can tell her you are busy."

"No, we are divorced now. There is nothing more she can say." And then Eugenio laughed, "But I would be very careful if I were you. As expensive as you smell, she may decide she wants you."

Mario just laughed and shook his head… "Mai, il mio amico."

"And never AGAIN for me, my friend."

When he walked outside, Alessia was wearing a low-cut dress and she was posed against the railing, knowing full well that her figure was revealing itself through the thin white material of her skirt. She walked toward him and gave him a hug. "Ciao, Eugenio," she whispered warmly into his ear. "I have missed you."

"Why have you come, Alessia? I go to the court, I go to the church, I sign the papers. We are divorced now."

"Eugenio, please. I do not want to fight with you. I need to talk. I have made a terrible mistake. I do not want this divorce. I can fix this while you are away and when you come back, we can be together. It will be different, I promise."

"It is too late, Alessia." He studied her face. She looked drawn and even the heavy make-up she wore could not conceal the dark circles under her eyes. "What are you not telling me?"

Tears began to flow and she sat down on the bench and buried her face in her hands. "He does not want me. I tell him I have a surprise for him, that I am free and we can marry. And he says to me I am foolish. He is already married."

"Alessia, this is not my problem." He started to walk away but she took Eugenio's arm.

"Please, listen to me. I'm pregnant."

Eugenio turned and looked at her. "Pregnant? Why would you do this? You do not want children. Did you think he would be sure and marry you if you were pregnant?"

"He said he loved me," she said softly.

"Did he ever ask you to marry him?"

"He said he loved me," she repeated.

"And you wanted to make sure he would not leave you. You ARE foolish, Alessia."

"Eugenio, please. Maybe this baby is yours, we made love the last time you were home, remember? You always wanted to be a papa. We could stay in our home and have this baby. Everyone would think it is our child. We could be happy again."

Suddenly Eugenio became angry. "No, it has been too long for this child to be mine. We were not happy for a very long time. I wanted a child of my own and you refused. I accepted that because of my love for you but it is gone now. WE do not have a home anymore. I have a home. You gave everything we had away because you thought your beauty would get you a rich husband."

Alessia tried to put her arms around him. "You still think I am beautiful. I can see it in your eyes." She pressed against him. "And I know you still love me."

"No, you are wrong. I do not love you. I see past your beauty and I do not like what I see. I leave soon and you are to leave my house as the court says. My cousin, Carmine, will be there to make sure you are gone and that you have taken nothing. It is just as you wanted. Is over, Alessia."

She stepped back and looked into his face. She did not see the hurt or the longing that had been there for such a long time. Instead, she only saw contempt. She had been sure he

329

would take her back if she offered him a child of his own. And once they were back together, maybe something would happen and she would not carry the child full term. But she would have her life back either way, with or without the burden of a child. Suddenly she was frightened. She had no home, no money, not even a car. She had signed it all away, knowing this new man would lavish her with all she dreamed of. She put her hand on the diamond necklace he had surprised her with on one of their secret meetings. So many times she had turned on the tears to get her own way but this time, the tears flowed in earnest. "What am I to do, Eugenio?"

Eugenio thought about Molly, who wanted nothing from him but his love. Molly, who was as beautiful outside as she was inside, although she never knew it. Molly, who had come halfway around the world just to be able to spend a few days each week with him.

"Eugenio, please, what am I to do?" she asked again.

"I don't care. But you aren't doing it in my home." He turned and walked away. He did not even turn around when she threw the car into gear and squealed the tires as she pulled out of the parking lot.

Eugenio went back inside and lit a cigarette. He took a long drag and let the smoke out slowly. He let out a sigh of relief. It had suddenly occurred to him. What he said was not about anger or getting even. He really did not care!

Just then there was a tap on the door. "You okay?"

"Yes, Mario, I am better than okay."

Just then they heard someone shout down the hall. "Bus is here. Thirty minutes, Gentlemen!"

***

"It's time, Molly. All set?"

Molly nodded at the doctor and looked at the IV in her arm. "Well, I am tethered so I guess there is no sense trying to get away."

"Nope, you belong to us now. Just relax...soon that heart of yours will be as good as the day you were born."

"Great, I was born with a heart murmur."

"Then you will be better than the day you were born." The nurse tucked the blankets tightly around her. "Just lay back and relax. We are going to take you down now."

Molly barely felt them move her from the bed to the cart. She had her eyes closed as they moved down the hallway because of the glare from the lights overhead. The meds were taking effect and it felt like someone was pumping warm wet sand into her body. "Fine, weight gain," and she smiled at her own joke.

At the door of the operating room the cart stopped and Molly opened her eyes. Andy and Nick and the Coopers and Amanda and Eddie were all standing there.

"Don't worry, Guys," she whispered when she saw the worried looks on their faces. "I got this."

"Molly?" The doctor was leaning over her. She opened her eyes. "Usually this is where I tell you to start counting backwards from 100, but I was given a special request."

"I don't understand."

"You will."

It was as if she was surrounded by slowly moving white human clouds with indistinguishable faces and then she heard the music. Vittori Grigolo! And the last thing she remembered was someone taking her hand and the air filled with that warm comforting aroma. "Watch over him for me, Sarah," she whispered and fell asleep.

***

Eugenio stood alone on the tarmac. Did Alessia really think she could just show up and dangle fatherhood in his face and he would forgive all those years? All the times he had talked about having children and how she had refused. And the minute she wanted to seal her relationship with her rich lover, she gets pregnant. What a shock it was for Alessia to learn that the money was actually his wife's and he never would have walked away from such a lucrative lifestyle.

He wondered what would happen to that poor child Alessia had tried to use as a pawn, not once, but twice, with a father who would not be there and a mother who was already regretting his or her very existence. Then it hit him! There was no need to even continue with this pregnancy. This child will never even be born! Guilt washed over him. Would God really expect him to walk away from Molly and take Alessia back to save this child. She certainly would not be any kind of mother and Eugenio would be handed another man's child to raise alone. Was this to be his lot for the rest of his life? He and Molly were so close. Only one more foreign crisis to deal with, her surgery, and a move halfway around the world and they would be together. He wondered what Molly would say to all this... No, he already knew what she would say. That was the difference between Molly and Alessia.

One more cigarette before getting on the plane. He pulled out his lighter but instead of putting it back in his pocket, he held it in his hand and read the quote once more on the front and then flipped it. "Love, Molly." He held it tight, pressing the words against his skin. He took one last drag, field-stripped the last bit, and climbed the steps to the waiting plane.

Chapter 23

"Daddy!" Amanda wailed into the phone.

"Amanda, calm down. What's wrong?"

"It's my mother! She is gone!"

"Gone? But she was doing so well after her surgery. What happened?"

"I don't know."

"Honey, I have to ask. Did she say anything about me…or the condo?"

"For heaven's sake, Daddy. She isn't dead. She is gone."

"I don't understand. What do you mean gone?"

Earlier that day, Amanda had gone over to Molly's to borrow her car. Amanda had Eddie drop her off in front of the condo and leave. She figured Molly could hardly say no to her request if she was stranded. She tried to let herself in but the key didn't work. She knocked impatiently, "Mother, open the door!"

But when the door opened, a tall young woman stood in the doorway. Amanda tried to move past her but the woman made no effort to move.

"May I help you?"

"Where is my mother?" Amanda demanded.

"Gone."

"Gone? What do you mean gone? Did she die? Why didn't anyone call me?"

"Calm down. Molly is fine. She just doesn't live here anymore."

Amanda looked past the woman into the living room. It looked pretty much the same. Wait, where are all Mom's books? Her bookcase was empty except for a few pictures.

"What is going on?"

The young woman smiled. "You must be Amanda. Nick and Adam said you would show up eventually."

"Let me in this instant. This is my mother's home. She wouldn't just move without telling me. I am her daughter!"

"This condo belongs to Nick and me. We bought it and moved in almost two weeks ago. But I believe Molly did leave a letter for you with Mrs. Cooper in 4B. Now if you will excuse me." As she closed the door, leaving Amanda standing dumbfounded in the hall, she smiled. "Wow, I thought Adam was kidding about his sister."

Amanda raised her hand to knock again but she stopped. Mrs. Cooper would know what was going on around here. She walked over to 4B and knocked. Mrs. Cooper answered the door and gave Amanda a big smile. She was going to enjoy this! "Why, hello, Dear, please come in."

Amanda stormed into the tidy little living room.

"Can I get you a nice cup of tea? You look upset."

"I am upset. I don't want any tea. I want to know where my mother is."

"Italy."

"What? Again?"

Mrs. Cooper took a manila envelope from the mantel and handed it to Amanda.

"I just don't know what is wrong with my mother. This isn't like her at all."

"Yes, and it is wonderful. I have never seen her so happy."

Amanda let out a noise that sounded like a moan. "No! It is not wonderful. When will she be back this time?"

"Dear, you need to read the letter. She isn't coming back. She sold the condo to Nick. He and Randi are getting married in the spring. And your mother has moved to Italy."

"Why didn't she consult me about this? And Daddy...and Adam. Maybe it is the medication she is taking."

"Adam knows. And since he has been transferred to Naples, it has worked out perfectly."

"Adam is going to Italy too? No, it is not wonderful and it certainly is not perfect. What about me? I will be alone."

"It is not about you at all, Amanda, not this time." Mrs. Cooper actually was starting to feel a little sorry for her so she walked over and put her hand on Amanda's shoulder. "Amanda, you will be just fine. Your mother said that you have been offered a great new job in California and you have Eddie and your father and Tiffany and a new baby brother."

"Eddie? Eddie?" She sobbed. "He doesn't even have a job; he spends all of his time in the coffee shop. And Daddy and Tiffany have Andrew. Mom is the only one I can count on and now she is gone. What am I supposed to do?"

Mrs. Cooper knew she should bite her tongue but she didn't. "Grow up, Amanda. It is time for you to grow up. Your mother had heart surgery and she needed you. And you were too busy to come. She didn't just leave; she has been gone for almost two weeks now. She wanted to tell you but you were too busy when she called and wanted to see you."

Amanda started to object but she knew the woman was right. Anything she would say in her defense would sound stupid even to her. Instead, she picked up the envelope and headed for the door. "Well, I need to borrow Mom's car. I see that is still sitting outside."

"Actually, Dear, it is my car now. I bought it from Molly."

"This just keeps getting worse by the minute. Well, Eddie left me off so you will have to give me a ride back to my apartment."

"I am sorry, but I have plans this morning. But the bus stop is right up on the next corner, you remember, don't you? Now if you will excuse me," she walked over and opened the door.

Amanda stomped out of the door. "I am going to call my father!"

Mrs. Cooper picked up the tea pot and poured herself another cup of tea. "And this is my plans for the morning," as she took a sip. She looked out the window to the street below. "Good for you, Molly," she said out-loud.

Amanda walked into the fire station on the corner. "Where is Nick?" she demanded. Three men were sitting around the table drinking coffee.

"Morning, Amanda," one of them said, "Just got back from a call so Nick was out all night. He headed to bed. What's up?"

Amanda plopped into a chair. "I need to talk to him. I went over to my mother's and she is gone. This woman answered the door and said she and Nick bought the condo and have lived there for two weeks."

"Yup, be two weeks on Saturday. We all helped Molly pack what little she took and we helped Nick and Randi move in."

"Would you PLEASE go and get Nick for me?"

"Only one reason I would…" but before he could finish his sentence, the alarm rang. "And THAT is the one reason," he said and he swallowed the last of his coffee and headed for the door.

Amanda watched the men scramble into their gear. Nick came down, boots in hand. He yelled at Amanda as he hurried by, "Hey, Kiddo, wish I had time to talk. Tell your mom we love the condo." He climbed into the driver's seat and started the engine. The doors opened and Nick waved as he headed out, sirens blaring.

An older man walked up and stood next to her. "Can I get you a cup of coffee and some cookies? Not as good as your mom's though."

"No," Amanda said quietly, "No, thank you." She turned and walked into the cold morning air. She pulled her scarf up and around her face and headed for the EL. She caught the train and headed into the city. She took a seat by the window and opened the envelope. There was a letter and an envelope addressed to Mrs. Cooper with a key.

"Dear Amanda,

I am not sure when you will get this. I had hoped to tell you all of this in person but you were always too busy for even lunch. I know you do not understand and I am sure you are feeling abandoned but honestly, my darling girl, this is not about you, any more than the choices you are about to make in your life should be about me.

We have so many memories of good times when you were growing up and now here you are, a college graduate, ready to go out and make your place in the world. I know you have always been your daddy's little girl and I came to

339

accept that, but you and I were always close and we will make new memories, you and I. I love you and I am so very proud of you. You are a smart lady, Amanda, and you will find your own way, and I am sure you will not let someone else control your decisions as I did for such a long time.

There are several boxes I have put in my storage locker for you. Everything is boxed and labeled. I told Nick that you would take what you wanted by the end of January and then Mindy would take the key and see that Goodwill comes and picks up what you do not want. There is a small blue box in one of the drawers of the small table in the back. It is my wedding rings from your father and some other jewelry he bought me over the years. I was sure you would want them.

I know you are angry but please know I am always going to be your mother and will love you and support your choices in life. When you didn't have time to meet, you told me we have Facebook and we can SKYPE any time you want to talk. So, I will tell you, as you have always told me, 'I am just a click away.'

Love, Mom"

Amanda leaned against the window of the train. The glass felt cold against her hot cheek. Why hadn't she gone to see her mother? Maybe she could have talked her out of all this nonsense. No, her mother was gone, moved to Italy to begin a new life with this man she barely knows. Amanda knew nothing she would have said would have changed that, but she should have gone and spent some time with her. If she had only known… instead she had… The train came to a halt and Amanda grabbed the envelope and got off. No sense going to see her father. She just wanted to go home.

When she opened the door, she was relieved to see Eddie standing in the kitchen. She burst into tears and he rushed over and put his arms around her, as he had in the hospital while they had sat in the waiting room during Molly's surgery. He told her to sit and he went to the kitchen and made her a most remarkably good cup of coffee. He listened to her pour out her tale of woe. When she was finished, Eddie said quietly, "Take the job in California, Mandy. It is such a good offer and I think we should go."

"We? You would come? I thought you didn't want to leave Chicago?"

"I have been thinking about it. I am tired of freezing my butt off four months out of every year. And I can't imagine being anywhere without you. We are ready for a change," and he reached over and took her hand. "Just like your mom, Mandy."

Amanda said nothing but she nodded. That night after dinner, Amanda called her father, but Tiffany said he wasn't there. Earlier she had tried his cell and there was no answer so she had left a message. "Tiff, is everything okay?"

"Well, you are going to hear sooner or later. We have split, Amanda, we are getting a divorce. This just isn't working for us. Baby Boy and I are staying here and I think your dad went somewhere downtown. He will be back in the morning for the rest of his things. I will make sure he calls you."

341

"Thanks, Tiff," she replied, her voice barely audible. She didn't even know what to say.

"And Amanda, stay in touch. Come and hang out any time, okay?" And before she could answer, Amanda heard her hang up.

She stood staring at her phone for a moment and then burst into tears again.

"Eddie! Daddy is gone!"

Chapter 24

Molly found herself back in the apartment that she and Eugenio had called home for a short time. She leaned against the kitchen counter, holding a cup of hot tea, looking out at the cold grey afternoon. It wouldn't have mattered what the weather was, she was back in Rome, back where she felt she belonged. And here she was now, quite content to wait out the last days of Eugenio's deployment.

The last five weeks had been unbelievable and even Eugenio with all his lists, would have been proud of the way she had gotten through so much in just five weeks.

Her surgery had gone so well; the doctor had put in three stints and in a week she was home and feeling great! Still carrying that tiny bottle of nitro in the necklace Eugenio had gotten her, but hopeful that she would never need it again. In August, she had returned to work and as much as she loved her job, she felt a sense of freedom when she went to the department chair and handed in her resignation. She had begun to make Friday nights at McGinty's a regular stop. She wanted to enjoy the company of the people she had worked beside so many years as long as she could.

Just before Thanksgiving break, Molly had been Skyping with Gina one afternoon, when Gina told her that their nanny was leaving. She had fallen in love and was moving to Florence to finish art school and be married. Gina was worried that they would have to step up their move to Sorrento if she could not find someone to take care of the children until May. While they were chatting, Alex crawled up on his mother's lap and held up a picture he had drawn for his Nomino Molly. It was the lemon tree in the backyard, the lemons now a bright yellow and ready to be picked. And when he leaned into the screen and said, "Come home, Molly!" she burst into tears. That night she sat down and wrote Gina a long letter and ended with "What do you think?"

The next morning, she found her answer waiting: "Yes, please come." It would all happen so quickly and there was so much to do. She walked down to the fire station and found Nick busy cooking bacon and eggs for the crew. Molly made the toast while he texted Randi and he came back in and announced, "Okay, guys, going to need some help in a couple weeks. Molly and I are moving!" From that point on, Molly's days were filled with lists of things to get done and her nights were filled with dreams of Italy.

Everyone from the college had all met one last time at McGinty's at the end of the semester to give Molly a proper retirement dinner. It was a warm and delightful evening and Molly had felt very honored to have worked with so many great professionals. Even Martin was on his best behavior. By 10:00 p.m., everyone else had headed out and Molly was the last to leave. A bag of lovely gifts sat next to her on the long padded bench. She ordered two shots of Limoncello and slid them together side-by-side on the table and sat looking at them. Then she made a silent toast and clicked them together and drank one. She picked up her coat and reached over for the bag when she stopped and looked at the single glass left on the table. Sarah wouldn't have liked her leaving it there alone. Molly raised the glass. "Sarah," she said out-loud and drank it down. She set it next to her own empty glass. Yes, better! She picked up the bag and walked out the door.

When she got home that night, she sat by the window and opened the manila envelope for the 100th time. Approved! She had a one-year VISA to live in Italy! All the paperwork and the trips downtown to the passport agency had been worth it! She thought about how excited she had been when she was finally able to write Eugenio and tell him.

On the last morning, Molly set her suitcases out in the hallway and turned to take one last look around. Deep in thought, she jumped a bit when Mrs. Cooper spoke to her. "Going to miss it, Molly?"

Molly took one more, quick look around the room and then closed the door. "Nope," she said and then slipped her arm around her friend's shoulder. "Just you."

When they pulled away from the curb, Molly didn't even bother to look back.

When they pulled out into traffic, Mrs. Cooper headed for the fire station. The guys were all standing outside. Molly rolled down the window.

"Can't believe you would leave us just to live in Italy."

"I know, silly me," she said, fighting back the tears.

Nick walked over and Molly reached out and handed him the keys. "All yours now."

Nick took the keys and then took her hand and kissed it. "We love you, Molly. Stay in touch."

This time when they pulled into traffic, Molly turned and waved. Some things she would definitely miss!

***

Molly refilled her tea and headed for the bedroom to finish unpacking. She had arrived that morning to find Gina, Marc and the kids waiting for her at the gate. Alex ran under the rope when he saw her and ran to give her a hug. Beatrice had a gift for her. It was a calendar and a marker. She said Molly could use it to count away the days until Eugenio came home and she would be happy again. Molly assured her that being back to help care for her and Alex already made her very happy.

Molly wrote Eugenio a long letter that night before she set her alarm and crawled into bed. She was exhausted from the long flight, but she wanted him to know she had arrived safely and that she was waiting for him to come home. She ended, writing: "I memorized everything about my first time in Italy and it is as I remember it, but it is better now. Now it is HOME!"

She pulled the soft duvet up around her and closed her eyes. Yes, she was home!

"Christmas in Rome, well, I don't even know where to begin." Molly began her letter to Mindy Cooper. "The streets are draped with red, green and white lights that go on forever. Each church has set out its own unique nativity scene and they have choirs and serve hot coffee. Some of them are hundreds of years old. There are over fifty churches participating, but I have only made it to five.

It is not often that Rome has a white Christmas, which is evident from the number of fender-benders I have seen. We had three inches of snow but it is warm so there isn't much left. After all those years of freezing cold Chicago winters, I love this!

Gina and Marc took the children to Sorrento for the week. They wanted me to come, not to care for the children, but as a guest, but I said I was quite happy here on my own. Eugenio's family made me promise I would come to the restaurant Christmas Eve to have lunch with all the cousins and aunts and uncles. I put up a tiny tree and put the gifts you sent next to it. Thank you for the lovely scarf and for sending along all the cards from the fire station.

I went to Marino's and had a lovely lunch, so much food and wine. And Carmine and his family bought me a beautiful Gucci handbag. I am so happy they have accepted me. When I got home, I baked cookies and decided to take a plate down to see if I could leave them for the young priest I told you about. Luckily, he was standing by the door, MASS having just ended. He peeked under the foil and smiled and said, 'Yes, is good, grazie.' I think his English is about as limited as my Italian but we both seem to be learning.

As I was walking home, I heard someone shout 'Mom!' and like every other mother in the world, I instinctively turned around. There was Adam just crossing the street! He reports for duty on January 1st in Naples. I was so happy I hadn't sent his gifts and then I remembered it was Eugenio who told me I should wait since they might get lost when he transferred. Later that night when I checked my mail,

Eugenio had left a message asking if his "gift" had arrived yet.

Adam will be here three more days, but waking up this morning and seeing him asleep on the couch was the best gift I could have asked for. I had decided I would cook a big dinner even if I was alone and enjoy the leftovers. I am so glad I did. Adam and I ate in the living room and watched our 'family tradition movie,' Christmas Vacation, which suddenly appeared from his duffle bag. He said Tiffany and the baby are living in David's condo and she has already moved in a new man, an up-and-coming young executive. David is staying in a studio that his firm owns, and feeling sorry for himself. When he asked Adam if he thought there was any chance that I might forgive him and take him back, Adam was quite unsympathetic. He told his father all about my books and Eugenio. I think after all these years, Adam has stopped trying to please his father and he is anxious to get to know Eugenio. It is amazing how things have worked out together, the last few months.

I finally heard from Amanda. She and Eddie moved to California on the 18th. She starts with a new company the first of the year and Eddie went right out and got a job. He is a barista and has discovered he quite enjoys being employed. I think Amanda is going to be okay.

Sometimes I miss the old neighborhood and of course, my dear friends, but honestly, Min, life here is good. And you know you are always welcome to come and visit once we get moved into our own house. Maybe I can tempt you with a promise to visit Venice and the Murino Glass factory!

Stay warm, my friend, Merry Christmas! -Molly"

She was just getting ready to close her computer when Eugenio sent a Skype message. She instantly answered and he appeared on her screen.

"Ciao, Bella. Merry Christmas. I am only allowed a very short time and wanted to send you a message but seeing your face is my best Christmas present. Did my present arrive?"

"Yes, it is asleep on the couch." Suddenly the tears began to flow. "What did I ever do to deserve you in my life?"

"Please do not cry. I cannot be there to take them away for you. You should be happy. You are in Italy and I will be finished soon and come to you. I tell Mario life will be good when we return. I will have you, and with his sexy expensive cologne, he will soon have a wife and we will retire, relax and enjoy life."

"I do so adore you. I am here waiting."

"Molly, I have to go, but am very happy to see your face. I love you."

"I love you too."

He blew her a kiss and then he was gone.

Molly walked over and stood watching Adam as he slept. She wanted him to take the bed, but he insisted on the couch. He said it was still longer and more comfortable than what he usually sleeps on. She couldn't resist leaning over and tucking the comforter up around his shoulder and

349

kissing his cheek before turning off the light and going to bed.

New Year's Eve they had gone down to The New Station for lunch and then Adam had come back to pack. He was taking the afternoon train to Naples because he was to report in at 9:00 a.m., New Year's Day. As they were finishing their coffee, Adam suddenly began to laugh. He reached over and took Molly's hand. "Who would have thought, Mom, all those years ago when we sat in the kitchen eating our leftovers from Dad and Amanda's nights out, that you and I would end up here. You had a successful teaching career and are now a writer, starting a new life with a dashing military Italian and me, a dashing American Marine about to start a two-year tour of duty in Naples. And who knows, maybe I will find myself a nice Italian girl and end up staying."

Molly started to cry. "Yup, look at us now."

An hour later, Molly had watched until the train had gone around the bend and was out of sight. She was waiting to cross the street when she saw the young priest standing in front of the church. "Saint Francis and Saint Catherine's has found itself a good man." Molly thought.

"Good afternoon and Happy New Year."

He walked toward her and reached out and took her hand. Then the smile left his face and in his very broken English, he said, "Be strong and have faith." Molly nodded, but as she walked home, she thought what a curious thing for him to say…and in English to make sure she understood. She walked back to the apartment and sat quietly looking out the window at the quiet street outside. In a few hours, it would be a new year, in a new country, with her son only two hours away, back with Alex and Beatrice, and with Eugenio soon to be home. Pretty damn good start!

It had been a mild January by Molly's standards. Molly was content with her occasional outings, but spent much of her time finishing up the teaching manuals, wanting to have all her spare time to devote to other things once Eugenio was home.

Alex went to school three hours each morning and Beatrice was gone all day. Molly and the children would walk the four blocks to school each morning on pleasant days or catch the tram when it looked like rain.

The school was a low grey brick building and Molly would return at noon and wait for Alex to come out. She didn't like that building for some reason. The only signs of life were the brightly colored pictures the teachers taped to the windows. When she was growing up, her school had a huge front lawn and playgrounds on both ends. She would ride the bus when the weather was bad, but she preferred to ride her bike every chance she had. Here the streets were not safe for the younger children alone and nannies and mothers accompanied anyone not riding the bus. No big yellow buses; however, there was a caravan of vans driven by nuns loading or unloading each time Molly was there.

At home, Molly and Alex would make lunch together and then read a story until Alex fell asleep. Molly tried to do things around the house and sometimes cooked dinner so Gina could relax when she got home from work and enjoy time with the family. Gina and Marc refused to take any kind of payment for the apartment saying, Molly coming was a God-send for them.

Once in a while, Molly would stay to eat with them, but usually, she just left them to be a family. She had a standing invitation to the restaurant now and when she did go, a family member would always join her so she did not have to dine alone. Sometimes, she would walk over to the supermarket, stopping by for coffee and a chat with Marcello. And, too often, she would walk down to The New Station when she felt like a big meal, still greeted with a smile from Alex.

Each night before she went to bed, she would take the marker and put a cross through the day. One less day she had to wait until Eugenio came home.

It was almost dark and Eugenio had been asleep for about an hour when there was a knock at his door. "Eugenio, it is time to go." Mario handed him a mug of hot coffee. "You are going to need this. It is going to be another long night."

Eugenio took the mug and took a drink to clear his head.

"Mario, sit for a minute. I want you to do something for me. I have a small box of things and a letter. If anything happens to me, I want Molly to have these things. Go to Rome and give them to her. She will ask but only tell her I died her hero. No details. She doesn't need to know. Stay and make sure she is alright. I am giving her my house. Help her settle in if she chooses to stay. But if she chooses to return to Chicago, please help her there as well. Will you do this for me?"

"Soon you will be in Rome and all this will be forgotten, but if it makes you at ease, yes, I will do this for you." Then he laughed. "I have nothing but a few personal things and of course, a very expensive bottle of No. 1. If I do not come back, you take it and wear it for your Molly. But now, is time to go."

Eugenio had received a letter from Carmine, telling him of the day Alessia had come to take the last of her things from the house. She had been very curt and when Carmine told her he was not surprised that she did not even ask about Eugenio, she said she had lost her child because of the stress Eugenio had caused her. Carmine said one day God would make her accountable for her own sins and had gone out and stood by the van to make sure each item she had the two young men carry out to load were hers. And before she left, he had demanded the car and house keys. She had wailed that she had no way to leave without the car, but in the end, Carmine had stood in the driveway and waved good-bye as Alessia left, wedged between the two young men in the front seat of the van.

Carmine and Eugenio had talked about the pregnancy and Carmine had written to his cousin that he should not feel guilty. His life was to be with Molly now, so he was not to feel accountable for Alessia's choices. But he added that he would go to MASS and pray for the poor child Alessia had tried to use not once but twice, and then threw away.

Still, Eugenio had gone to the small room in the compound set up as a makeshift church and asked God to forgive him. In those quiet moments, alone with only he and His Maker, he decided not to tell Molly of the "lost child." The burden of guilt he felt would be his own to deal with.

Within the hour, Eugenio climbed into the Hummer next to Mario and felt it lurch forward. No headlights! Eugenio said, "Doesn't matter if we have lights or not, the enemy will smell Mario's cologne and know we come." They all laughed as they moved into the darkness and made their way along the dunes and up into the hills.

Chapter 25

The morning was over-cast but was unusually warm for February. Eugenio stood silently, watching as they brought the coffin from the hold of the plane. The pain in his shoulder was intense but he took a deep breath and raised his arm in a salute as the coffin was wheeled past him and placed into the back of the waiting hearse.

There was no family so Eugenio stood alone and waited until the doors were closed and the honor guard had silently marched away. "It wasn't supposed to be like this," he thought. "You were supposed to be part of my new life, you, Molly, and I."

Molly! Suddenly he wished she was there with him. She had wanted to come to the airport but he did not want her to worry about finding her way out of Rome, much less travel halfway across Italy. And he did not want their first time together in eight months to be full of such sadness. No, it was better he do this on his own.

Later that day, he would attend the graveside service and then check himself into the infirmary for yet another check-up. But in just four more days, he would pack one last time and leave for Rome.

***

Carmine had come to the apartment late one evening. Molly remembered the fear that had engulfed her when she saw the look on his face. But Carmine had stepped quickly inside and taken both her hands, feeling them turn to ice.

355

"No, Molly, come and sit down. I speak with Eugenio and he is going to be good, but he has been wounded in his shoulder. He is in hospital now but he is very worried for you. He says I come to Molly and tell her. But his friend, Mario, he was not so lucky. He did not survive."

"What happened?"

"They were on patrol and were attacked."

All Molly could think was how Eugenio must be hurting, not just from injuries but from the loss of his friend. They had talked many times about Molly and Mario finally meeting.

Eugenio said they needed to find Mario a good woman and the four of them would have good times together. Molly thought about Sarah. She wished Eugenio could have met her. And who knows, maybe she would have found in Mario what Molly had with Eugenio.

Carmine made a pot of strong tea and stayed with Molly until he had assured her that Eugenio would recover and was safe now. His unit would be returning to Italy as soon as they were able to travel...sooner than planned. Before he left, he made Molly promise that she would come to the restaurant the next evening and have a late dinner with him.

It was almost a week later that Molly finally found a long letter waiting for her from Eugenio. He told her what he could about the attack and he said wounded or not, he was going to put both arms around her and never let her go again. He said very little of his own injuries but wrote of his

356

many years with Mario as a friend and comrade. He said his unit would be returning almost four weeks earlier than originally planned and he would let her know as soon as possible. She could hear the pain in his words but he ended with, "Soon, Bella, soon we will be together. Your Eugenio."

She wanted to be there when the plane landed, to welcome her eroe home but he asked that he would come to her in Rome. He would worry more about her traveling alone and Molly had to laugh. She had made two trips to Italy on her own and she was pretty successful on her own these days, but she agreed to wait.

***

At 2:00 p.m., Molly stepped off the tram and took a deep breath to calm her shaking hands. Spring was still weeks away but the air was warmed by the sunshine and the sweater she wore was more than enough. He had asked her to meet him on the bridge. His family called it Marino Bridge because it was such a big part of all their lives for generations. So, she crossed the street and began to walk slowly up the bridge, scanning the faces of those walking toward her. But her steps quickened when she saw that familiar face emerge from the crowd.

Seven months, three weeks and four days all seemed to melt away. He looked tired and his arm was in a sling, but his face brightened when he saw her. Despite the pain of lifting his arm, he took her face in his hands.

"I have thought of this moment so many times." And he kissed her...softly and gently, as he had done that first time at the apartment.

"Let's go home," Molly whispered against his cheek.

"Yes, but Molly first, there is something that must be done." He started to kneel.

"Eugenio, please don't. You are hurt."

"No, it must be done. I say when the time is right I would do this properly." He held up the gold band with a single amethyst stone he had taken from his pocket. "Molly, I promise I will make you happy, I will always kiss away your tears, and always buy you gelato if you will marry me."

"Yes," she replied quietly and held out her hand for him to slip the ring on her finger.

Just then the breeze blew Molly's sweater back from her shoulder, exposing the thin pink scar that was visible above her neckline. She quickly covered it but Eugenio took her hand.

"Eugenio, please, it is so ugly."

"No, Bella, is beautiful to me, because of scar, I have you and your heart. Besides..." He pulled down the shoulder of his jacket and exposed a large bandage. "Now this is going to leave a scar!"

"Let's go home," Molly repeated.

At the foot of the bridge, a quiet figure stood watching when a man spoke to her. "I am sorry, my English is not so good, but you are American, yes?"

"Yes."

"Are you alright? You look very sad."

"No," she answered, wiping away her tears with the back of her hand. "I am actually very happy."

He nodded toward Eugenio and Molly. "Do you know these people?"

"Oh yes, she is my best friend. I have been worried about her for such a long time, but you can see, she is happy now."

"You are Molly's friend?"

"Do you know Molly?"

"I know many things of Molly. Eugenio spoke of nothing else for many months. I too worried, but is good now."

She smiled warmly at the handsome man in uniform who stood before her. She held out her hand. "I am Sarah."

"I am Mario. Eugenio and I are friends. We served together for many years until..."

"I am so very sorry."

"Not how I think to end my military career. Eugenio and I were to retire now. I have no family, only an elderly aunt and uncle who raised me. But Eugenio and I, we speak of my visiting his home with Molly, always to be welcome."

"I was to retire as well." She continued to look into Mario's deep brown eyes. "Would you like to come with me?"

"Where do we go?"

"Well, we will have to look in on Eugenio and Molly from time to time but have you ever been to Atlanta?"

"No, but yes, I would like to come with you." She reached out and took his hand.

***

When Eugenio and Molly reached the foot of the bridge, they stood waiting for the light to change when an American couple walked by. The woman stopped and asked, "What's that wonderful smell?"

It was not the usual comforting smell for Molly. Something was different, still comforting, but now there was something else. Whatever it was, it was a perfect combination. Eugenio took her hand. "Focaccina and No. 1."

"You know?"

"Yes and now is good. Come, Bella, is time to go home."

The young priest stepped out on the steps of the church after afternoon MASS. He raised his face to the warm sunshine and nodded. "Grazie."

Read More with the Second Chances Trilogy.
Coming Soon. . .

Molly was glad the airport security line moved quickly. She really did not mind the wait. She well understood the need in these scary times but she was happy she had gotten through in time to sit and enjoy a much needed cup of coffee before her flight.

She was balancing her carry-on and a tray with her cup and a doughnut when she heard someone call her name. She turned to see a familiar face motioning for her to join the two ladies already seated at a table.

"Molly, sit with us. This is Juliet. Met her in the security line."

Molly knew Kate from her years at McGinty's. Another teacher who found the pub a quiet refuge from the city rush.

"Kate, great to see you again. And, Juliet, nice to meet you. Where are you headed?"

"London."

"Business or pleasure?"

"A little of both. I am going back a much older and wiser woman than my first time as a student," replied Juliet.

"Molly, It's been a while. I am so sorry about Sarah. Where are you off to?" Kate spoke up.

"Italy. I am running away from home for a month."

"Good for you. I'm headed to Ireland on a search."

"And what are you looking for, Kate?"

"I have absolutely no idea. A second chance at life, I think."

Molly and Juliet nodded. Molly raised her coffee cup.

"LADIES, here's to second chances."